Ready or Knot

JILLIAN RINK

Copyright © 2023 by Jillian Rink

All rights reserved.

No part of this book may be reproduced in any form or by any electronic or mechanical means, including information storage and retrieval systems, without written permission from the author, except for the use of brief quotations in a book review.

*To my thirteen year old, fanfiction writing self:
Turns out you still like weird shit, girl.*

Before You Read

This is a work of fiction intended for adult audiences. While there is a happy ending for Faedra, this book does include violence, explicit sexual content, and discussions of potentially triggering events.

Please consult the trigger warnings in the back of the book before reading. Your mental health matters most.

All names are used with the intent of fictional usage and any similarities are coincidental.

Playlist

Welcome to New York (Taylor's Version)
  Taylor Swift

Crowded Room
  Selena Gomez

Say Something
  Pentatonix

Home
  Phillip Phillips

What My World Spins Around
  Jordan Davis

Tenerife Sea
  Ed Sheeran

PLAYLIST

I Guess I'm in Love
    Clinton Kane

Gravity
    Sara Bareilles

Falling like the Stars
    James Arthur

Give Me a Sign
    Breaking Benjamin

You Got Me
    Gavin DeGraw

Chasing the Sun
    Sara Bareilles

One

FAEDRA

My hands shake enough that it takes me two tries to get my earrings situated. I don't even attempt to touch up my lipstick, though I grab the tube and shove it in my clutch. My phone pings with a new notification across the room.

"Violet, I think the car's here," I call as I rush to grab my phone. Sure enough, there's a notification from the app and a text message from the driver double checking. I send a quick response and then rush out to the shared living room of the hotel suite.

"Violet?" I ask, realizing she's not waiting for me.

"Coming," comes her frantic reply a moment before she steps out of the adjoining bedroom. My eyebrows rise as a smile stretches my lips. She looks up from putting last minute items in her own clutch and proceeds to blush a deep red. "It's probably too much, isn't it?"

I shake my head. "It's perfect," I assure her. The floor length bodycon gown is a metallic green, shimmering in the waning sunlight illuminating the space. It almost seems to be living, moving with her as it hugs her generous curves.

"Don't know how I'm going to survive wearing these, but I guess the Council will just have to factor that into their decision," she says as she waits for me to open the door. Her hand pulls the hem of her dress up just enough to show the strappy black heels she's wearing. The three inch heel is just as thin as the straps. I raise my eyebrow again before shaking my head and laughing.

"Of course you'd wear something that would jeopardize your safety."

Even with the heels, she stands a few inches shorter than my average height.

"They're fucking perfect, and you know it." She's adamant, just like she was when she insisted on packing a full suitcase as well as a carry-on for the short one night visit. But that's Violet, always prepping for the best—and worst—case scenario. My phone pings again, and I send another text letting the driver know we're almost down. "Besides, Alphas are almost always ridiculously tall. The last thing I want is for them to think I'm some dainty, virginal eighteen year old. The idea of ending up with a pack that idealizes that makes me want to vomit."

She scrunches her nose and pushes the call button for the elevator. I manage to keep from flinching at the virginal comment. Violet is bold, daring. She knows what she wants from the world, and she's not afraid to demand it.

I'm...not.

I've always been quiet, cautious. Not that I won't try something. I'll do anything once if someone suggests it. But I'm not the life of the party—or friend group.

Even our outfits exemplify our differences, her bold, draping gown outshining my beaded black satin dress. If not for her, I wouldn't have even picked out this one with its single shoulder and open back. Which she knew, of course. Nothing gets me to try something faster than someone daring me or suggesting I can't. Her black hair is done up in one of those updos women always save on Pinterest while I'm happy to just manage decent curls for once. One side is pinned back and the rest drapes over my shoulder, bright red against my pale skin.

The idea of having to try to stand out tonight is overwhelming, but I know it's the reality of being Omega. The Council puts on one of these lavish parties every three months for us, and only registered packs are allowed to attend. Violet and I are both older than the Council prefers. She knew from the moment we were freshmen roommates that she didn't want to join a pack until she had graduated. It was one of the reasons we bonded so quickly. Packs mean babies, and there was no way I was going to try to balance being a parent with my undergraduate degree. So here I am, waiting for an elevator in the middle of Manhattan, a mere month away from graduating with honors.

It only cost me suppressing two heats.

Violet steps onto the elevator, hips swaying, her entire body exuding confidence. My only goal is to keep my hands from trembling, but I manage, and then the elevator is dropping, moving at a wicked speed to navigate all twenty floors between us and the lobby.

My parents aren't this kind of rich. I know Violet's are well-off, but she refuses to take anything from her mother, so she lives similarly to me—and these kinds of hotels are definitely outside of the budget. I suppose the Council wanted to sweeten the pot for us finally picking a Matching Gala.

Or maybe this is how they treat all Omegas.

I only get one of these, so it's not like I'm an expert at knowing what comes standard.

"Deep breath, Faedra. Alphas are going to be interested in you, I promise," Violet says as the elevator finally opens into the opulent lobby.

We step out, heading straight for the main doors where a doorman pulls one open ahead of us. I smile as we pass, murmuring a thank you, and he nods. The car is pulled against the curb, hazards flashing, and we rush to settle into the backseat. The driver nods once as we pull away from the curb and starts navigating Friday evening traffic. The car, too, is a courtesy of the Council.

"You're even more quiet than normal," Violet points out, and I shrug. She frowns and grasps my hand, lacing our fingers together. "Once the awkward first round of mingling fades, it'll be good. The first ten minutes are always uncomfortable at big events like this. And by the time the dancing starts, I'm sure you'll have found at least one Alpha that you like."

Violet was raised by a pack, her mom being an Omega, too. Her older sister has been with her Alphas for almost as long as I've known her, and her younger brother plans on attending the next ball. She grew up surrounded by all of this: the Council, the paperwork, the suppressants.

My parents are both Betas—normal, happy people that fell in love and had two happy children in the Midwest. My brother's a Beta, too, a few years older than me and doing his final year of medical school in Boston. When I turned seventeen and designated as an Omega, it was a shock to us all. In a lot of ways, I still feel like a Beta, especially with the suppressants I've been taking the last few years to keep my heat from emerging.

"I had to switch to the big suppressant," I tell her, looking out at the city moving past us.

"Oh shit, Fae." Violet's eyes are wide, and I grimace. "Is this your third?"

A single nod has her grimacing, too. I sigh. "I just worry that

I won't be Omega enough, Vi. I don't crave touch the way you do. I don't desire to be around people all the time or want to hear compliments, either. What happens if no pack wants me and I have to go through a heat alone?"

Heats are intense stretches of time where Omegas become hyper fertile. Everything rational clicks off in their brains, and they become the craziest, horniest people in existence. They tend to happen every six months, but there are suppressants to keep them from being as intense—or stop them altogether. Doctors warn heavily against those ones though, especially for long term use. Each heat suppressed means the next one will be even more intense.

I've been warned that the effect is exponential, so the consequences of suppression are substantially worse the more you do it. But no way in hell was I going to go through a heat—something I've only ever read about—while in the middle of college and surrounded by mostly strangers.

Violet squeezes my arm and tightens her fingers around mine. "They'll want you, Fae. You're witty, smart, graceful. Not to mention a fucking bombshell. Don't worry. There'll be good packs there that you'll fit with."

I soak in her words, trying to let them soothe the bone deep worry within me, just as the car pulls to a stop along the curb.

"I know this is practically impossible for you, but try to turn off that analytic brain and just have fun tonight. That's what the Council wants to see—it's part of why they don't show up here in person," she says before stepping out into the night. With a shake of my head, I follow closely behind her.

People swarm the sidewalk around us. There's a line of people with cameras pointed towards the cars, flashes going off every few seconds. Some others stand near the curb with microphones, videocameras held behind them, trying to catch a few words from those trying to get inside. I take a deep breath and smooth my hands over my hips.

The Council makes these parties a huge deal for Omegas. And I suppose I can be appreciative of it. Unlike the Alphas, it's the only one I'll get, so it might as well be a once-in-a-lifetime experience.

"Clutch," Violet says, nestling the small piece of fabric in my hand.

"Oh shoot," I mutter, and Violet chuckles.

The line of cameras turn towards us as our car pulls away from the curb. Violet smiles, letting her body relax even as she pushes past the line of media people, and I laugh as I follow. One reporter is brave enough to step in front of Violet, but I continue around them. She looks at me, winks, and then turns back to the woman holding a microphone out.

I don't hear the question, but Violet happily responds, "Oh, I'm just excited to have a night of fun. It's a once-in-a-lifetime experience, and I'm ready to make the most of it!"

I step closer to the door, trying to be subtle about my taking in everything around me. There aren't any Alphas out here. The Council is careful about who works this part of the parties, making sure they're either Betas or bonded Omegas. Something about making us comfortable as we adjust to all the attention.

The Omegas attending are gathering around the entrance, slowly moving into the ballroom, chatting amongst themselves in groups of two or three. There's an even split of men and women, and most seem to be younger than me. I breathe a sigh of relief as I realize I'm not underdressed.

Violet catches up to me a moment later and bumps her shoulder against my arm.

"You're welcome," she says, smirking, and I laugh.

"Owe you for that one," I tell her. We brush past several

groups, being more intentional about getting inside than most of the people mingling.

"Let's get you your one allowed drink and then find a spot to see the Alphas. I'm sure there will be someone that sticks out to you."

Violet is always the one with a plan, and I'm grateful for it now more than I've ever been. It's still a foreign thought, not yet taking root, that this party will decide where I end up living for the rest of my life—and with whom. I take a deep breath, messing with the gold chain I added to my orbital piercing, and nod.

"And what about you?" I ask.

She just smiles and winks.

"Don't you worry about me, Fae. You know how I am."

I'm laughing as we take the first steps into the lavish ballroom, and I can't help but feel like maybe it's a good omen for the night ahead of me.

JUDE

The light catches the white gold cufflinks as I adjust them before I drop my head into my hands. How are we already back in Manhattan at one of these? Wasn't it just January?

"Doors just opened," Logan says, and I groan, sitting back up to find him standing behind Carter and me, adjusting his suit jacket, running a hand through his hair and messing up his gelled style. Carter grunts but doesn't say anything, looking at his phone.

"Let's get our drinks before the lines get inundated," Logan says after a moment.

I'm not going to oppose that decision. Standing, I fix my tie, making sure it's sitting flat against my shirt and under my vest, following wordlessly behind Logan and Carter as we cross the room. As we wait for our turn at the bar, Carter checks his phone again, shaking his head and cursing under his breath.

"What happened now?" I ask as my own phone vibrates in my jacket pocket. He's been working longer days than normal, trying to secure a new contract for his start-up, Mountain Tech.

Carter's look is dry, his lips pulled into a flat line. "The same shit that happens every time we fly out for one of these," he says, and I sigh.

Nothing about the contract, then.

I can't decide if it's good or bad that it's unrelated to the company.

"I suppose that explains my own phone going off," I mutter. I don't bother reaching to double check.

Where Harper goes, Melanie follows. It's unfortunate but infinitely better than if Melanie moves first. Harper, for all her flaws, is significantly less cruel in her methods of keeping her claws in Carter. I intentionally don't think about the last time Melanie moved first.

My phone vibrates again, and I hold back another sigh so it can't turn into a scream. Neither woman was so insidious when Iris was involved. Or maybe they had been, and Iris diffused it. It didn't really matter now.

The third vibration has me pulling out my phone and shutting it off, but not before I see a flash of a picture. Melanie's in a racy set of lingerie, posing for the camera, her lips a bright red. I linger on it longer than I care to admit before deleting it.

That'll be a problem for tomorrow.

"What can I get you three?" the bartender asks, a smile still on her face, the purple pin on her collar sitting in stark contrast to the shirt's crisp white.

"Three whiskeys, please," Logan says. "Neat."

She nods and grabs three tumblers from below the workspace, grabbing a mid-level whiskey from the rows of alcohol options behind her and pouring a generous knuckle's worth in each glass.

Carter hands her the green tickets before we take the drinks, and I hand her a moderate tip. Her eyebrow ticks up before she can control the reaction. Moderate tip for us, at least. I suppose four hundred in cash is large for some packs in attendance tonight.

"How do we want to do it this time?" Logan asks once we're out of the way of other Alphas trying to get to the bar. Most are vaguely familiar at this point in the same way the thousands of students on campus are. You pass them enough times, and you're almost sure you remember their names. "Same as usual?"

I take a sip of the alcohol, letting the burn distract me from the fact that this *has* become the usual. Every three months we fly out to Manhattan and do this. Most packs only attend a handful before the Council puts them out of their misery, but we've had the *esteemed privilege* of being at more than ten of these events.

"I think I'd rather start on the edge," Carter says, tucking his hand into his pocket, the TAG watch he wears just visible. "See if anyone is brave enough to venture near us."

Logan, in his own sign of fatigue over these damn things, doesn't argue, following Carter to a spot along the far wall, about halfway between the bar and the string quartet. From here, we have a good view of the entryway as well as the smattering of cocktail tables set out near the dance floor.

A rush of sound precedes the first wave of Omegas, and Logan throws back his whiskey all at once, not even flinching at the burn.

"Fuck, I'm getting tired of these," Carter mutters.

That makes two of us.

Two

FAEDRA

"Can I just get a soda right now?"

The Omega in front of us looks around, clearly nervous, and fiddles with his jacket buttons.

"Of course," the bartender replies, eyes softening a bit. She pulls a tall glass with ice from behind the bar and sets it in front of him a moment before she opens a soda and pours it in. "Just keep that drink ticket with you until you want something with alcohol, alright?"

The guy nods, takes the drink with a shaky smile, and then turns towards the room. I can't help but watch him, my chest clenching at how uncomfortable he clearly is.

"Here," I say, handing my ticket to Violet. "Can you grab me my usual?" Her eyebrows furrow, and she glances at the bartender.

"I heard her, so it's fine. What can I get you, ma'am?" she replies, and I turn around, taking quick steps until I'm next to the Omega. My hand touches his forearm before I can think better of it. He pauses, looking at me with a frown, and I smile.

"Want to hang out with us for a bit?" I ask, nodding towards Violet. The frown smooths out, and he offers what seems to be a genuine smile.

"I'm alright, ma'am. Thank you." He rubs the back of his neck, cheeks reddening.

"I hope you enjoy the night, then," I say, and he smiles again.

"I'm sure I will," he assures me before turning toward the back corner of the room, his eyes quickly assessing the groups of Alphas around the edges.

Violet steps up to me in the next moment, and I take the copper mug from her hand.

"Honestly, Fae, only you would try to help out someone else at your own Matching Gala."

I blush and duck my head, but she laughs and leads me towards the center of the room, having clearly decided on a spot perfect for her perusing the packs. She steps up to the empty cocktail table with ease, setting her glass tumbler on the table while she surveys the entirety of the party for the first time.

There's a large dance floor taking up the center of the room, a DJ booth set off to one side, the speakers subtle where they perch at every corner. A large spread of various finger foods lines the wall behind the DJ. Cocktail tables line three sides of it, two rows offset from each other to facilitate easier movement of people around them. Beyond them, another few rows of round tables, and then a moderate band of space around the edges functioning as both mingle space and walkway for the catering staff. Everything is draped in white linens, small white lights, and white flowers that seem to coordinate with the late April date—tulips, peonies, and hyacinth the ones I can name.

Violet leans into me as I set my drink on the cocktail table.

"I'm honestly shocked that so few Omegas are wearing black," she says. "Really expected to be more ostentatious, you know?"

I roll my eyes, lifting one corner of my mouth. "Vi, the entire room looked when we came in. I don't think you'll have any problem with garnering attention tonight."

She waves off my comment, still scanning the space with sharp eyes. While she decides how best to conquer the evening, I set my clutch next to my drink, unclasping it from my wrist for the moment and grabbing one of the pieces of chocolate I'd tucked into it.

She catches the movement and shakes her head. "An entire dessert bar, and you bring Rolos from the airport?"

"Emotional support airport Rolos," I say, popping a second into my mouth and then washing it down with a bit of the drink. She gives a reluctant half smile before her gaze sweeps the room again.

"There's more Betas here with packs than I expected," she admits after a moment. My raised eyebrow serves as question enough. "That's what the blue lapel pins mean. Alphas wear red, Betas wear blue. They'll have the official pack name on it, too. Didn't you read the information they sent a couple weeks ago?"

Another drink while shaking my head. "I was too busy trying to finish my final paper for my Comparative Early Modern Literature class."

Violet scrunches her nose in distaste. "The people working have purple lapel pins, in case you need to make sure." She blows out a breath and takes a small sip of her drink. "Betas being part of packs is pretty rare. They don't have the same need to be surrounded like we do or to take care of someone, like Alphas. And the bond doesn't quite work the same for them, either."

Bonding is one of those things I haven't really thought about. At least not beyond the basics: a visceral emotional connection formed through a bite during knotting. More lasting than any vows offered at the altar of a traditional wedding, the scars left behind on the Omega a bolder statement than any engagement ring. One of the informational packets the Council sent that I'd actually read talked about how most packs end up forging one.

"Do you think you'll bond with your match?" I ask her. We haven't had much time to talk about any of the *after* parts of attending tonight. School's been hectic, and her second job has her working most nights while the baseball tourism starts back up.

She scoffs. "Absolutely not," she says, twisting one of the golden chains of her necklace around her finger. "That's way too intimate, you know? I may be Omega, but I still need some space to myself."

"Totally get it," I say.

She scans the room again, and I let my gaze wander, trying to see it the way she does. Now that she's mentioned them, I notice the pins everywhere. And she's right, there's at least a dozen blue pins—a dozen Betas that are registered as pack. It's a small number, nearly inconsequential statistically compared to the hundreds filling the room as more Omegas work their way inside, but it's surprising nonetheless.

My eyes catch on a man standing across the room, back pressed against the wall, shoulder touching another man's, a small red pin resting on his left lapel. His brown hair is flecked with silver, and so is his well-groomed beard. The distance is too much to tell what color his eyes are, but the way he assesses the room has my chest going hot. The man next to him points to someone behind me, and he follows the gesture, eyes settling on someone for a moment before moving away again.

I duck my head, turning so that my ribs press into the table, and pick at the chain attaching the star pendant to my orbital piercing. Violet's breath catches, and I focus on her, frowning when I see that she's biting her lip, her hands holding her clutch to her belly in a death grip.

"What's up?" I ask, scanning the room for a problem. She shudders out a breath before looking at me.

"Just didn't expect to recognize anyone, that's all," she says. I raise an eyebrow, and she huffs. "Remember I dated that Beta in high school?"

I look around the room again. "Oh shit. Jasper is here? Is he part of the string quartet?" I ask, trying to see the seated musicians across the room, their playing offering an undertone to the space that's becoming progressively more drowned out as people start mingling. She shakes her head.

"He has a pin." For the first time tonight, Violet looks unsure. Fiddling with one of her gold earrings, she looks just behind me, sizing up the main entrance to the ballroom.

"Do you want to go chat with him?" I take a small sip of my drink, trying to gauge how she feels about him being here as a potential pack match. Her lips pout, and she takes another pull from her Old-Fashioned.

"I don't know," she finally says, her eyes on the tumbler in her hands. "Not yet." She takes a deep breath and then looks back up at me, the usual spark in her eye. "Did you notice anyone while you were looking?"

My cheeks heat, and I give a single, small nod. Her grin turns wicked.

"Should I guess? Or do you just want to point him out?"

I can't help but laugh. "Go for it, Vi. Let's see if you still know my type."

I haven't seriously dated anyone since high school, and we haven't had a chance to sit at the pier and people watch since the fall, but if anyone can pinpoint the type of man that gets me thinking about recreating the scenes I've read in my contemporary romances, it's Violet.

She raises an eyebrow and turns away from the table, a hand still on her drink. Her eyebrows furrow as she looks around the room, her eyes moving slowly from one group of Alphas to another. She hums as she stops, her eyes drifting back over someone, and then she smirks. My heart rate picks up, but I offer her a half smile when she turns towards me.

"I think I found him," she says. She glances down at her drink, fiddling with the glass, and then uses a finger to point towards the back wall—right where that Alpha had been standing. "He's older. Brown hair and beard with just enough gray for it to be a salt and pepper vibe. Standing with another guy. Probably his pack mate."

I can't help it. I blush, fiercely enough that it seeps onto my neck. I trace my piercings and cast a quick glance just to make sure it's the same man. My breath catches in my throat as his eyes lock with mine. His lips close around the rim of the tumbler in his hand, his throat moving with a swallow. The move carries so much sensual impact that my belly clenches.

The faint trace of my scent permeates the air around us.

"Oh, hell yes, that's him," Violet snickers. I force my gaze away from the man, eyes wide, and flush again, my chest going hot.

Even with my attention off of him, the way his lips moved over the rim of the glass burns into my mind. He probably kisses with that same confidence. I loop my clutch around my wrist again, intent on seeing who the man is, when Violet stops me, her hand on mine for a brief second. "Let's see if he makes the move first. You have all night, Fae. No need to rush right now."

There's no way I can explain this feeling to Violet, this sensation in my chest telling me that he's the one. I'm itching to find out his name if just to hear his voice say mine for my fantasies. Violet flexes her fingers, and I sigh, taking a sip of my drink.

"Trust me, Fae."

I can't help but smile. "You know I do, Vi."

JUDE

"I swear to God, he's getting faster every party we attend," Carter gripes before taking a sip of his whiskey. I chuckle and sip my own. "Seriously, Jude. It's been fifteen minutes since they arrived, maximum. Most of them haven't even gotten their damn drink. And we agreed we'd see if anyone was bold enough to approach us first."

His shoulder brushes mine as he adjusts his bow tie, his eyes locked on the third man in our pack. Or, rather, on his back, since he's currently cutting a quite impressive straight line through the crowd, clearly intent on getting to one of the Omegas that just recently came inside.

"That's Logan for you. Each party, he becomes more sure of what he wants—and what will work for us as a pack." I blow out a breath and lean against the wall. "And maybe he knows we're exhausted and wants to cut the night early. Let's see how he does this time before we start giving him shit," I say, and Carter nods once. I take another sip of whiskey and track Logan's progress, trying to figure out which woman caught his eye.

"Should we bet?" Carter asks, and I laugh.

"I'm always shit at this, man, especially when you spend all day reading people," I gripe. "Might as well just give you the four hundred dollars now."

He raises an eyebrow, and I roll my eyes, waving him on before he decides to tell me anyway.

"I think it's that blonde near the entrance. She didn't come in with anyone and that doesn't seem to be worrying her," Carter offers with a subtle point using the hand holding his whiskey.

"She could probably handle the few events I actually go to a year without it being a huge stressor."

I take in the woman—she's gorgeous with legs for days and generous curves, but honestly younger than I'm comfortable with. She's probably only eighteen, for fuck's sake. I grunt before scanning the room at large.

"Oops. Too late," Carter says before I can offer up a guess. He points towards the cocktail tables near the dance floor, and I spot Logan carefully leaning against one of them. His hands are clasped in front of him, resting on the table, and his foot lightly taps to the beat of the string quartet playing in the corner. His smile is polite but guarded.

I shake my head. I may be shit reading people compared to Carter, but I know Logan. "That's absolutely not where he was headed."

The women at the table laugh, and one of them runs her hand down Logan's arm. The warmth leaves his smile, and he's quick to disengage from the table.

Logan's odd like that—an Alpha that doesn't appreciate unsolicited touch from an Omega. It's part of why he fits so well with Carter and me. It's not that we don't like being around Omegas and their need for contact. It's just that we like to be in control of when and with whom. We're not so desperate as to take anything offered up, even at these blasted parties.

My eyes roam the room again, trying to remember where he was headed before he was pulled to the group of Omegas. My eyes catch on a short woman wearing a slinky green dress but quickly move to the woman standing next to her.

Her dress is a simple black that catches the light when she moves. It's tailored well, hugging her breasts and hips before cascading to the floor. One shoulder is bare, and I can see from the way she leans against the table that most of her back is, too. Her hair falls in waves over her shoulder, a sea of fire against her skin, and her jewelry is tasteful, draping around her neck perfectly, drawing my eyes to the hollow of her throat. Her gaze flicks across the room, locking on mine, hitting my chest like a punch. I take a sip of my whiskey as my heart rate accelerates, the urge to get close and feel her skin rising in me.

It's been a long time since I felt that need.

After a moment, she drops her gaze and takes a drink from a copper mug.

Who the hell under the age of 25 actually drinks Moscow Mules?

Pointing her out to Carter, I say, "Probably wishful thinking, but I think it's her. And she's not eighteen, thank fuck."

Carter takes her in, head tilting a bit to the left, and eventually nods. "Yeah, definitely a bit older. So is the woman she's standing with. Not our age, but probably the closest we'll find since the Council pushes Omegas into packs so fast."

I make a derisive sound deep in my throat, and Carter chuckles.

We've been officially registered as a pack for just over four years, and it feels like each one goes by faster. We're not the oldest Alpha group here, but we're close. Fate does that to people sometimes. We didn't find Logan until we were in our early thirties, and the Council's paperwork is a bureaucratic nightmare. Now I'm forty, Carter not far behind, and still attending these hellacious parties in the hopes of the Council deciding we'll make a good pack for one of the attending Omegas.

Logan stops next to their table, and I smirk. His hands are in his pockets, shoulders relaxed, as he says something to the women. Neither tense as they reply, and he steps in a bit closer.

Fuck, are my hands actually clammy?

I take another sip of whiskey, closing my eyes and focusing

on the burn of the alcohol down my throat. I hate these goddamn parties.

"Holy shit, I actually owe you. What the hell?" Carter complains, and I look over at him, managing to smirk a bit. He digs his wallet out and pulls the bills, scowling at me as I pluck them from his fingers.

I flick a quick glance at the table before focusing on the rest of the whiskey in my snifter. A waiter walks through the edge of the crowd, a half full tray in one hand, and I signal to him with my empty glass. It takes a bit to navigate the space between us, but he's nice enough about taking the empty drink from me, and I hand him the money I won from Carter. His eyes widen before he shuts it down and thanks me while turning to walk the perimeter again.

"Shit, man. He might have actually found one this time," Carter says a few minutes later.

My eyes snap back to the table. The woman in green leans into the other, hand grabbing her elbow, and says something. The redhead smiles and nods, holding up her small purse. A moment later, the woman leaves the table and starts to wander through the crowd. Logan takes the opportunity to move closer to the woman I'd noticed, his hands still in his pockets.

"Think he's drawing it out just to torture me?" I ask. We always let Logan pick the first woman we talk to at each of these. He's younger, more outgoing than me, and is more into pop culture than Carter. But he's been standing with her for nearly five minutes without giving us any kind of signal. Carter rolls his eyes.

"This seems different, J. Logan doesn't fuck around at these, remember? If he didn't see something, he'd move on and let us pick someone out. Give him a bit longer."

I know Carter's right. But the reality is that I'm going to need another whiskey if he takes much longer, and the Council restricts everyone to one alcoholic drink at these things. Which, for what it's worth, is perfectly reasonable—admirable, even. They don't want inebriation to factor into their placements.

Too bad my nerves are already stretched thin.

The woman turns into Logan and drops her hand from her drink, resting it on the table top. He doesn't miss a beat, mirroring her movement as he says something to her. She glances around, and he gestures towards where we're standing. Her gaze looks across the crowd without pausing, and then she turns back to him. She smiles, and my throat closes.

Fuck. When was the last time I was actually nervous about talking to a woman? Over a decade, I'm pretty sure.

Logan taps his finger on the table twice, his eyes flicking towards us before returning to the woman across from him. Carter raises an eyebrow as he looks at me, and I blow out a breath.

Showtime.

Three

FAEDRA

"Pretty big party. Is this what you'd dreamt it would be?" a man asks, stepping up to our table, his voice smooth with just enough bite to make my fingers tingle.

The man's hands are in his pockets, bow tie impeccable, a red pin labeled Bennett on his lapel. His sandy blonde hair is more unkempt than I'd expect at this kind of function, and I find it intriguing. Was it intentional? Or had it been styled and then ruined by running his hands through it?

Violet answers easily, "Yes."

He smiles and then looks at me, his blue eyes raking over my dress. "And you?"

"I'm not sure what I thought it would be, but it's certainly big," I answer, the truth falling out of me before I have the sense to come up with something witty or demure. He chuckles and takes a step towards me while his gaze coasts over the table between us. His eyebrows raise even as he grins.

"Please tell me that's an actual Moscow Mule and not just a bartender too lazy to grab a fresh glass for a daiquiri."

I can't help but laugh, my hand tightening on the copper mug. "It's an actual one. They're my guilty pleasure."

He nods, his gaze intense on me, and I feel my chest darken with a blush. "I'm Logan," he offers after a moment. Violet gives a one-sided smile, leaning into the table a bit more.

"I'm Violet," she offers, looking at me.

"Faedra," I say, playing with my piercings Logan's eyes are sharp, watching the movement with an intensity that makes my thighs clench. My question is breathless. "Where's the rest of your pack?"

"Around," he offers, shrugging a shoulder, not deterred by my reaction to him. "They're not as outgoing as I am. I'm sure they're trying to stretch their one glass of whiskey until I manage to convince them to come mingle."

"Honestly? Same."

Violet huffs and rolls her eyes. "You're ridiculous, Fae. I just had to talk you down from trying to go find that Alpha that struck your interest."

I shrug, blushing when Logan quirks an eyebrow.

"It's nothing," I manage to say, and Violet laughs. I shoot her a glare. "It isn't. The whole point of the Council putting together these damn things is to match us up with packs. Why not make the first move?"

Logan takes another step towards me, rounding the table without pulling his hands from his pockets. Was that a good sign?

"It'd be a shame if you had to make the first move with all these Alphas around naturally hardwired to give Omegas what they want."

His words make butterflies swim in my stomach, but I don't hesitate away from the unspoken proposition.

"Are you offering?" I ask, and he takes one last step towards me, eating up the last bit of space before our distance officially crosses into *improper*.

Violet leans over until she can whisper in my ear. "Have a good time," she says. "Make sure your clutch stays on your wrist and text me if you leave, ok?"

I work the strap of it onto my wrist again before I can forget, holding it up as proof as I promise to text her, and then she grabs her half-empty Old Fashioned and disappears into the growing crowd around the dance floor. Logan doesn't move his gaze away from me.

"So, Faedra," he says, and goosebumps race down my arms at the way his voice curls around my name. "Where are you from?"

"Do you want the honest answer, or my attempt at impressing an Alpha?" I ask, giving a small half-smile. His attention grows more intense.

"How about both? What would you tell me if you're trying to impress me?"

My breath catches. "I'd say that we just flew in from Los Angeles."

He quirks an eyebrow. "Is that where you're from?" I shake my head, gripping the mug tighter. "Then why did you fly out from the other side of the country?"

"School. I'm almost finished with my bachelors," I say.

He hums, a small tilt to his lips that makes me think he's amused.

When did it get so hot in here? I hope this isn't my heat breaking through the suppressants.

"Which school?" Logan asks.

"UCLA."

He leans into me, eating away the bit of distance between us, his voice dropping until it's practically a purr. "So where are you from, then, Faedra?"

"I grew up in Iowa," I breathe.

"The Midwest?" When I offer a shrug, he grins and says, "I grew up in Madison."

"Oh, it's gorgeous up there," I say, smiling, the tension building between us suddenly gone. Was that a bad sign? "My family'd go up there every summer. My mom is from Green Bay, and she loved taking us up and down the coast any chance she could."

"It is beautiful," he agrees, setting a hand on the table. "Some days I miss it. But I enjoy where my pack is more, so I don't find myself overly homesick."

The soft notes of the quartet fade out, replaced by a recently released pop hit pulsing through the speakers as the DJ takes over. I drop my hand from my drink, letting it rest on the table between us, and turn towards him. He mirrors me before leaning in the rest of the way, his face inches from mine as he taps the table a few times.

"In all actuality, Faedra, the other guys in my pack are hiding on the other side of the room, waiting to see if you want to meet them," he whispers, pointing towards the back wall. My eyes sweep over the crowd, but no one in particular jumps out at me —not the way the Alpha did earlier. It's hard to focus on trying to find them when Logan is so enigmatic in front of me. "I'd love to meet them," I tell him, taking a long drink of my cocktail.

If I don't enjoy the other members of his pack, I can always excuse myself and go looking for the man that had caught my attention.

Logan says, "Have to be honest, Jude's been in a shit mood most of the day. He hates these parties, and it's just about finals season, which makes it worse."

"Finals season *is* awful," I admit on a whisper, laughing, and Logan smiles, a mischievous look lighting his eyes a moment before a heavy presence settles behind me.

"Come on now, Logan. Don't turn her off from Jude before he has a chance to put his own foot in his mouth. At least that way he can't complain to us later."

A man steps up across from me, one hand in a pocket, the other resting on the table top, gripping a tumbler full of amber liquid with a relaxed hold. The tux he wears is well-tailored, draping across his body like a glove, giving a subtle highlight to what seems to be significant athleticism. His golden skin glows against the black fabric, and his gaze conveys a level of self-confidence that has me clutching my mug tighter. Short waves of black hair combine with a narrow chin and high cheekbones, reminding me of—

"Has anyone ever told you that you look like a bulkier John Mayer?" The question falls from me before I can pull it back.

He tilts his head back and laughs, eyes closing as he grabs Logan's bicep. Logan grins, looking me over like I did something surprising but exciting.

"Holy shit, Logan. You actually found someone who knows our era of pop culture." The man chuckles before wiping his eyes. After a deep breath, he looks at me again.

"Can't make any more promises on that front," I say, letting my voice dry out a bit. "I only really know him because of Taylor Swift."

Logan grimaces. "Does that mean it's a strike against us that he looks like John Mayer?"

I shrug, adjusting how I'm standing on my short heels, cocking my hip a bit. "As long as he isn't taking advantage of nineteen year olds, it should be fine."

"Definitely not doing that," the man says, taking a drink before stretching his hand across the table. "I'm Carter."

I take his hand in a light hold even as Logan rolls his eyes.

"Good grief, man. It's a meet cute, not a board meeting. What the hell are you doing?" Logan gripes, and I laugh, tightening my grip on Carter's fingers. He raises an eyebrow, eyes growing more intense, the brown seeming to darken.

"Does it matter as long as she likes it?" he asks, voice turning husky, and I clench my thighs instinctually. An eyebrow raises before he drops his hand, his eyes flicking just behind me. He tips his chin towards the man stepping up next to me. "And this is Jude."

I turn and smile to the new man, trying to be polite, but my breath catches in my throat as I take him in, my hand tightening on the drink in front of me.

He's the man I'd noticed across the room.

Up close, I can see there's more silver flecking his beard than I'd originally thought, leaning almost silver fox instead of salt and pepper. His eyes are sharp, his lips set in a deep frown. His hands are in his pockets, his shoulders held more stiff than his pack mates.

"You would dread finals season, too, if you were stuck with an introductory class full of non-majors, Logan," he says, bypassing any greeting towards me. His voice reminds me of caramel, flowing over my skin and leaving me breathless despite the social faux pas.

"Correction: I would dread finals if I had to do them all on shit I don't really care about. Nothing sounds more dreadful than having to write a timed paper about Mesopotamia," Logan snarks, leaning forward, resting an elbow on the table while keeping his body angled toward me.

"I can think of at least three finals that were worse than my Ancient Western Asia paper," I argue, frowning.

Why was I coming to the defense of a man who hadn't even acknowledged me?

Carter raises an eyebrow. "Like what?" he asks before I can answer my own question.

"Statistics." The shudder is automatic, and all three men laugh.

Something deep within me sits up and takes notice, enjoying the combined attention.

Logan nods, tucking a hand back into his locket, the exact image of suave gentleman. He could have been in a shoot for some luxury yacht brand.

"That's true," he says. "That's way worse. At least I can fake my way through a paper that doesn't have a right answer."

Jude rests his elbow on the table, his hands still tucked away. "Which final was your favorite?"

Logan relaxes. I'm not entirely sure how I can tell since he's been the picture of comfortable from the beginning, but there's something in the way he looks at me that has me realizing Jude was the pack mate he was nervous about me meeting.

I frown, looking down at my drink, sorting through various answers that will win me interest points. I'm not really the one for bullshitting, though, so I give the men the truth.

"I'm not sure any final is really all that great, especially when the professors make it more than half the overall grade. Who wants one day to be representative of their entire outcome?" I pause, glancing around the room once, taking in the overstated opulence of the entire place. "Which I realize is pretty ironic considering I'm an Omega at my Matching Gala."

I shrug once, running my finger around the rim of the copper mug, and then glance back at Jude. His eyebrows are furrowed, head tilted just a bit to the side, his gaze intense on me—like I'm a problem he needs to solve. For some reason, it feels like he's stripping me bare. The nervous swallow is instinct.

"But, um, I enjoyed my class about Dante's Divine Comedy. It's tied with my Tolstoy focused Russian literature class," I manage to say, only a little breathless.

"What was your major?" Jude asks after a moment.

"European studies," I admit, looking back down at my drink. "Completely useless degree since, as an Omega, there's no way I could end up being a delegate for any Embassy. But it's what struck my interest the most at the time."

When the men don't immediately respond, I chance a glance up at Logan. His eyes are wide, shoulders dropped in what I'm pretty sure is surprise. I feel the blush creep down my throat before I can drop my head again.

Carter chuckles a bit under his breath.

"Hot damn, Jude. Logan managed to find someone that can keep up with you," he mutters.

I turn to the man next to me, head tilted a bit, trying to ignore the growing ball of nerves in my belly.

"I haven't heard someone discuss Dante outside of required classroom discussions in years," he murmurs, the corners of his lips tipping up. The blush spreads across my chest in a heartbeat, but I'm nearly positive it isn't from nerves. Not entirely, at least.

Logan groans. "Don't even start, Jude. Tonight's supposed to be *fun*."

Four

LOGAN

Jude rolls his eyes, and Faedra laughs, the sound of it knocking me on my ass just like it did the first time—light and airy without being too delicate.

"Not an English major then, Logan?" One perfect eyebrow arches over her green eyes. I grimace, shuddering, and she laughs again. Jude's shoulders relax, just a bit, and I mentally high five myself.

"Definitely not," I tell her, leaning closer. Her breath catches for a second, her hand tightening on the edge of the table, and I smirk. "I'm way more interested in the way bodies move."

I intentionally drop my voice and grin when she scents—just a little bit. There's too many people in the room for it to be much more than a faint trace, but I breathe it in all the same, letting that intrinsic part of me roll in it before the movement of a group to my side stirs the air and dissipates it. Her lips part, her tongue tracing over them. Freckles dot across her cheekbones and smooth down her arms, and I want to trace them—first with my hands and then with my tongue. The vision of it hits me hard enough that I scent, too, and Carter chuckles beside me.

Faedra glances at him, her head tilting in silent question. The movement highlights the opal pendant resting just below the hollow of her throat. I need to figure out a way to get her body under my hands—get her close enough that I can bask in her scent again without people ruining it.

The universe must hear my scheming because the DJ changes the song and the heavy bass of a Taylor Swift song fills the room. Faedra gasps.

"Oh, I love this song," she says. She throws her head back as she brings the copper mug to her lips, finishing the drink in three quick gulps. It shouldn't be as hot as my body decides it is, and I find myself quickly adjusting my boner so she doesn't notice it. Her lips tick up in a soft smile as she asks, "Does your interest in moving bodies include dancing, or just dirtier things?"

God *damn*.

Jude's eyes widen, and Carter takes a last drink of his whiskey, setting the tumbler on the tabletop. I close the distance between us, holding out my hand in invitation, and she raises an eyebrow.

"Who said I can't make dancing dirty?" I ask her with a smirk. Her blush is instantaneous, and I bask in it as she takes my hand.

"God damn it, Logan," Jude grumbles.

I pointedly ignore him, focusing instead on guiding Faedra to the edge of the already crowded dance floor. She doesn't hesitate, turning so that her back is pressed to my chest and moving to the beat of the music, her hands above her head. She hums the melody under her breath, and I smile. The dance floor becomes more crowded as the song's chorus plays, several women giggling behind me. Faedra doesn't hesitate, pressing into me, taking up less space, and I bracket her waist, enjoying the feel of her curves under my palms. The longer she dances, the more relaxed she becomes, and I'm content to watch her grow more comfortable as the DJ moves through a reasonably modern discography.

When the song changes, morphing into a slow melody clearly meant to be something that encourages people to pair up, Faedra turns in my arms, a soft question in her gaze. Her smile is bright, and her cheeks are flushed, and I don't hesitate to bring her closer into my arms, taking a half step into her and moving my hand to the small of her back. Her hands are gentle where she laces them together behind my neck.

As we turn in a slow circle, she asks, "How many of these have you gone to?"

The dreaded question.

It comes up every gala, and every time it gets harder to answer with the truth. Something about the extended time makes Omegas wary, and they find a way to move onto another group of Alphas soon after I tell them.

"A lot," I offer, holding my breath, bracing for the guarded eyes and feigned interest to appear.

She tilts her head, her eyebrows pinching, her lip between her teeth.

"How many is a lot?" The question is soft, almost pitiful, but her hands stay locked around me, her body still pliant against mine.

I pride myself in being the optimist, especially compared to Jude's general dour outlook on life. But disbelief has me biting the inside of my cheek to keep from saying something sarcastic. I offer her the truth. Best to rip the band-aid so we can see if there's someone else here that might work for us.

"We've been officially designated for four years. I think we've missed two galas," I explain before leading her into a spin as the music starts to fade. I blow out a breath, prepping myself for the inevitable polite disengagement. Instead, she steps back into me, a thoughtful look in her eyes, her shoulders relaxed. A second slower song begins to play, and she follows my lead to continue dancing without hesitating.

"That must be really draining. Just one is a lot—and I know I'll end up matched with a pack." Her cheeks flush, her teeth digging into her lip again. "It must take a lot of courage to keep showing up."

There's no way. This is unreal. How many times have we managed to find someone that enjoys the three of us just to find them suspicious of how long we've waited to match? Or the opposite, too. They're understanding of the extended selection time but then don't get on with Jude or Carter or even me.

And yet, by some miracle, Faedra seems to be both.

"Can I kiss you?" The question falls from me before I have the good sense to keep it where it belongs—in my goddamn head.

We don't get physical at these.

The first few galas were different. We were still optimistic. But it grew tiresome to have what would become one night stands without the lack of emotional attachment. So the most we do is dance and chat. Anything more, and we politely decline and move on.

So why the hell am I asking this woman if I can kiss her?

She giggles and leans forward, her lips pressing against mine, her tongue tracing my bottom lip. I pull her tighter into me, enjoying the feel of her body, and the faint smell of jasmine floats around us.

Her scent.

I groan, low in my throat and so quiet the music drowns it out. Our tongues tangle, sharing an unspoken language that I'm not sure I understand. Whatever the question, though, I like the answer. I trace her spine and twist my hand into the hair at the nape of her neck, and she hums. I vaguely hear the song change again, the moment of intimacy giving way to another bass heavy hit. Her chest is flushed when she pulls away with a smile, and her face is radiant as her fingers twist around a lock of hair at the nape of my neck. She's gorgeous. I'm struck speechless.

Carter steps up beside me as my shocked silence continues, and thank whatever higher being that he does. She turns to him with a wide smile.

"Mind if I join?" he asks.

She giggles, adjusting so she stands between us, bringing her hands over her head again.

"Can I call you Red?" I ask, my lips pressed against her ear. Goosebumps rise along her neck. "Or is that too on the nose?"

She laughs, twisting to look up at me. "I like it," she says. My grip tightens on her hips.

The night flies by, song after song spent with her between us, and I can't honestly remember the last time one of these galas has been so fun. A woman taps on Faedra's shoulder as the next slower song starts, her gaze intent, a sly smile gracing her lips. She leans into Faedra, asking a question, and Faedra glances at us both. Carter steps back, and I follow his lead.

The woman has Faedra in her arms, whispering something in her ear that makes her giggle, before we manage to get off the dance floor. Jude's chatting with a few Omegas, hands in his pockets but his stance relaxed. We join him.

"Denver's on my bucket list, actually. I'd love to summit a few of the fourteeners," one woman says, adjusting her hair over her shoulder, bringing attention to the low neckline of her dress. Stifling a sigh, I glance at the dance floor, catching sight of Faedra's red hair in the mix of people. Carter leans in.

"You going to find her again?" he whispers, keeping his lips turned away from the others at the table.

I nod, offering a polite smile to the group while Jude keeps up a decent flow of conversation. The moment the group of women has moved on to the next table, I scan the dance floor again. And then the room at large.

I frown, and Carter sighs, rubbing his neck.

Faedra is gone.

∼

FAEDRA

I fiddle with the envelope, opening it and then tucking the flap back in as I try to summon the courage to read whatever is inside. It's small, much smaller than I'd really expected for correspondence from the Council about the party a few days ago. The person who had delivered it had given soft, simple instructions: read through it and submit my response within twenty-four hours.

Simple enough.

Except I can't seem to manage to open it to see what, exactly, the Council is wanting me to give a response to.

With a sigh, I unfold myself from the lounge chair in the dorm living room, stepping up to the closed door across from me and tapping on it once.

"Vi, I know you're there. Can I come in, please?"

There's the sounds of someone moving around, followed almost immediately by a soft curse before the door swings open just shy of violently. Violet's hair is pulled back, a messy bun sitting atop her head slightly askew, and her cheeks are flushed. I raise an eyebrow, and she grimaces.

"Don't act like you haven't been hot and bothered , too, Fae," she says.

I lean against the doorframe, fixing the waistband of my skirt. "Wasn't going to, Vi. Just didn't realize that you were busy. You could have told me to wait."

She waves a hand, walking to her desk.

"Did you get yours, too?" she asks, grabbing an identical letter, similarly unopened, from the corner of it.

"Yeah," I say, holding up mine.

She stares at it, the flush in her cheeks growing darker, and she groans under her breath, her shoulders slumping.

"Finally. I've been staring at mine all morning, but I didn't want to open it alone."

She settles onto her bed, and I sit next to her, crossing my legs. Balancing the envelope on my knee, I make quick work of pulling my hair into a haphazard braid.

"What is it? I don't remember reading about this step."

"They've settled on a list of packs for us and want us to rank them," she says, ripping her letter down the side and pulling out two folded sheets of paper. With a frown, I do the same, smoothing the first sheet on the bed in front of me.

Five small lines of text: Omaha, Denver, New Orleans, Louisville, Ceour d'Alene.

"These are cities," I say, the confusion and accusation clear in my tone. Violet laughs, setting her list next to mine.

None of them match.

"The Council tries to keep outside influences from interfering with the matches," she explains. "By giving cities, it decreases the chance of someone outside of the packs manipulating potential final pairings."

"Outside influences like your mom?" I ask after a pause, and Violet purses her lips before nodding once.

I look her over as she takes back her list. Her shoulders are rolled forward, and her fingers tap on her knees.

Clearing my throat, I ask, "What's wrong, Vi? You've been a nervous mess since we left the party. Did something happen that you didn't mention?"

She'd texted me while I was in between dance partners, trying to decide if I wanted to try and find Logan again and see if he was interested in more than just a kiss. When I found her, her makeup had been worn off, her eyes puffy, but she hadn't offered an explanation other than her desire to leave—and I hadn't pushed.

She gives a half-hearted sigh of a laugh. "Yeah. I met an Alpha, just like you."

I shove her. "Why didn't you tell me? Did he make you cry? Because I will find him and make him regret it."

She shrugs, and I snarl. She shoots me a glare, her hands running across her list of cities, pressing it into the mattress.

"He didn't make me cry," she says after a minute. "Jasper did."

My chest tightens. I grab her hand and squeeze tightly. "I'm sorry."

We're quiet for a bit.

"Did you like his pack?" I ask.

"He didn't introduce them," she admits in a whisper. She seems so unsure, and it takes me by surprise. I lace our fingers together and press my lips to her temple until I feel the tension in her body slowly melt away. "I really liked him, but I'm worried about why he didn't want me to meet the others. But he told me where he lives. And it's on here."

I'm quiet for a moment. "Do you want advice, or do you want support?"

She gives a smile and leans against me. "Just support. Did your guys mention where they live?"

I shake my head and glance at my list again. "I suppose it'll be fate alone that pairs us together. I'm going to take the day to think about it and then rank them on where I'd like to live."

"Good plan, Fae," she says, and I hold her hand just a bit tighter.

Five

CARTER

"Come on, man, hurry the hell up," Logan groans, leaning against the doorframe of my room.

I roll my eyes. "You already got me out and on the side of a mountain at the literal crack of dawn, Logan. Forgive me for dragging a bit in getting changed so we can go to lunch." I shake my head even as I pull off my shirt. Running my hands through my hair, I sigh. "Remind me again why we let you pick our Saturday outings? I know I like sunrises, but it's a bit much even for you this time of year."

Logan chuckles, a grin plastered on his smug face. "The Omegas seemed to appreciate that I keep you both in shape. Maybe the benefits outweigh the irritation, yeah?"

Damn it.

The last thing I want right now is to be reminded of the party last weekend. Every time I think about it, all I can focus on is Faedra's long, red hair draping over my hands, her freckles darkening with her blush, her curves pressed against me as she danced with us. And *that* always leads to—

"Holy hell, man. You need to calm down, or I won't be able to take you anywhere," Logan grumbles, and I scowl. I walk into my closet and take a deep breath, hands rubbing my shoulders. The distance doesn't deter Logan, though. "You scenting is nearly as bad as an Omega. And I, for one, do not have the patience for you trying to secure a hook-up today."

I grab a new set of clothes, walking straight toward the ensuite, not commenting on whether or not I should fuck someone just to try and get Faedra out of my head.

Instead, I say, "You're the one that brought up last weekend as if you haven't been jerking it out every night, too."

Logan scowls.

"Both of you need to get a move on. This was just delivered by some poor intern for the Council," Jude growls, filling the rest of my threshold. I pause, turning to him, an eyebrow raised. He holds an envelope up so we can both see it. My throat is suddenly dry, a leaden weight settling in my gut. We haven't gotten a notice like that in years.

"No way in hell am I opening this thing without a decent amount of liquor in me," he growls, his scowl lines around his mouth etched deep. "Let's go."

He leaves just as quickly as he appeared, feet falling lightly on the hardwood of our home. Logan quirks an eyebrow and follows almost immediately afterward, closing my door with a soft click. Blowing out a breath, I rush through getting ready after our morning hike. Hair adequately styled and my hiking gear replaced with a polo and khaki shorts, I grab my phone and wallet and then head out to meet the guys.

"Fuck me, we've really been shortlisted?" Jude asks, surprise and dread weaving together, making his voice drop until it rumbles through him. "Part of me was convinced they were notifying us to stop trying."

Ignoring Jude entirely, Logan grins and sets the letter on the table between us, using an empty cup to keep it from folding back up. I scan it, devouring the information, and then take a long pull from my Irish coffee, reminding myself to be prudent. My body isn't interested in prudence, though, happily reminding me of the feel of Faedra's skin and the soft timbre of her voice as she sang along to the songs while we danced. Pine mixes with the smells of the restaurant.

"Carter," Jude groans.

I grunt, rubbing my eyes with my palms before taking another drink.

I'm not sure I can do this again, to be honest. This isn't the first time we've been shortlisted for matching after a gala. In the early days, we were shortlisted after every single one. But a week later, we always received a packet with a single page in it, notifying us that we weren't matched. By the third time, I was ready to never be shortlisted again. It probably won't be any different this time, too. When I say as much, Logan purses his lips.

"We're going to be optimistic, Carter. Jude's cynicism is enough for all three of us."

Except I'm the realist between us, the one that looks at whatever is happening and sees it as it is. And the reality is that our numbers are absolute shit for this. If I were looking at this like a business deal, I'd walk out with zero remorse. There was nothing but shattered dreams at the end of this.

Logan shoves me, pulling me from my thoughts, and then unfolds the second sheet of paper. My palms go clammy, and I tip my head back, staring at the pendant lights hanging from the ceiling, unfocusing my eyes and then refocusing them, counting back from ten in my head.

"Is she on there?" Jude asks, the question practically *shy*, and I drop my head just in time to see him take a long pull from his beer, his cheeks red under his beard.

Logan's brows are furrowed as he looks it over, and then his lips quirk into a barely there half smile.

"She's listed second," he says. "It's been long enough I don't remember if the order they're listed actually matters."

Jude shakes his head. "They're alphabetical by last name. That's what Doug said, at least, and he'd have a pretty good idea of how the internal process works."

Doug, Willa, and Mark matched with Brianna nearly three years ago. We'd gone to the gala where they'd met. Willa worked for the Council shortly after graduating college, so she knew it could take a while to be matched. Turns out, the first time was the charm.

Part of me still holds a measure of jealousy over it.

I shove the memories aside and clear my throat, moving my empty glass to the edge of the table for the server to take when they're able. I ask the necessary question without preamble. "Do we consent to being shortlisted?"

Logan sets the list on the table in front of him, smoothing it out. Jude leans over, reading the names.

"I'm not sure," he says after a minute, his scowl firmly in place again. "I can't place another name off this list from the gala, and I didn't spend half the time with her that you both did."

I press the base of my palms into my eyes again, trying to turn off the part of my brain telling me this was all just a waste of time.

"If we don't, will you be haunted by the possibility of what might have been?" I ask when the others don't say anything. I pull my left wrist far enough away that I can read the small Latin script.

Remember to live.

Logan runs his hands through his hair before nodding. "Absolutely. I'll always wonder if it could've been her."

"She intrigued me," Jude says instead of a simple yes or no. We've been friends long enough that I don't need to ask for more. He wants a chance to interact with her for longer.

"We talked about choosing to withdraw in January," I say, pulling the sheet of paper toward me. "How are we feeling now? Because I think I'm ready to consider it."

"Let's wait until after this one. Kick the can down the road another week. If…" Logan trails off, even his enthusiasm waning.

Jude clears his throat. "If it doesn't happen this time, we'll submit the paperwork to deactivate."

I pull a pen from my pocket, filling out the requisite information and then signing at the bottom.

Logan regains some of his pep. "I'm going to choose to hold out some level of optimism."

"Good," I say, handing him the information so he can get it sent off. "One of us needs to be."

FAEDRA

"Thirty minutes remaining."

The announcement jars me out of my daydream, and I internally groan while attempting to refocus on the final exam in front of me. It's my last one—and my most difficult. Which is unfortunate because my mind can't seem to be bothered with the nuances of Dostoevsky's works.

In hindsight, I probably should have decided to attend the Matching Gala the council is holding in August. But I hadn't honestly expected to meet a pack that enthralled me so thoroughly. Or to be so consumed with anxiety while I wait for the Council to inform me of their decision. Two weeks seems like such a short time on paper, but it's wholly different experiencing it drag by in real time. It doesn't help that Violet got her papers yesterday.

I jot down what is hopefully halfway coherent concluding thoughts and then gather my things, prepping to beg Martha for an early release from the final. I'm ridiculously hungry and in desperate need of another date with my vibrator. Not that it does much, not since meeting Logan, Carter, and Jude at the party, but taking the edge off is imperative when you are an Omega trying to avoid unwanted attention from Alphas. Especially since I'm already on the maximum dose of suppressant doctors are allowed to prescribe.

The door at the back of the class opens, and everyone looks up from their tests. A man walks between tables, intent on Martha sitting at the desk in the front. She looks up from her stack of papers, a scowl already in place, but she quickly drops to a neutral expression.

There's no mistaking this man is from the Council. He's dressed in a well-tailored navy suit, a simple black tie held in place with a silver tack. Tucked under one arm is a large white envelope, conspicuously devoid of any writing. And on his lapel is a pin of the Council's insignia. My heart races. My hands are shaking as I shove the rest of my supplies in my bag. The man leans across the desk, setting the envelope carefully on the surface, and whispers something to Martha. Her eyes flick to me and then she nods.

"Faedra, are you finished with the final?" My professor's voice cuts across the room.

"I am."

I'm surprised that my voice is steady. She nods and reaches out a hand, and I focus on keeping my hands steady as I cross the room and give her the essay.

The man turns towards me, hand pressed against the

envelope. "Ms. Wilson, it's a pleasure to meet you," he says, holding out his other hand. I take it with a smile, and he nods before handing me the unmarked envelope. "You'll have forty-eight hours to review the information and respond to the Council using the official letterhead enclosed. If you consent to the match, there's a video call tentatively scheduled for Friday night with the pack. My contact information is on the first page, and you can notify me if you are accepting of the appointment, as well as to address any questions or concerns."

"Thank you, sir," I say, taking the envelope from him and holding it against my belly. With a nod, he turns and walks out of the room, paying no one else any attention.

"Faedra, you're more than welcome to leave," Martha says, her voice quiet, keeping the rest of the class from hearing. "I won't make you wait the last twenty minutes to find out your pack. That's just cruel."

A small smile. Martha is an Omega, paired with her pack over a decade ago. "Thanks, Martha."

She smiles, too. "Of course." Her face grows serious. "The Council doesn't talk about it much, but know that you are allowed to request a different pairing. Appeals from family might not always work, but an appeal from the Omega is always taken seriously."

I nod, clutching the packet tighter. "Thanks for the reminder. I'll see you at commencement," I say. Grabbing my bag and draping it over my shoulder, I leave the class at just shy of a run. I keep my head down, the packet still held protectively against me, as I navigate the halls of the history building. My phone pings with a text just as I step out into the courtyard.

I check the text on the way towards my preferred quiet area on campus, and I smile a bit at Violet's name.

> Saw a Council rep just leave the science building. Think they're delivering another round of papers. Did you get yours?

> Yep. Want to read it with me? I'll be at the tree.

> Give me five.

'The tree' is actually a small collection of trees that grow around one of the main walkways through the campus. But Violet and I always sit under the same one, tucked towards the back away from the sidewalk. It's across campus from me, so I do my best to not panic as I head over to it.

By the time I see Violet standing under it, my heart is in my throat and I can't quite manage to pull in a full breath.

"Oh shit, Fae. Were you in the middle of that final?" Violet asks as soon as I'm within a few feet of her. I nod, and she grimaces. "Did you at least get to finish it?"

"As much as I was going to be able to even without the papers. My brain is fried right now, Vi."

She grimaces again. "A couple more weeks and you'll finally be able to come off the suppressants."

"Yeah, and that was my last final. So at least the only thing left is not falling on my face walking across the stage." I set my bag under the tree before settling on the ground and tilting my head towards the sun. "I didn't expect to really want a specific pairing, Vi. That's the worst part of this. If there had been multiple packs I had fun with at the party, I feel like I wouldn't be so nervous now."

Violet shakes her head and sits down next to me, stretching her legs out in front of her, her hands rubbing the denim of her shorts.

"Scarlett was a mess, and she didn't feel any special interest in any of the Alphas at her party. Pretty sure the nerves are just part of the whole experience." She rolls her eyes as she says it, and I can't help but laugh.

"When's your video call?" I ask, picking at the seal on the packet.

Violet raises an eyebrow. "Stalling?"

My cheeks heat, and she laughs. "I haven't seen you since you got your papers. Maybe I'm just trying to be a good friend and check in on you."

She rolls her eyes again, shaking her head. "It's tomorrow night. When did they say yours is?"

"Friday," I admit.

She hums. When I continue to pick at the seal, she sighs.

"The sooner you open it, the sooner we can go get drinks. And once we have drinks, I'll tell you the pack I matched with," Violet says, and I grin. Trust my best friend to know how to get me to do something. They say curiosity kills the cat—they wouldn't be wrong to say that of me, too.

My hands shake as I rip the seal and pull the large packet out. The informational letter from the Council chairman sits on top, printed on the official letterhead, the watermark of the Council insignia taking up most of the page. I read carefully, aware of Violet watching me.

"Why do they include a letter when it says all the same things the process server told me in person?" I ask, sighing, and move the letter to the bottom of the stack.

A small paper slips out as I do, and I grab it off the ground before dirt can ruin it. My heart races as I realize it's a picture. With a deep breath, I flip it over. My breath catches in my throat.

"Oh shit! That's definitely the guy that chatted with us towards the beginning of the party." Violet's laughing. "That's them, right, Fae?"

And then I'm laughing, too, grinning. "Y-yeah," I manage to say, trying to actually take in the photo of the Alphas.

It's a candid shot at a restaurant of some kind. Jude stands in the middle, dressed nearly identical to how I met him at the party, his beard a bit less gray, a tumbler of whiskey in one hand, eyes on Carter and a small smile on his lips. The others are both dressed more casually, in simple Oxford shirts and black ties. Logan's hand is on Carter's shoulder, head thrown back in laughter, and Carter's rolling his eyes even as he's smiling.

My smile stretches as I trace the lines of each of the Alphas. The memory of Carter's hands on me has me clenching my thighs.

"What's their pack name? I didn't bother to read his lapel pin at the party," Violet says, breaking me out of the daydream.

"Bennett," I rasp. I flip through the packet of paperwork, looking over the basic information before pulling the response letter out.

Violet hums. "You know, Faedra Bennett has a pretty good ring to it." I giggle like I'm twelve again, and she grins. "I'm ready to find hearts all over the dorm with FB in the center, girl."

"Only if you draw your own next to them," I say, sticking out my tongue. I set the paperwork on my lap and dig through my bag, finding a pen that I'd shoved in haphazardly after the final.

Violet squeezes my knee and sets her head on my shoulder. "It's early enough you could get that sent to the Council and have everything official before their offices close tonight."

I nod, quickly signing the bottom of the acceptance letter before grabbing my bag and standing back up. "Want to come with me to drop it off and then we can go for those drinks?"

"Hell yeah, Fae. Let's go."

Six

JUDE

My heart pounds, my chest tightening with each minute that passes, each floor that the elevator climbs in our building. I glance at the text from Logan again, halfway convinced it's a figment of my imagination. Maybe I *want* it to be from my imagination.

> Council member just left.

I don't know if I'm ready to face the reality of us deactivating with the Council. The last five years have been difficult, and I hate the idea of walking away from all of this with nothing to show for it.

Fuck, that sounds terrible, as if being matched with an Omega is nothing more than an item on a proverbial checklist. In reality, it's one of my most ardent desires.

The elevator opens, and I brush off the train of thought, forcing my mind to stillness as I work to get into the condo. I bypass the drop tray just inside the door, and head deeper into our home. A nondescript manila envelope sits on the kitchen island, and I clench my hands tight enough for my nails to bite, breathing through my nose to keep my heart from racing. Logan sits in one of the lounge chairs, his elbows on his knees, his fingers steepled, focused on the windows lining the living room. He flicks his gaze to me.

"Carter called the girls," he says, forgoing any niceties.

Good. If we're going to close this part of our life out, I don't want us to be alone. Gina and Ashlynn will keep us from sinking too low. Will they want to separate all the assets? The idea of living alone is about as appealing as hiking Zion in the heat of summer.

"They're almost here?" I ask, keeping my thoughts to myself.

When he nods, I drop into the other armchair, focusing on the city outside, the mountains standing tall, the sun just starting to creep into the condo as it ticks over into the afternoon, burning a wide strip of light across the living room. It's another ten minutes before they arrive, Gina and Ashlynn holding hands while they laugh about something, Hallie asleep where she's strapped to Gina's chest in a star decorated carrier.

Ashlynn catches my gaze. Whatever she sees must be pretty haggard because she lets go of Gina's hand and crosses the living room before I can even manage to say something. She perches on the edge of the chair, grasping my arm, and I lean against her.

"It'll be worth it," she murmurs, and I cover her hand with my own.

Carter rubs his shoulders before setting his phone on the island, picking up the packet without a word to any of us and walking over.

Does it seem thicker than the other ones were? I'm not sure. The others all had a single piece of paper, one small paragraph informing us that our dreams would have to wait for the next gala.

In a sign of willpower I don't possess, Carter's hands are steady, breaking the seal and pulling the small packet of papers out before I can manage to take a fortifying breath.

Wait. *Papers?*

Tears well in Carter's eyes as he pulls the informative letter from the top of the pile and passes it to me. Logan moves to look over my shoulder. There's a collective breath as we read the decision together.

Pack Bennett,

It is with great pride that we are able to inform you of being selected for matching with Ms. Faedra Wilson of Los Angeles. Please find enclosed...

The rest of the letter blurs as tears flood my eyes. Gina whoops, startling the baby, but she doesn't apologize as she rushes around the back of the chairs to wrap her arms around Carter. Ashlynn laughs, hugging me. Logan and I share a shell shocked look while I try to process what I've read.

Selected for matching.

Four years of galas. Five years of torment from Melanie. Six rounds of being shortlisted to be told *no*.

We've matched.

We have a chance to prove worthy of an Omega.

CARTER

"Fuck, but this feels like an interview," Jude mutters, settling into the seat next to me. His hair is styled, pulled off his forehead with gel, his beard trimmed within an inch of its life. "And I haven't had to do one of those in almost a decade. How the hell do you do this all the time, Logan?"

Logan shrugs, clicking through the joint pack email until he finds the link to the video chat the Council sent yesterday. "It hasn't ever bothered me. But they don't feel like interviews to me. They're pretty chill. And the sporting world is small, especially the semi-pro circles. We all mostly know of each other already."

I lean forward, resting my elbows on the desk in front of me. Logan's office is bright and carefree, the perfect reflection of the man. My gaze skates over the large canvas portrait he has hung behind the desk, aligned just right to be seen on his work calls. The three of us stand at the precipice of a canyon, hiking backpacks peaking over our shoulders.

I wonder if Faedra enjoys camping, too.

The video chat loads after a few moments, but it's not Faedra's face I see at first. A young man sits in the main window, his white shirt offset by a dark grey tie, the council's insignia serving as his tie clip.

He smiles and says, "Hello Pack Bennett. Faedra should be joining any minute now. Do you have any questions for me while we wait?"

Logan and I shake our heads. Jude leans forward and asks, "What's the timeline after this call? The information was vague beyond due dates for paperwork."

The man nods once like he was expecting the question, and I figure it's probably pretty commonly asked. I tap my fingers on the hard maple top of Logan's desk.

"After this, the Council steps back and lets you interact organically. Final paperwork to either request a different match or make this selection permanent is typically due thirty days from now." He shuffles some papers around in front of him. "However, Ms. Wilson has requested an extension." Jude grunts, and the man glances up, nodding again. "The Council granted it. Instead of thirty days, you'll have sixty."

Logan and I share a look. Why would she ask for such a long extension?

"Are we allowed to know why she did?" Jude asks.

The man nods, pulling a piece of paper from the stack and setting it atop the pile.

"She cited her inability to facilitate a move in the next two weeks, which would decrease the effective Window of Exploration to fourteen days. She requested an extension to forty-five days to accommodate this, but the Council opted for a longer extension to alleviate time pressures regarding cross state moves."

I roll my shoulders, closing my eyes to recalibrate. Nothing about that screams that she regrets the decision of the Council.

"As you don't currently reside in the same city," the man continues, "it'll be up to you all to decide how you want to navigate that. If you choose to move where she is currently—or if you as a group decide to relocate to somewhere entirely new—you'll need to file the necessary paperwork with the Council. Her moving to you doesn't require any additional paperwork."

"Does she know all this?" Logan asks. The man nods. He glances somewhere else on his screen, and a moment later a small chime sounds.

"Ah, here she is. Let me get her added, and then I'll leave you all to it," he says.

Another half minute passes, and then Faedra's on the screen, her red hair pulled away from her face, a few short pieces framing her cheeks. Her eyes are framed by slim winged liner and thick lashes, black from mascara, and her smile makes her freckles stand out along her nose and cheekbones.

"Good evening, Ms. Wilson," the man says, smiling again. Faedra blushes and offers a small greeting back. "I know you've already been briefed, but before I log off and let you all chat, is there anything you need from me?"

Faedra shakes her head. "Thank you, Matthias," she says, her voice the same mellow, sensual cadence that had captivated me at the party. Jude sits up straight, dropping his hands to his lap, and Logan mirrors me, elbows resting on the desk.

"This call will automatically end in an hour," Matthias says. "So don't panic if it cuts out. I encourage you to start by exchanging contact information."

We all nod, and Faedra glances off screen for a moment, shaking her head.

"Perfect. Have a good night," he says before his square on the screen disappears.

Logan clears his throat. "Everything alright, Faedra?"

She blushes again, looking at us, and nods. "Yeah, just trying to convince Violet that I don't need her here for emotional support." There's a sharp noise from somewhere in her space, and then she laughs, shaking her head. "Don't even start, Vi. We both know you were way more nervous than me. I'll be fine."

"What if I just want to meet the rest of them?" a woman says, her voice almost sharp but tinged with humor.

Faedra rolls her eyes. "I'm positive you'll get to meet them in person—which is way more up your alley, anyway." She pauses. "When I'm done, we can go to that new pinball bar," she offers, her cadence dropping to one of persuasion.

Violet makes a noise, Faedra laughs, and the soft sound of a door closing comes through the video chat. She glances back at the screen, biting her lip.

"Sorry," she says. I shake my head, and Logan chuckles. "Vi is really protective of me."

"If I hadn't met her at the party, I'd be convinced she's an Alpha," Logan jokes, and Faedra nods.

"We've confused people when we're out and about. They assume she's an Alpha, and I'm a Beta."

Jude tilts his head, frowning. "Who could possibly mistake you for a Beta?"

She shrugs, looking down. "I don't crave touch the way most Omegas do," she admits after a moment. Logan nods.

"Well that fits right in with us," I say, and her eyes cut to me, an eyebrow raised. "We don't crave touch that way, either. At least not to the point where we solicit for it from anyone. We like being in control of when and how."

"Before we start down any more conversation, can I have your number so I can text you?" Logan asks as Jude is about to say something. Faedra smiles, just a bit, and my chest warms. She nods and rattles off a number, Logan putting it in his phone and then sending off a group text that includes Jude and me. We quickly respond with our names so she can tell which number is each of ours. She taps on her phone for a few more minutes before setting it face down next to her.

"So..." she says, letting her voice trail off. "I'm not all that great with this kind of thing."

Logan gives a half smile, running his hand through his short hair. "That's alright. Neither is Jude," he says, chuckling, pointing at Jude. Jude grunts and rolls his eyes but doesn't discredit Logan. Faedra smiles. "How did your finals go?"

She shrugs. "They went alright. I haven't gotten my scores yet, but I did get the official notice saying I've passed well enough to graduate, and that's most important right now." She perches her chin on her open palm. "Would you be interested in coming to that?"

"Absolutely," I answer for all of us without hesitation. "Send us the information, and we'll make sure we're there."

She grabs her phone and taps a few times before setting it down again. My phone vibrates a moment later, and I take the opportunity to set a reminder to discuss the trip with Amanda on Monday. Two weeks is more than enough time for her to adjust whatever needs to change in my schedule.

"So you all live in Denver," she says after another stilted pause. Jude blows out a breath and nods. She looks at Logan. "I understand better what you said about not being overly homesick. Everything I've seen of there looks gorgeous."

"I love it," Logan says. "There's so many good hiking and camping options within an hour or two, and the backpacking choices are phenomenal as well. Anything outdoorsy, really. We try to get out every weekend, especially in the summer since Jude doesn't have the same amount of workload as he does during the rest of the school year."

Her head tilts a bit, eyes skating down Jude.

"I know," he mutters, gruff. "It's not what most people expect me to enjoy. But being out in nature with people I like is significantly better than being surrounded by people I don't know."

"Which is why my date to sporting events is always Carter," Logan jokes, sighing dramatically. "Not that he really cares, but he's good at amusing me."

"I haven't camped since I was a kid," Faedra admits. "But Vi and I have been to a few hockey games since living in L.A. I've always enjoyed them."

Logan grins, and I chuckle a bit.

"Maybe we can go camping this summer," I offer. "Nothing too intense, just something far enough away to feel removed from everything."

Faedra gives a soft agreement, and I tap my fingers on the desk. She looks over at me, eyebrows furrowed a bit.

"What's wrong?" she asks, growing quiet. A low growl comes from Jude, and Logan raises an eyebrow, looking him over, the surprise evident in his dropped shoulders.

I shake my head, giving her a half smile. "Just trying to decide the best way to ask you about moving out here. Do you share a place with Violet?"

"We're both R.A.s, so we share a dorm suite. Move out is the same weekend as graduation."

Jude nods. "We'll help get everything sorted while we're out there, then. I can have a moving truck scheduled for the day after commencement, and then you can fly out when you're ready later that week."

She smiles, her countenance lighting up, and I can't help but lean towards her, even knowing that a screen and a thousand miles separate us.

"That sounds perfect." She pauses, and her cheeks darken with an intense blush, maroon against her pale complexion. "I'm excited to see you all again."

Even Jude grins at that.

Seven

LOGAN

About the same time my eyes start blurring from staring at the two different spreadsheets the accountant sent me earlier in the week, my phone rings. I groan, rubbing my eyes as I dig it out of the drawers behind my desk, not bothering to look at the name as I swipe to answer the call.

"Bennett," I say, setting the phone in front of me and looking at the spreadsheets again.

"Logan?" Faedra's warm voice fills the office, and I curse, grabbing my phone.

Faedra's sitting on the ground with her computer on her lap, her phone propped somewhere to give a view of her and a gray sofa that she leans against. Her hair is pulled back, and she's wearing the necklace she wore at the gala, the opal nestled in the hollow of her throat.

Hell, I never thought I'd be jealous of a piece of jewelry, but here we are.

She smiles as I say hello and lean my phone against the computer monitor.

"Is this a decent time?" she asks, biting her lip. "I can call back later."

I shake my head. "Just trying to sort through some payment information the accountant sent me."

She grimaces, and I laugh.

"What are you working on? I thought your finals were done," I ask, closing out of the spreadsheets and pulling up my client schedule instead.

"I'm looking up quilting patterns," she admits, her cheeks dark with a sudden blush. I raise an eyebrow. "I picked up the hobby about a year ago. I really enjoy it because you can have these super small pieces that can fit in your bag but they end up becoming intricate projects. It's very satisfying."

Her face lights up as she offers the explanation, her eyes brightening. It's the same look she had at the gala when her and Jude were talking about literature. It makes me want to kiss her. Everything makes me want to kiss her.

Next week can't come fast enough.

"Are you starting a new project then?" I ask.

She nods, turning the computer screen just enough that I can see a picture of a blanket with a wreath of flowers around the edge. "I'm going with Violet tomorrow to get some fabric for it. I was thinking about using all of your favorite colors, actually. I was going to ask the others tonight."

She pauses, turning the computer back towards her, her eyebrow rising as I hesitate to respond.

"Do you not have a favorite color, Logan? I know some people don't."

I shake my head. "Not necessarily," I say. Though that copper of her hair is quickly becoming one. "I tend to gravitate towards greens and wood tones, though."

She nods. "Like your office," she says, typing something before grinning.

"So what's your favorite color then?" I ask.

"Blue." Her answer is immediate.

My email chimes, and Faedra glances at me. "Do you need to go?"

I shake my head, opening the email. A moment later, I grin.

"What is it?" she asks.

"Remember that college contract I told you about a couple nights ago?"

She nods and leans forward.

"I just got offered it."

∼

FAEDRA

"Alright, Faedra Rose. Put the guys to work and then tell me about these Alphas."

My mom stands on the threshold of my shared dorm, a bright smile lighting her face, her red hair pulled back into a no-nonsense braid, a large bag of Chinese takeout in one hand. Dad and Aiden stand just behind her, dressed down in cotton shorts and t-shirts. Aiden rolls his eyes at Mom's comment, but Dad chuckles and steps around her to give me a hug. His lips brush over my hair, and I smile into his chest.

"How about we start with some lunch? We came straight from the airport, and Aiden has been cranky since we left Boston," Dad offers, guiding me into the shared kitchenette and living room. Violet sits on the couch, scrolling through her phone, but glances up with a grin as we walk inside. "There she is! I was wondering if we'd get to see you or if you'd be out of here already."

Violet laughs and gives my dad a hug. "I thought I told you two years ago that you're stuck with me for life, Jay."

He hums as he starts pulling food from takeout containers. Aiden stands next to me, and I smile, giving him the stereotypical sibling one arm hug. "How was your last semester of med school, then?"

"Fine," Aiden offers. He stands at least six inches taller than me, but his voice has always been soft. "Settled into the new apartment and ready to start internship in July."

He brushes by me to get to the food, clearly finished with the conversation. Anybody else, and I'd be halfway convinced they were upset with me. But Aiden has always been slow to words, absorbing the world around him before choosing to interact.

"So who are these men my daughter is going to be living with?" my mom asks as Dad grabs plates and then settles into the living room chair with his food. She wastes no time getting her own food while Violet fills two plates with the Kung Pao my family hasn't touched and brings one to me. "They live in Denver, right? And you said they're really into camping. What are their names? What do they do for a living? What—"

"Elizabeth," my father cuts in, a touch of humor in his exasperated tone. She huffs but doesn't continue, looking at me with an eyebrow raised.

"The pack name is Bennett," I offer after a few bites of food. Violet giggles, shaking her head as my mom scowls. I can't help but laugh, pointing my fork at her. "How do you know I've gotten a chance to really get to know them?" I joke, and Mom rolls her eyes.

"Because you're *you*, Faedra Rose. Curiosity might as well be your middle name."

My cheeks heat. She's right, of course. We've spent nearly every evening on video calls, getting to know each other—and I spend a lot of it blushing like a damn maiden, but I try not to let that bother me. Logan's taken to calling me during the day, too, when he's catching up on his admin work.

"Logan's an athletic trainer that works mostly with semi-pro athletes, especially ones that are trying to make the jump to professional. He said he mostly does baseball," I explain before my dad can get his hopes up. "Though he mentioned he just got selected for a contract with one of the downtown college hockey teams."

My dad grins. Mom clucks her tongue, and I continue. "Carter owns a tech start-up. I don't really understand it, but it has something to do with drone mapping of farmlands. And Jude is tenured at CU Denver."

"He's old enough to be tenured?" Aiden asks, and I blush. "I thought the Council paired everyone up so there weren't huge age gaps."

Violet snorts. "Every year the Council pushes Omegas into matching younger and younger. We were some of the oldest ones there this time."

My mom frowns. "Just how old are they, Fae?"

My blush darkens, and I focus on my food for a few minutes to avoid answering.

"Faedra," my dad says, warning clear in his tone. I take a deep breath and keep my eyes down.

"Logan is 35. Carter turns 40 in August, and Jude turned 40 in February," I say in one quick rush. "His birthday is a week after mine."

Aiden's eyes are wide, and Mom does her best to hide her surprise by fussing with the takeout containers, shuffling them around and setting a couple in the fridge. Dad hums, head tilted just a bit, and I can tell he seems to be the least upset about the age gap.

"Well, the Council has been doing this for a long time. I'm sure they had a reason for selecting this pack for you." He gives a pointed look at my mom as she huffs, clearly ready to start an argument. "We'll reserve any judgment until we meet them."

Relief floods me, and my shoulders drop. My mom sighs, glaring a bit at Dad, and starts interrogating Violet instead.

"So tell us about your match, Vi. Where are you moving to?"

Violet leans against me. "I'm actually staying here."

"That's fantastic!" Mom gushes. "Have you gotten to spend a lot of time with them, then?"

Violet nods. "It's been great. Way less stressful than Faedra's current set up."

I scoff and shake my head. "Liar. You're nervous every time you go to meet up with them."

"You would be too if the Beta you had a fling with in high school was part of the pack you've been matched with," Violet says testily.

I can't help but giggle as Aiden chokes on his bite of food.

"Betas aren't that common in packs, though," he sputters after a moment. His eyes are wide as he looks over Violet. "How the hell did you manage to draw that match?"

"The Council works in mysterious ways," she jokes, and I giggle. She shrugs after a moment, standing to set her cleared plate on the counter. "Reconnecting with Jasper has been the easiest part of it, actually. It's one of the Alphas that's making me consider appealing the match."

A thread of vulnerability runs through her comment, and I'm quick to come to her rescue before my family can bombard her with Beta-typical advice. Not that my family isn't incredibly supportive. Omegas are just wired differently—or so I've been told. Their advice has always made sense to me.

"They're flying in tonight for the ceremony tomorrow morning," I say. "They're supposed to get in sometime around seven, and they're staying in one of the hotels near the airport."

We'd chatted lightly about going out tonight, but I had

hesitated in confirming anything until my family had gotten out here. I wanted to make sure I spent enough time with them, too. And part of me doesn't want to have my first time knotting with an Alpha to happen in a hotel. Everything I've read and heard about the experience impresses the idea that it's life-changing. Certainly not something you could really ever prep to feel—though the toys on the market try to argue otherwise. And, honestly, if I'm going to have some world altering moment with an Alpha, I'd rather it happen somewhere I can revisit.

I know. It's cliché as hell. But I am who I am. And *that* is as sentimental as an old lady remembering her first love.

Mom gets that glint in her eye that tells me she's about to hatch a diabolical plan, and I feel vindicated in waiting to tell the guys we could do something alone tonight. My dad must notice it, too, because he intervenes before she can say anything.

"We're excited to meet them *tomorrow*."

The emphasis causes my mom to pout. "But tomorrow is going to be impossible between the ceremony and getting everything situated for the move."

Aiden sighs. Dad stands up, sets his plate on the counter, and then surveys the space, hands on his hips. "You said the truck will be here tomorrow?"

I nod, not commenting on him sidestepping what Mom said. "The goal was to have it come Sunday, but cross-country movers are at a premium right now, and they only had a slot left for tomorrow afternoon."

"Sounds like tomorrow's going to be hectic. Let's get this done so that your mom has enough time to actually breathe instead of just bombarding your pack with questions, yeah?" he says, hugging me again, and I smile. Violet laughs, and my mom rolls her eyes even as we all set about getting the dorm packed for the final time.

My fingers tap on the counter, my eyes glued to the phone next to them, my heart in my throat.

"Still nothing?" Violet asks, stepping out of what used to be her room. Her pack helped her get everything moved to their place yesterday so that my family was only tripping over one set of boxes. When I shake my head, she sighs and steps up next to me, wrapping an arm around my waist. "The flight probably just got delayed. It's only been half an hour since they were supposed to land."

I nod, biting my lip.

"Jasper's outside. Want me to have him come in? We can stay until they call."

I swallow and nod. "He won't mind?"

She gives me that half smile that tells me she thinks I'm ridiculous. She pulls her phone from her back pocket and taps out a quick text. My eyes invariably land back on my own dark screen. We don't break the silence as we wait for Jasper to come in, and when he opens the door a few minutes later, he doesn't offer any kind of empty greeting. He simply comes to stand on Violet's other side, setting a soft kiss against her hair.

Each minute that passes ratchets my nerves tighter, coiling in my belly until I'm pretty sure I'll be sick if I try to say anything. Violet and Jasper are having a soft conversation, the murmurs blurring, and I'm too distracted to try to figure out what they're saying. Forty-five minutes after they were supposed to land, Logan's picture finally shows up on my phone as it vibrates with his incoming call. I let out a hard sigh, swallowing twice to try to settle my stomach, and then answer it.

"Faedra?" Logan asks, frazzled, the drone of voices surrounding him filling the background.

"Hey," I answer.

"Sorry, we just finally got off the plane. It left Denver late and then there were storms over the mountains." He explains, and I hear Carter murmur something near him, like he's trying to buy something. "Are you still wanting to meet up with us tonight? We understand if you'd prefer to stay in."

Violet lifts an eyebrow in question, and I nod, hugging her with my open arm. Jasper grabs her hand and leads her out of the dorm while I collect my purse, the small bag I'd packed, and my dress and robes for the commencement.

"Yeah, I'd love to see you all," I say. "Where should I meet you?"

He rattles off the name of the hotel they're staying in, and I switch him to speaker so I can request a ride share.

"Um, Logan?" I ask, my voice growing breathless from my worry.

"What's up?"

"Can I stay with you all tonight?" I ask, biting my lip. "The dorm's completely packed, and Violet's already moved out."

There's a short pause, and I hear one of the other men laugh in the background.

"Of course, Red. We'll see you in a bit, alright?"

Eight

JUDE

The flight to Los Angeles is a complete dumpster fire.

There's a mixup with our tickets, so instead of being in business class, we're offered standard economy tickets with free food and a hefty refund. But naturally the seats aren't together, so I'm wedged next to a woman in her mid-thirties that spends the first hour clearly trying to work up the courage to start a conversation with me. And since the flight leaves more than half an hour late on account of the plane hitting a bird on its previous flight, her deciding to make a move on me ends up being in the first half of the flight—which means the second half was spent in awkward silence due to me turning her down. Why can't this shit happen to Logan since he's the one that actually enjoys talking to strangers? And to put salt in the wound, there's turbulence over the Sierra-Nevadas that's bad enough to make me seriously reconsider if I, in fact, do get motion sick.

By the time the three of us arrange ourselves into the rental

Carter's assistant booked for us, I'm ready to just lay low at the hotel until the ceremony tomorrow. I'm no stranger to commencements—I sit through two a year, after all. But I can confidently say I haven't been so nervous for one since awarded my undergrad. Blowing out a sigh, I pull out my eReader, intent on finishing the book I hadn't been able to read on the flight. Carter pulls his phone and chuckles.

"She text you?" Logan asks, keeping his eyes on the road.

"Yeah, she wanted to make sure you'd asked us, too."

Logan huffs. "Don't see why I need your approval. You're my pack mates, not my damn parents."

I set down the tablet. "Asked us what?"

Carter turns in his seat, holding up his phone to show me the text.

> Hey, Logan seemed really frazzled. Just wanted to double check he made sure it was ok with you that I stay at the hotel tonight.

> I don't want to intrude. It's just that the dorm is empty and packed.

My eyebrows raise, and I attempt to rearrange my mind so that I can actually enjoy her presence tonight.

"Are there enough beds?" I ask when Carter turns back around.

Logan grunts. "You really think I would tell her she can stay if there wasn't enough space? Good God, Jude. What has climbed up your ass the last week?"

"Same thing that's climbed up yours," I mutter, tilting my head and shutting my eyes. "You just handle it with excessive humor and extra workouts."

"Don't forget calling her in the middle of the day, too," Carter says. A hard smack sounds from in front of me a moment before Carter curses. I shake my head and do my best to tune them out for the rest of the drive, focusing instead on the remembered sensations of Faedra's soft skin and silky hair. Logan groans from the driver's seat, but I ignore him, using the time to become excited for my Omega.

～

The sight of her knocks the breath from my lungs, and I can't help but stand on the curb like a dumbass teenager, staring at her from across the patio. Her skin is aglow under the warm lights of the hotel, the oversized shirt she's wearing falling off one shoulder, highlighting the curves of her collar bone and throat. Her freckles stand out against her pale skin, and her hair is pulled away from her face. She glances up as Carter closes his door and Logan chats with the valet. My chest clenches as she smiles, a carefree moment that radiates joy. Carter starts across the space, and I follow close behind, closing the distance between us as if we are magnets unerringly attracted to each other.

"Hey," she says, shy, her cheeks darkening with a quick blush. I hold out my hand, a silent request for the garment bag folded over her arm, and she hands it over after a brief hesitation. Carter hesitates, eyebrows furrowed, and Logan steps up between us a few moments later, not pausing as he pulls Faedra into his arms.

"Hi, Red," he murmurs, and Carter looks over at me, eyebrow raised.

What I wouldn't give in this moment to be the outgoing man that Logan is.

She pulls away from him and turns to me, blushing again.

"How are you?" I ask in lieu of another greeting, offering my arms, and she moves into me without pause, settling her palms across my upper back and pressing her cheek against my chest. I can't help but brush my lips across the crown of her head, and she relaxes further into me, her Omega nature responding to the physical touch.

"Tired," she admits before pulling away. "I know we talked about going out. We still can if you want. Santa Monica is beautiful."

Carter shakes his head. "Only if you want to, Faedra."

Shaking her head, she steps into him, too, a rueful smile playing at her lips. He takes her bag from her as she pulls away, slinging it over his shoulder before grabbing the handle of his suitcase.

"Let's get checked in and settled, then," Logan offers, leading our group—pack—into the hotel.

"You're sure you're alright with me taking that entire half of the suite?" Faedra checks again, like she has the last three times since we settled on the sleeping arrangement.

An unspoken agreement between us guys means that we're not bringing up knotting until she's in Denver. And that means there's no way I can sleep in the same room as her. Some men might have better control, but I don't, and I'm honest about it. Logan and Carter seem to understand, too, because they adjust so that it doesn't just look like me that has a problem with sharing a space with her.

Logan nods. "It's fine, Red. One of us was going to end up sleeping out here anyway. Now Carter and Jude just get to relive their undergrad days. No big deal."

She smiles, closing the door to the connected bedroom after setting her bag carefully on the ground just inside the threshold and turning off the light.

"Feel free to grab whatever from the minibar," Carter says, coming back into the living space, running a hand through his hair. He's swapped his business casual for a pair of grey sweats and a thin blue shirt that stretches across his chest. Faedra looks him over, her eyes skating over him twice before she clears her throat and grabs a lemonade from the small fridge.

It strikes me that she doesn't scent despite her obvious attraction. Especially when she scented twice at the party strong enough for me to notice it, and that was in a room filled to the brim with people, diluting exponentially any reaction she gave. Logan tilts his head, glancing at me, and I raise my eyebrow in silent question. He shrugs and runs a hand through his hair.

Sitting next to me on the couch, she takes a deep breath and a long swallow from the drink. Logan settles on her other side, and she smiles. Carter grabs the small bottle of whiskey offered by the hotel for a small fortune and pours three tumblers, neat. As he hands one to me, Faedra breaks the silence.

"I'm not really sure how much eggshell walking I should be doing with you three. Can I just be blunt?"

Her eyes are clear, her shoulders back, no sign of worry or shame. It's second nature to smile at her self-confidence, her surety, and Carter notices.

"Damn, Faedra, that's the second time you've gotten him to smile after a really shitty day. If I didn't know any better, I'd argue that you're magical."

I roll my eyes, and Faedra giggles.

Logan says, "No eggshells. If you're nervous to say what you want, then we've done something wrong."

She nods and pulls her hair from where it's piled atop her head in a messy bun. The waves cascade down her back, and my fingers twitch with the desire to wrap them around my hand while I run my lips across the delicate skin of her throat. Logan grunts as my scent fills the space, but Faedra doesn't react at all.

"I'd really like to do a formal Pack Celebration, especially in the fall," she says. Carter settles into one of the chairs across the coffee table and nods. "My family, especially the extended portions, doesn't really understand pack dynamics, so it might be awkward, but it's important that I have a chance for my family and friends to celebrate with me. And it'll probably help if we do some of the traditional wedding practices, like engagement photos and vows, even though those aren't typical for these types of things."

"That sounds great," Logan agrees. I take a sip of the whiskey.

"Alright. Second, you should know that I've been on suppressors since before I started college," she says.

My eyes widen at the same moment Logan mutters a soft, "Seriously?"

When she nods in confirmation, I slam the rest of the alcohol, using the burn down my throat as a momentary reprieve to collect my thoughts.

No wonder she didn't fucking scent to Carter. Did she even notice when we did at the party? Did she notice now? Not to mention her being misdesignated when in public. If she's been on suppressors for—at minimum—four years, then only Alphas would have a hope of noticing that she isn't a Beta. Most Omegas probably wouldn't even be able to tell.

Carter leans forward, resting his elbows on his thighs, letting his half-drunk whiskey hang from his fingertips.

"How many heats has it been?" he asks, his voice keeping low and soothing, trying to hide his worry. Logan glances behind Faedra and catches my attention, frowning. I purse my lips in response, mirroring his concern.

She swallows before admitting, "Three. The last one was during the Matching Gala."

"Holy shit. It's a miracle I even managed to get you to scent that night," Logan murmurs before throwing his own whiskey back. "I thought it was faint because you wore scent blockers."

"I wasn't required to wear any because I'm suppressed." Faedra ducks her head, a blush creeping down her throat. She blows out a breath. "I didn't designate until the spring semester of my senior year. It was life-altering, you know? I begged my parents to let me start on a low dose as soon as the Council member left our house. I didn't want to go through a heat while at school. And I didn't want to match until I was finished with college. My degree is important to me."

"Makes sense," Carter assuages her. "What else is important to you?"

She looks up at him, biting her lip. "I'm not comfortable knotting until I've moved in with you. And I think I'd like to be in control of when my heat starts. I know there's a medication I can use to trigger one."

I run my hand down her spine, reacting on instinct, and she leans into the touch.

"Alright," I say, twisting a strand of her hair around my finger. "We're more than happy to make both of those happen."

She smiles, and I can't help but lean in and kiss her temple. When her breath catches, the faintest trace of her jasmine scent hits me, and Logan groans, low and deep. I don't move my hand, even as we settle in to a card game of Carter's choosing—that Faedra manages to win twice, despite her helping Logan start and finish the bottle of rum from the minibar. When we finally decide to call it a night, my hand slides from between her shoulder blades down to her hip, and I growl just a bit at her soft tremble, her slight catch of breath.

Even as I head to sleep in the spare bed in the other room, my hand still seems to feel the heat of her skin, and my scent blends with Carter's in the small space.

Nine

FAEDRA

The morning comes too soon, and I roll off of the plush hotel mattress while quietly cursing the headache making me wince at the soft sunlight filtering through the half-closed blinds. Digging through my bag with half-opened eyes, I manage to find the forest green bralette I'd left out in the hopes of staying with them last night. I pull it on, readjusting my pajama top, and then run my hands through my hair, twisting it up onto the top of my head. As quietly as I can manage, I open the door to the shared portion of the suite. I vaguely remember seeing a coffee maker tucked into a corner of the bar area last night, and I intend on using it ASAP to help with what is shaping up to be a wicked hangover.

The door to the hall opens as I pass where Logan sleeps on the couch, sprawled on his stomach, an arm hanging over the edge. His short blonde hair is mussed, sticking up in different directions, and I smile.

"Oh, you're awake," Jude says, his voice quiet despite his

surprise. I twist to see him standing in the doorway, and I flinch as my head pounds, reminding me of the hangover quickly settling into place. He frowns, setting the drink tray on the little table just inside the suite. "What's wrong?"

My cheeks heat, and his eyes trace them, his eyebrows furrowing. He crosses the room with large strides, tucking his hands into the pockets of his grey sweats. The blush intensifies as the reality of his being only a few inches away from me settles on me.

And my head pounds enough that I can't really enjoy it like I want.

"Did something happen?" he asks, his voice still a quiet murmur.

Licking my lips, I admit, "I have a hangover. I was going to see if there was any coffee to try to curb the headache."

He nods. "I'll be right back."

He's gone before I can ask what he's doing, disappearing through the slightly ajar door to the room he and Carter slept in. I walk to the minibar, careful to keep my head still, the throbbing in my temples growing worse. The door closes with a soft click, and I see Jude move back into the room from the corner of my eye. I rummage in the drawer under the single-cup coffee maker, looking through the small cups.

Are they seriously all hazelnut? Who decided that was a good idea? For some reason, tears well and make my eyes sting.

Jude steps up next to me as I'm still digging through the drawer, hoping to find something I actually like. Or at least will tolerate.

"Here," he murmurs, holding out his hand. He drops four small pills into my palm, and then sets a disposable plastic cup in front of me, the straw still half-wrapped. "It's a vanilla macchiato."

I offer a small smile before taking the pills and drinking half the coffee.

"Thank you," I murmur when I'm done, turning towards him. He's leaning against the counter, his hands tucked into the pockets of his sweats, his hair disheveled.

"Give it about ten minutes," he says. With a nod, I lean my hip against the counter and sip on the remaining coffee. He's content with the silence, his gaze rapt on me as the minutes pass and my headache becomes more manageable.

When I'm nearly positive it won't hurt to talk, I say, "Sorry you had to see me like this. I didn't mean to drink quite so much last night."

Jude shakes his head. "We've been matched, Faedra. Seeing you handle a hangover is par for the course."

I tilt my head, moving slow enough that it doesn't ache, and bite my lip. "You're an expert on matches, then?" I ask with a soft smile. "I didn't realize you were hiding a previous Omega from me."

He scowls, crossing his arms over his chest, bringing attention to a tattoo I hadn't noticed before. It's a small, flowing script across his rib, just under his heart and half covered by his arm.

"What does that say?" I ask, reaching out and tracing the words I can see.

Non amoris.

Without love?

Jude moves his arm without answering my question.

Finis vitae sed non amoris.

My hangover is bad enough that I can't manage a decent translation, even with the headache mostly gone.

"What's without love?" I ask, tracing the rest of the words. His stomach muscles tighten, but he doesn't back away. He also doesn't pull me closer. I try to not be worried about what that might mean.

"It means end of life but not of love," he says, voice gruff, before grabbing my hand and pulling it off of him. He wraps my fingers in his grip, looking at me with an eyebrow cocked. When I don't ask an immediate follow up question, he murmurs, "I got it after my sister's funeral."

"I'm sorry," I whisper, pulling my hand out of his grip. Jude nods once and then covers the tattoo completely when he crosses his arms again. I look around the room, biting my lip as the awkward silence extends. Eventually, I mutter, "I'm just going to go get ready then."

He blows out a breath and grabs my hand.

"How's your head?" he asks, looking me over, his gaze intense, his jaw ticking under the clean lines of his beard. My belly flips, my thighs clench, and he breathes deeply as a soft trace of my scent surrounds me. His hand flexes around mine as he pulls me closer.

It takes me two tries to answer. "Better. Thank you."

"Good," he says and pulls me even closer, my feet stumbling over his and crashing me into his chest. My hand splays wide on his stomach to keep my balance. He lifts my chin with one finger before telling me, "I've never matched. I've never bonded. I've had one serious relationship that was less than ideal and that was with a Beta."

I swallow. "It was a joke."

He nods, his thumb running along my jaw. Despite everything, my scent increases, and he groans under his breath. "That doesn't mean I haven't been with enough Omegas to know what a half decent Alpha should do. It's instinctual, Faedra. The day I don't want to take care of you is the day you know to put a gun to my head. Understand?"

His voice skates over me, rough and low, and I bite my lip to keep from making an embarrassing noise. His grip tightens as the moment stretches, his eyebrow rising.

"Yes," I manage to whisper.

His hand moves from my chin and runs down the length of my throat, his thumb nestling into the hollow above my collar bone. I lick my lips, and his gaze flicks down, growing more intense as he watches.

I want to kiss him. I've already kissed Logan, and Carter's had his hands all over me. But both seem to pale in the light of Jude's attention fixed on me, his singular focus making heat pulse in my core and my scent grow stronger even with the suppressors. He turns us before I can decide to make the first move, pressing me against the counter, encouraging my legs apart and stepping into the space created between them.

"You smell like jasmine," he mutters, lowering his lips to mine but not quite kissing me. "It's so fucking faint, but it's all I can focus on. It makes me wonder what you'll smell like when you stop the suppressors."

My pulse throbs in my ears. "I've...never been off of them."

He brushes his nose with mine, moving his hand until he can run his thumb along the column of my throat. "You said that last night."

I manage a breathless laugh. "Yeah, I did."

His lips part like he's going to say something else, but I close the minimal distance between our mouths, pressing into him as my eyes flutter shut so I can focus on the feel of his lips. He takes a half step into me, his hips pressing into my belly, and deepens the kiss, tracing the edge of my lower lip with his tongue until I open for him. The spicy scent of musk permeates the air around me, overwhelming my soft jasmine, and I groan, leaning into him and wrapping my hands around his neck.

I'm thoroughly breathless when he pulls away, cupping my

face in both hands, his green eyes intent on me. His voice full of desire, he says, "You didn't want to knot here. I need to stop."

My thighs clench even as I nod. His nostrils flare as another small bit of jasmine layers in with the musk, and he groans, pushing his erection harder into my belly. I scrape my hands down his chest, enjoying the way he groans and tightens his grip on my face.

"God damn it," he mutters before kissing me again, his movements dominating my own. He trails his touch down my arms and thighs, gripping them and lifting me onto the counter without hesitation, guiding my legs around his hips. The change lets him grind into me, and I moan into his kiss, clutching at his sides. He palms my throat, his thumb and finger resting just under my ears, and a wave of heat rushes through me.

"Not to be the asshole," Carter says from behind Jude, "but she has somewhere to be in an hour, and she absolutely cannot be late."

Jude mutters a curse against my lips as he pulls away. My cheeks are warm, and the blush spreads down my neck when I see Carter standing next to Logan a few feet away, arms crossed over his chest, already dressed in an expertly tailored navy suit. At least Logan isn't ready yet. Jude kisses me again, a lingering press of our lips that makes my heart race and my scent surface again.

One of them groans, and I blush even as Jude whispers in my ear, "Good morning." He runs a hand down my thigh, tracing some of the darker freckles on my knee before stepping away. Without a glance to his pack, he flips off Carter and closes the door to the other room. Logan shakes his head and grabs his suitcase from beside the couch.

"Go get ready, Red," he says after grabbing a toiletry bag. "You'll have to save our greetings for later."

I laugh and slip off the counter, heading towards the other

half of the suite and the bathroom where my dress has been hanging all night.

Before I close the door, I glance over my shoulder, catching Carter messing up Logan's hair as they both laugh.

Smiling, I say, "I'll make sure to write down the rain checks so I don't forget."

∽

"I should warn you that my family can be overwhelming," I say. I twist a strand of hair around my finger as the line of cars inch forward, following the poor faculty stuck on traffic duty.

Logan smiles as he pulls into the parking garage, his fingers tapping on the steering wheel.

"Can't be any worse than the parents I deal with," he says. "Especially the ones that are convinced their kids should go pro when the kid isn't interested in the sport half as much."

I grimace but shake my head. "Aiden is a wildcard, though I think he's tired enough from med school still that he'll be decent. Dad is pretty relaxed unless something makes him worried about me or my brother. But my mom is a lot. She has been for as long as I can remember."

The words tumble out faster the farther into the explanation I get. Sighing, I pull my finger from the looped hair and comb it out before tucking it behind my ear and pulling down the car's mirror to check my makeup again.

"You look great, Red," Logan says, grabbing my knee.

"Your family sounds pretty normal, Faedra," Carter says, tucking his phone away while Logan pulls into a spot and turns off the car. "We're excited to meet them."

Nerves flutter low in my belly. "Um... You should know that my mom's really worried about the age gap. My dad was nicer about it but was still pretty shocked."

Jude grunts. "How old are they?"

I close my eyes. "Forty-seven and forty-nine. They're two years apart, almost to the day."

Carter curses. "Should've seen that coming."

Logan talks over him, taking my hand in his and squeezing tightly. "Let them be worried, Faedra. They're trying to make sure you're safe. Nothing wrong with that. We'll all get used to each other."

I give a tentative smile, and he kisses my knuckles. Carter and Jude get out of the car, and Jude opens my door, helping me get out and holding my elbow while I put on the small heels. Logan drapes the gown over his arm and holds the cap with a careful grip.

"So family aside, what are you hoping to achieve this year?" Carter asks, taking my hand while Jude sets his palm against the small of my back.

I frown, and Logan runs his knuckles along my cheek before turning around and leading us across the courtyard and into the pavilion.

"I'm not entirely sure," I admit after a few minutes of quiet. "I hadn't really let myself think past being matched. Some packs are...very strict in what they allow their Omega to do, and I didn't want to get my hopes set up to be crushed."

Carter squeezes my hand. "Well, we aren't like that. There's more to you than just being an Omega."

Logan nods, turning around and grinning while he walks backwards. I smile as a piece of hair drops onto his forehead, the soft breeze messing up his carefree styling.

"And don't pick something based on income," Jude adds. "The Council has robust requirements for what packs have to bring in so they can qualify for matching. We've got it covered."

"Pursue whatever you love to do for a career. Or don't pick a career at all and stay home with me." Logan grins and winks. My cheeks flame, and he laughs, grabbing my other hand and kissing my palm before turning back around.

"I'll think about it," I tell the men. "You're serious about anything?"

Jude nods, but Carter says, "It would be pretty difficult to move from Denver permanently. Not just with our jobs, though mine can be picked up and taken anywhere with some planning. It's the Council that makes it challenging."

I squeeze his hand, smiling as we come to stand with the rest of the people trying to get in the building for the ceremony. Someone calls down from the other end, but I ignore it, the crowd starting to make me nervous.

Jude steps closer to me, encouraging with his soft touch for me to stand right behind Logan, the three of them making a makeshift wall between me and the swarm of people.

"Faedra Rose! There you are!" My mom's voice carries over the din of the crowd, and I turn towards it, finding my family walking towards me, Violet and Jasper with them. Violet shakes her head in warning but keeps smiling as she waves.

The look on my mom's face has me swallowing as I step around Jude to greet them.

Ten

CARTER

Faedra's entire demeanor changes as she steps around Jude and drops my hand, waving once at her family. It's subtle. Certainly not anything her mother seems to notice. But where she had been relaxed against us, leaning into our touches and moving close enough to scent us, she's now more closed off, her posture rigid and her hands fidgeting with the ends of her hair where they cascade over her shoulders.

Jude glances at me, and I lift one eyebrow.

"Betas, remember? And she's been suppressed for the last four years. They probably have no idea," Logan says under his breath, keeping Faedra's cap and gown in his hold. "Especially since I don't think she even does."

I blow out a breath. "And she mentioned they were leery of the gap."

Jude takes a minute to recalibrate, closing his eyes and adjusting the sleeves of his suit jacket. When he turns around, he gives us each a subtle nod.

"Alright, alright, enough with the greeting. Introduce us," her mother says, her eyebrow cocked as she looks me over.

Faedra blushes but comes to stand between us again. She points to Logan, who steps forward and offers his hand to her mother.

"This is Logan," she says, then points to me. "This is Carter. And this is Jude." She finishes by holding her hand out to him, and he nods once.

"Guys, this is my mom, Elizabeth."

A man in his late forties steps forward, his red hair fading into white, his freckles nearly as dark as Faedra's. The man beside him is a mirror image despite the dark red hair the younger man sports.

"This is my dad, Jay, and my brother, Aiden."

We all do the customary exchanges, and her father relaxes as we offer small bits of information about ourselves over the next few minutes. The short woman beside Aiden clears her throat. She's unfamiliar to me, but Logan waves with a small smile.

"Shit, sorry, Vi," Faedra says, stepping around her parents and grabbing the woman's hand. "Everyone, this is Violet. She's my best friend and has been my roommate for the last four years." She smiles, her gaze sizing up Jude. Faedra clears her throat and continues. "And this is Jasper. He's part of Pack Montegue, which Violet matched with at the same gala as we did."

Logan shakes his hand, striking up a conversation easily enough. Jude and I step back, our natural dynamic becoming more apparent as the time passes.

"Betas aren't common. I'd love to hear your story if it's something you're comfortable sharing," Logan says, and Jasper laughs.

"Sure, man. It starts with me being bi," Jasper says, grinning, and I laugh.

Jay clears his throat. "Where do you need to be, Faedra and Violet? Last thing we want is you girls to be late."

Another man walks towards us, his attention on Violet, a cap and gown held over one shoulder. His eyes are sharp, his other hand tucked in the pocket of his slacks. His black hair is wavy, and there's a tattoo tracing up the side of his neck and disappearing into his hair.

"Hey, Vi," he says, coming up on her other side. "Here it is. Sorry, it took me a bit to find parking."

She reaches for the items, but he shakes his head, helping her into the gown instead. Logan turns to Faedra, and I swear they can communicate telepathically because she's already moving to stand between the three of us again. Logan helps her with the gown before Jude gets her cap placed and then centers the three different cords she's been awarded. Elizabeth adjusts a few tendrils of hair before smiling.

"We're so proud of you, Faedra Rose," she says, and Faedra hugs her before turning to us. Her blush is bright, but her eyes are sharp, no shyness to be found in them. Logan kisses her cheek, and she hums. I squeeze her hand while Jude presses his lips just under her ear and whispers something, low enough I can't hear it. Faedra laughs again.

Violet disentangles from the men beside her and stands next to Faedra, subtly wedging between her and Logan. With a wave, she locks arms and turns them towards the side entrance where the other graduates are grouping together.

"Alright. We'll see you after."

~

FAEDRA

My mother grills all three men throughout lunch, barely taking time to eat her own food. She is especially keyed in on Jude—probably because he's gruff and aloof, though plenty attentive to me. He hands me the ketchup before I can ask for it, helps move my plates around to help accommodate the extra appetizers my brother orders, and subtly adjusts my drink so that the server is always refilling it before it's even halfway empty. But with each thoughtful gesture, my mom grows more concerned, the corners of her lips pinching and her eyebrows lowering.

The men handle it all with more poise than I can muster, humoring my mother by answering every ridiculous question she manages to ask. By the time Carter helps me into the passenger seat of their rented SUV, I'm ready to lay low and let everyone else deal with managing the move out of my dorm room.

Logan reaches across the console while putting on his seat belt. "You good, Red?"

I close my eyes and lean back against the headrest, pulling the pins from my hair and letting it cascade over my shoulders.

Carter hums. "You can stay in the car if you'd like, Faedra. All the paperwork is in my name anyway."

"Did you guys notice how my mom got *more* concerned the nicer you were to me? Or was that something I just imagined?" I ask, glancing back at him instead of taking the easy way out. Logan pulls out from the restaurant and eases onto the road, his phone perched against the SUV's screen to show him the way to the dorms.

"You mentioned that all of this is new for your family, right?" Jude asks instead of answering my questions. I frown but murmur an affirmative. He continues. "Then what is typical Alpha and Omega dynamics is likely being perceived as us being overbearing or controlling. Add to it her concerns with our age difference, and she's probably worried we're going to coerce you into doing something you don't want."

My frown deepens. Logan palms my thigh, running his hand along the edge of my knee. For some reason, the small touch calms me, and I lace my fingers with his.

"But you aren't. And I'm more than capable of telling you to back off if I'm uncomfortable."

Carter nods. "But she doesn't know that. Many pack dynamics are seen as worrisome from people outside of the experiences."

Logan adds, "It's just her trying to protect you again. We aren't bothered by it, and she hasn't said anything nasty. It'll take some getting used to for all of us."

The other men murmur agreements. I blow out a breath and run my hands through my hair, adjusting it now that it's down from the partial updo for the graduation ceremony.

"You fly out tomorrow?" I ask to break up the silence.

Logan nods, glancing at me with a smirk before focusing on the road again. "Have some bold plan for tonight, Red?"

I blush but roll my eyes. "Just double checking I don't need to beg my parents for a spot in their hotel until tomorrow."

Logan laughs. "Don't want to spend the time with Violet?"

"I can only imagine what's happening in that house right now. I'm good," I say, shaking my head.

Violet and Jasper have been *very* excited about being reunited. And Rylan seems interested, too. I would rather spend what little I have in my savings than stay at their place the next few days after the guys fly back to Denver.

"We can extend the room if you want," Carter offers.

I glance back at him and frown. One night at that hotel is more than I have in my savings. Carter shakes his head before I can say anything.

"Don't worry about the cost," he says. "We've got it covered. Do you want us to extend the room for after we're gone?"

I blow out a breath as Logan pulls into the crowded dorm parking lot, taking the first available spot instead of hunting for something closer. As we head towards the dorm, I see my parents. I grab Carter's hand and lean into him, a small ball of nervousness unwinding in my belly when he hums and kisses the top of my head.

"Let me chat with them. We can figure it out tonight, right?"

"Of course, Faedra."

~

CARTER

"I'm ready to get out of this dress," Faedra says once Logan gets the hotel room door open and we filter inside. She heads straight to the bedroom she stayed in last night, shutting the door quietly behind her without a glance back toward us.

Logan grabs his bag and heads into the other bedroom, Jude right behind him. He glances back at me, but I shake my head, pulling off my tie and tossing it to him. He catches it without missing a beat, shutting the door once Jude is inside.

I grab one of the waters from the restocked minibar and settle on the couch, pulling out my phone and going through some emails. There's two from the Hawkins Corp. pushing back on the contract the team had offered. I notice I'm not actually the intended recipient—they've been forwarded to me by one of my upper managers. I mark them to come back to later. Amanda has sent me one, too, explaining the problem with the whole negotiation, and I sigh. I shoot back a quick email requesting her to set up a direct meeting between me and the administrator they've assigned to the deal.

The door opens, and I glance up, finding Faedra has changed into a set of athletic shorts and a cropped black hoodie, the creamy skin of her belly flashing with each small movement. She blows out a breath but offers me a smile, and I bask in it.

"Come join me?" I ask. She's quick to cross the room.

"At least dinner was better than lunch," Faedra offers as she sits next to me, a careful three inches between us.

"Logan seems to have been right with giving her some extra time," I say. Putting my phone facedown on the coffee table, I turn toward her, adjusting so that my arm stretches across the back of the sofa.

Faedra rolls her eyes as she pulls her hair into a high ponytail in one fluid move.

"I'm still not convinced," she says, leaning against me, messing with the cords of her hoodie as she rests her head on my shoulder. "Pretty sure my dad said something after the movers to make her back off."

Her boldness in seeking touch is still surprising considering what she's told us about not craving it, and it takes me an extra moment before I twist a lock of her hair around my finger. She hums, moving until her feet are tucked under her.

"What's something you're looking forward to in Denver?" I ask after a minute. She hums in thought, leaning into my touch when I start tracing shapes along her neck before sitting up and biting her lip.

"The different landscape," she says after a moment. "I've taken so many pictures of the ocean and the city here, and I love them, but I'm excited to have new things to capture."

"You're a photographer?" I ask. It's not something she's brought up when we've talked late at night.

She shrugs, tracing my knee. "It's something I enjoy."

"I can't wait to put your prints up at home, then," I say.

Her eyes brighten, and my control snaps. I put a finger under her chin, tipping her head up, and I kiss her. Her response is immediate, her tongue tracing my lip in silent question that I'm happy to answer—thoroughly. When I finally pull away, her breathing is choppy and I'm hard enough that it aches. The soft, subtle notes of her jasmine scent make it even more impactful. She traces her lip, her cheeks flushed, and I groan, kissing her again.

Before I can get lost in it, though, the other door opens and the men walk back into the living area. Faedra pulls away, offering me a soft smile before resting her head on my shoulder again as Logan takes the chair across from the sofa.

While Jude pours a generous three knuckles of whiskey, Logan asks, "Did you bring that project you showed me? Or is it packed?"

Faedra lifts her head, twisting to look at Logan. I finger comb her hair, luxuriating in the feel of her subtle relaxation into me.

If she's this responsive suppressed, I can only imagine how much touch she'll need when she comes off of the medication. Good thing there's three of us.

She nods. "Do you want to see it?" she asks. I press a quick kiss to her shoulder when Logan nods and she twists her legs off the couch, sitting up in a smooth movement that has my cock twitching.

Fuck, but the next several days without her are going to be long.

And hard.

Eleven

FAEDRA

The sun is warm on my skin as I drag the hotel's lonesome chair onto the balcony and arrange it in the corner to look out over the water. The sunset is gorgeous, and despite living here for four years, I find myself wanting to take photos of it again. So instead of settling in with the quilting project I showed Logan last week, I unpack my camera from the bag near the front door of my new hotel room, adjusting the lens and settings to make sure it's capturing in a high enough resolution for large printing.

My mind quiets as the time passes, the nervous energy I've had since the guys left early this morning calming. Once the lights along the walkway below turn on and the sun is completely behind the ocean's horizon, I drag the chair and camera back inside, locking the balcony door before I forget. I pull a few of the photos off the memory card and onto the shared server so that I can post them on my social medias before tucking the camera bag into the larger suitcase and nestle the whole thing under the desk.

As I stand back up and reach for the small batch of hexagons I'd planned to finish tonight, my gaze catches on the credit card Carter handed me once they'd helped me into the new hotel room. It sits on the desk next to my bag, seemingly innocuous, but my attention continually draws back to it as if a beacon shines down on it, demanding me to acknowledge its presence. The soldier gilded in gold makes incredulity thread through me again.

A black fucking Amex.

He gave me a black American Express with a shrug of his shoulders and an easy half grin as if it weren't one of the single most significant signals of extraordinary wealth known to modern culture. Blowing out a breath and shaking my head to clear it, I gather up the quilting supplies and settle on the floor in front of the sofa, putting in one of my headphones and listening to my favorite Harry Styles album.

I'm snipping the thread on my third seam and belting the chorus of the fifth song when my phone rings and Logan's picture flashes across the screen. My music pauses, and I close it out before setting aside the project and answering the phone, propping it against the coffee table leg a bit to my left.

"Hey, Red," Logan says, and I smile.

He glances behind him, dropping the phone to lower how loud his shout is as he lets the others know I answered. There's movement behind him, but he ignores it to ask about my day. While we chat, Carter and Jude come up behind him, and Logan sets the phone down in front of him, far enough away that I can clearly see the three of them.

"Your day was good?" Jude double checks.

I offer a nod and say, "I spent most of the day with my mom while my dad and brother hiked. She loves walking the beach. And then Violet and I got lunch. It's been good."

Carter grabs his shoulders, stretching his neck, and I can't help but focus on how his black tee stretches across his body, moving like it's been painted on. I clear my throat, ignoring how hot my cheeks have gotten. There's nothing wrong with being turned on by them. I know that. But my lack of experience still makes me embarrassed more than I'd like.

"I actually wanted to ask you guys about something," I say after a moment. Carter drops his hands, focusing on me, while Jude lifts an eyebrow.

"What's up, Red?" Logan asks.

Biting my lip, I twist a piece of hair around my finger before gathering it up and securing it in a claw clip. All of their gazes follow the movement of my throat as I swallow, and my breath stutters for a moment.

"Going off the suppressors is something I'll need to start doing soon, right?" I pose it as a question even though I don't wait for them to answer. "I have a doctor out here already. She's actually the one that's kept my suppressors up-to-date and has seen me through all three suppressed heats. Would you mind if I saw her before flying out to work out a plan for coming off of them?"

Jude hums before shaking his head, running a hand over his beard. "Of course not, Faedra. Your body is yours, not ours. Do what you feel is best."

"Alright." I run my tongue over my bottom lip. "I realize this was something we probably should have discussed while you were out here, but do you want me to go off my birth—"

Logan cuts me off, gaze growing sharp. "That's not our choice, Faedra."

His using my actual name makes me pause.

Carter is quick to step in, smoothing over my surprise. "Is that something you were wanting to do?"

I shrug before shaking my head. "I'd like time to settle in. But some packs are..." I blow out a breath. "Well, you know. You've spent more time around them than I have."

Jude makes a derisive grunt, rolling his lips together. Carter adjusts how he stands, tucking his hands into the pockets of his jeans.

Logan is the one who manages to break the silence.

"Any kind of long term family planning shouldn't happen until you're out here and settled. If you want to come off of it, that's fine. We'll make sure we have other options available." I blow out a breath. Logan continues before I can say anything. "And you should also know that we're clean. We all get tested regularly, and I have the results from the most recent time—which was after we got the news of our being shortlisted."

Relief has my shoulders dropping, the nerves bleeding away from me. I manage a true smile. "Thank you. I, um, am clean, too," I say.

Being a virgin with no history of partners will do that. The three of them nod.

"I'll chat with her about options." I continue before I can blush again. My lack of experience is *not* something I want to bring up over a video chat. "I've been on the shot, but it actually lapsed because it was finals when I needed to get it redone and I didn't have time."

"Sounds good, Red," Logan says, a small smile curving his lips.

The conversation lightens, and I find myself laughing for most of it, my cheeks aching from how much I'm smiling.

"We'll see you at the airport on Wednesday, alright?" Carter says, his voice dropping to a smooth, soothing baritone that washes over me. When I nod, the three of them murmur soft goodbyes, and then I get ready for bed, wrapping myself in the shirt Carter left in my bag, luxuriating in the pine and smoke scent that clings to it.

I need to figure out which cologne he wears. It's delicious.

∼

The pharmacy takes a bit to get their shit together, so I'm running late by the time I make it out onto the main thoroughfare heading towards one of my favorite cafes where my family is meeting me for brunch. I'm tucking the new medications into the inner portion of my messenger bag when I round the corner and hear my brother call my name. I close my bag, a slight blush warming my neck, and glance down the street. My dad stands from the patio table where my family is looking through the brunch menu. The hostess starts towards me, and I smile, recognizing her from campus. She smiles and waves.

"Hey, Faedra, I thought you'd be long gone by now since move out was over the weekend," she says, tucking away a stray piece of her blonde hair. "Especially since you posted that sunset last night. I figured it was your final goodbye." I laugh as she unlocks a piece of the fence and a gate opens. She says on the same breath, "Here, just cut through."

Shrugging, I walk through the gate and close it behind me. "We decided to make a mini vacation of it."

"Well, have fun!" she says with a short laugh. "I'm excited to see all the photos you post of Denver. It's on my bucket list!"

I'm still smiling as I take a seat between Aiden and Dad, tucking my bag under the metal chair. Dad wraps an arm around my shoulders and pulls me into his side, kissing the crown of my head before looking back at the menu.

"We ordered you an iced vanilla latte," my mom says, setting aside her menu. She glances over her shoulder. "It should be here any minute."

My phone buzzes with a text, and I grab it from my bag before my parents can lay down a no phones rule for brunch.

> How was your appointment yesterday?

I smile at the simple question, biting my lip as a weightless, giddy feeling swells in my chest. Aiden grunts, but I ignore him, texting Carter back.

> Good. We came up with a plan for getting off the suppressors and switched my birth control. Excited to see you tomorrow.

> Can't wait. See you soon, gorgeous.

The endearment has me smiling as I tuck my phone away again. Dad and Aiden are chatting about something involving hockey, and Mom is shuffling through her purse. It takes me a minute to realize there's still empty seats at the table. I frown, looking over my shoulder towards the road.

"Did you invite Violet?" I ask.

Aiden laughs, and my mom curses, quiet but vehement.

I turn back around. "What did I miss?"

Dad's voice is full of restrained mirth. "Your mom and brother had a bet about how long it would take you to ask if Violet was invited, too. Your mom figured it would be in the first minute of sitting down. Aiden thought it would take a few minutes for you to realize anything was off."

Rolling my eyes, I punch my brother in the arm hard enough that he actually flinches.

"Fuck off, Fae," he grumbles, rubbing the spot on his bicep where I hit him. "Not my fault you've been ridiculously clueless the entire weekend. I didn't think they'd fuck you senseless so soon."

"*Aiden*," my mom gasps, smacking his hand with a menu.

He doesn't even flinch.

My cheeks heat, but I manage to look the server in the eye as they drop off the drink my parents ordered for me.

"Faedra?" my mom asks after a minute, too much concern laced with the curiosity.

Shaking my head, I sigh. "Don't ask, Mom. I'm twenty-two for crying out loud."

Her look grows hard, and I grimace, rubbing my face before cursing my brother under my breath.

He has the audacity to fucking *laugh*, and I punch him again, making sure I hit the same spot. His curse is more colorful this time. Mom makes an unhappy sound, and I turn to her, pursing my lips.

"Nothing happened," I tell her quickly. "I'm on my period. Now stop asking. It's none of your business anyway."

There's laughter behind me. "First time you've seen them in a month, and you're on your period? Tough break."

I glance over my shoulder, catching Rylan's gaze as he approaches alongside Violet and Jasper.

"Whatever, man. Periods don't bother me," Jasper says, laughing, shoving his pack mate in the shoulder.

Groaning, I drop my head into my hands.

"Rylan," Violet chastises, but there's no venom in her voice. She even has the audacity to snicker when I cock an eyebrow, incredulous. "It's not like it'll be a problem for long. You're only getting them because you're suppressed."

My dad intervenes before I start punching Violet, too.

"You bring that project you started? The inspiration picture you sent the other week looked really impressive." He takes a drink of his coffee and turns to me, the movement subtle but intentional as he blocks my view of my mother.

Violet sits across from me while I grab my bag and dig out the small group of hexagons.

My mom leans around Dad, taking a drink, and says, "This is for that flower wreath quilt you texted me a couple weeks ago?"

When I nod, she takes a couple of the hexagons I've started assembling into what will be the flowers. She hums as she turns it over and looks at the stitching along the seams, a small smile curving the corners of her lips.

"Interesting choice of colors," Jasper says, taking one of the menus and smacking Rylan's hand where it rests on Violet's thigh.

"Fuck off," he grumbles. But he moves his hand, lacing his fingers with Violet's on the table instead.

I clear my throat and arrange some of the hexagons to form another flower.

"I'm doing the flowers out of their favorite colors," I explain. "But I thought the small patterns would be pretty when seen as a whole. And I'm not following the pattern exactly since I didn't want to keep track of hundreds of white hexagons. So I'm just going to quilt these onto a large white background and then quilt it all together."

"It's going to look great, Faedra," my mom says, her voice gaining that lilt she gets when she's trying to not be overly emotional. I glance up at her, my cheeks warm, and she smiles around my dad's arm, setting the half-done flower down in front of me.

Bless the waiter because he appears at that moment, keeping the moment from becoming a cry fest at a public restaurant. The reprieve doesn't last long, though.

Once we've put in our order, Violet asks, "Did you look up where they live yet? I can't believe you've managed to not look."

I shrug. "I don't know Denver."

The reality is that I'm trying to temper my expectations. I don't want to build up some fantasy in my head just to have it crushed by whatever the guys actually have.

She arches an eyebrow, and I sigh, pulling out my phone before she can even ask.

"Aiden, switch," she says, standing up and moving around the table. My brother doesn't hesitate, switching spots with her and striking up a conversation with Jasper while Violet settles in next to me. I type in the address Jude gave me before they left and pull up the first search result, loading a real estate website while Mom and Dad discuss something quietly between them.

My jaw drops at the same moment Violet laughs, the lilt growing more unhinged the longer she does.

"Holy shit, Fae," she says, gasping, grabbing my arm in a tight grip.

My dad leans over, and I tilt the phone screen so that he can see. He murmurs his own surprise, and then Violet is passing my phone around the table, each person expressing their own level of excitement before she eventually takes it back and flips through more photos. She offers them to me, but I close the program instead, slipping my phone back into my bag.

"Eight million dollars?" Rylan says, a note of disbelief threading through his voice. "Damn, Faedra. Does one of them have a black Amex, too?"

I blush and duck my head.

"No fucking way," Jasper says, nearly giddy when I pull the card from my wallet, the black and gold blazing in the mid-morning light. Violet gasps, and Aiden grunts. Jasper laughs, tossing his head back. "Damn, I need to find me an Alpha with that kind of connection."

Rylan shoots him a glare, pushing his shoulder. "You did," he grunts. "He just has a stick the size of Texas shoved up his ass right now."

"He still doesn't have a Centurion, Rylan." Jasper laughs, grabbing Rylan's hand and kissing his palm. "And to be fair, Sienna has that effect on most people."

Violet clears her throat, shooting a pointed look at both men.

"Wait. What has your mom done this time?" I ask, and Violet glares at me, flipping her hair over her shoulder and twisting the industrial piercing in her ear.

Rylan is the one who answers. "What *hasn't* she done to Dominic at this point?"

Violet reaches across the table and covers his mouth. "I don't want to talk about it," she tells me, looking over her shoulder. Rylan bites at Violet's hand, the look on his face making me think it's playful. Her soft giggle confirms it a moment later.

Jasper says, clearing his throat and sitting forward until his elbows rest on the table, "Sienna has decided that Dominic's *pedigree*," his lips curl back as he spits the word, "is not nearly as perfect as she would like. She's filed three different motions with the Council to have Violet reassigned."

Oh shit. My gaze stays locked on Violet, and she gives a subtle shake of her head, a brittle look crossing her face for a brief moment as she resettles next to me.

"Please tell me you're going to buy something ridiculous with that card, Faedra," Jasper says after a bit.

I roll my eyes but laugh, the heavy feeling of a moment ago gone.

Twelve

JUDE

My eyes ache as I close the laptop and pull the connector that allows me to run a second monitor. Summer is typically a lighter workload, but with Faedra flying in tonight, I've been trying to finish a week's worth of work in two days, and it has my head pounding. Two graduate thesis evaluations, one undergraduate senior study plan development, and submissions for potential additional classes to be added to the fall docket.

I blow out a breath and stash my laptop, cleaning off my desk.

I'm two goddamn seconds away from being able to leave and prep for Faedra arriving when she walks in. I swallow a groan but don't hide my displeasure.

"You're leaving early," she says, leaning against the door frame, her arms crossed. Her blonde hair is down, curled into perfect waves that hit just below her collar bone and accentuate the neckline of her white blouse.

Fuck. The last thing I want is to have to deal with Melanie.

"Prior arrangement," I say, finishing packing my bag and slinging it over my shoulder. "Did you need something?"

Her lips bunch into a pout, her eyebrows lowering. "You never leave early. It's your *thing*. What's suddenly so important now?"

Good fucking hell.

I cock an eyebrow but don't offer a response, standing behind my desk and using it as a barrier between us. It's been five years, but somehow she can still manage to get my head in knots tight enough that it takes Carter, Logan, and a solid weekend somewhere outdoors to get me back to normal. If I weren't tenured, I would seriously consider looking at another position at one of the other universities.

I wonder if Faedra would be opposed to camping this weekend. The look in Melanie's eyes tells me I might end up needing the open air to try and remember who I was—*am*—without her claws in me.

"It's not another of those stupid parties, is it? I thought you just had to go to one of those," she says, scrunching her nose in disgust. "Doesn't the Council know that they're wasting their time? If you were going to match, it would have happened years ago."

It takes all of my control to keep my expression the one of bland disinterest I've become a master at over the last decade.

"What do you need, Melanie?" I ask instead of answering any of that bullshit.

She's been pissed at me for five years over our decision to register as a pack. I'm not about to tell her we were selected and that our Omega is literally on a plane as we speak. God only knows what she would do with the information.

Nothing good, I'm nearly positive.

Her pout becomes more pronounced, and she flips her hair

over her shoulder. The movement makes the neckline of her blouse pull taught, her breasts pushing against the low line. I grit my teeth, keeping my eyes on her face. When I don't respond to the practiced invitation the way I did five years ago—and to my chagrin much more recently—she pushes off the door frame and walks away without a word.

That's a nightmare brewing.

It'll have to wait until later though.

My phone alarm goes off, the soft chirp cutting through the silence of my office. Shutting off the light, I double check the door is locked and run a hand over my beard. A text message from Carter flashes across the screen as I head towards the public transport train station.

> You ready?

> Absolutely.

~

FAEDRA

I'm a decent flier. It's not my favorite activity, but I'm not someone who dreads it like my father. For whatever reason, though, this flight was rough, and my nerves are stretched thin. My alarm goes off for the new suppressant medication, so I step to the side and dig it out of the small zipper pouch in my messenger bag. As I take it and then a drink of water, I look around—and then frown.

What the hell is wrong with Denver's airport?

There's some construction, but what's odd is the lack of signage. Did they really take down all the information to accommodate whatever they're working on?

I turn around, trying to get my bearings, pausing the music in my headphones as if that will make this weird terminal make more sense. Finally, a sign catches my eye, and I breathe a sigh of relief when I see the arrow pointing in front of me for getting to the main concourse.

Why is there only one little ass sign?

Grumbling, I turn the music back on and grab my bags, slinging the messenger bag over one shoulder and wheeling the other beside me as I make my way across the thirty something gates this concourse has. As I get closer to the central point, more people start to crowd around me, and I readjust my bags so I take up less space. The odd train that goes between the concourses isn't any better, and I end up wedged between two people, holding one of the rails to keep from falling. By the time I manage to get onto the final escalator that the signs promise will dump me into the main portion of the airport, my skin is crawling and I'm filled with an unfamiliar anxiety. The feeling gets worse when a person shoves past me and knocks me off balance while I'm trying to walk out into the atrium, and I have to breathe slowly through my nose to keep from crying.

"Faedra?"

Carter's familiar voice is a wave of comfort. The tension in my limbs releases, but the nervous energy I've been feeling for the last hour clogs the back of my throat. I glance up as a hand grabs my carry-on and blow out my breath when I lock eyes with Jude. His mouth is tipped down, the corners of his lips tight, and his eyebrows furrow as he takes me in.

"You alright?" he asks.

I shake my head before I even realize that I'm *not* fine.

The three of them move faster than I can process, closing in around me and helping me to a bench nearby. Carter guides my messenger bag off my shoulder and slings it onto his own while Jude sits next to me on the bench, moving my carry-on so that our legs press together. Logan crouches in front of me, his hands on my knees, and the look of concern on his normally smiling face has me leaning into him and resting my head on his shoulder. The contact calms me, a foreign need for them to hold me settling in my bones. After a minute, I'm able to lift my head and focus on the men.

"Better?" Logan asks, and I nod, swallowing the lump in my throat.

Carter's frown is deep, his hands tucked into the pockets of his slacks.

"That's never happened before." I explain while pulling my hair from its claw clip and readjusting it to fall around my shoulders and down my back. "I'm normally fine in crowds."

"Did you start the new medication?" Carter asks.

When I nod, Jude curses, and I frown.

"Why is that bad? We all agreed to have me start weaning off of the suppressors."

Logan murmurs an agreement.

Carter asks, "When did you start them?"

"Yesterday." My answer is immediate. "Once a day for four days and then every other day for a week."

Jude palms my thigh and presses his lips to the crown of my head. He murmurs, "Aspects of being Omega are becoming more pronounced with the new medication. Struggling in high contact experiences can be one of them."

My mind catches on how they formed a barrier at graduation, and it's like a layer of film has been pulled away from the memory. Logan pulls his hands away, but I'm quick to lace my fingers with his, that deep-seated part of me still craving contact.

Craving contact.

That's what this is.

"Oh." It's all I can manage under the weight of the epiphany.

Needing touch is one of the cornerstones of Omega nature. And it's something I've never really experienced before—certainly not to this level. "Will it become...worse when I've gone off the suppressors completely?"

Logan shrugs and stands, helping me up from the bench.

"Probably," Jude says, walking beside me, his hand on the small of my back as Carter leads us through the airport and to the parking lot. "But it's possible this is presenting all at once and the other aspects will do the same. We won't know until you're off of them."

LOGAN

Nerves are something I'm accustomed to dealing with. The first time I came face to face with one of my favorite professional baseball players and had to tell him he couldn't go back on the field for six weeks really forced me to figure out decent coping mechanisms.

Breathing. Calm walks. Visualizing. Counting backwards.

But hell if none of them are working right now.

Faedra sets her bag under the entry table, tucking her shoes next to it before looking down the hallway and gasping. Her hand tightens around mine, and I follow her as she crosses the condo, stopping in front of the wall of windows that look over the mountains. The sounds of the others moving behind us echo around the living space.

"Wow," she whispers, her smile wide and her eyes bright. She glances at me and blushes. "This view is gorgeous."

I don't even think.

"Yeah, it is," I murmur, keeping my eyes on her.

Her blush darkens. I only have a moment to enjoy it though

because in the next heartbeat she's kissing me, her lips soft against mine.

"The airport is still weird," she says when she pulls away, turning back to the windows. "That horse is something else. If I see it again, it'll be too soon."

Jude laughs, the coarse sound filling the space.

Biting her lip, Faedra looks over her shoulder.

"Can I have a tour before dinner?" she asks.

Carter pauses, looking up from where he's adjusting the bags from one of our favorite local restaurants left at our doorstep when we'd gotten home. I squeeze her hand as Jude agrees. He steps around the island and crosses the living room, his hands tucked into his pockets.

"Kitchen and living room, obviously," he says, nodding behind him. "That side is for play." He tips his head to the right. "And that side is for sleeping." He tips his head the opposite direction. "Which would you like to see first?"

Faedra smiles, looking at both options. "Play," she says. Carter joins us as we pass the kitchen, resting his hand on the small of her back. Jude opens the door in the corner.

"Logan's office," he explains.

Faedra gasps again before turning to me. "You didn't tell me you had this kind of view!" she says, eyes wide.

"Most of the rooms have this kind of view," I say with a shrug. Her eyes get wider, and she turns to Carter.

"Really? Even my room?" she asks.

He smiles as he nods.

She's surprisingly quiet as we show her the rest of the condo.

"It's more rooms than I expected," she admits as we cross the space. "Aren't most places like this open all the way?"

Carter nods.

"We had a designer add rooms to make it more usable for us.

We can always have them come back and change something if we ever need to."

She nods, her gaze thoughtful, though her eyes get wide when she realizes there's two staircases. She turns around in a circle as we finally step onto the landing of the first one, the walls of the loft filled with Jude's bookcases. Her eyes catch on the large leather chair in the corner, a small table next to it with two books currently open, bookmarks tucked into the spines.

"What's through here?" she asks, crossing the loft and setting a palm on the door.

"Your nest," Carter says. Her eyebrows furrow, and she hesitates to open the door. "If you'd like it here, at least. We had to designate a space for the Council to approve, and this was the room that made most sense. But there are a few others, too, if you want to decide between them."

Faedra shakes her head, blowing out a breath before opening the door and taking a careful step inside. The room itself is basic, a large bed taking up the wall to the left and a small dresser nestled next to the door. The blackout curtains are pulled back, the sunset staining the room a warm orange. While there's no closet, there's a door on the right that leads to a moderately-sized ensuite with its own washer and dryer to help accommodate the linens that heats typically require. Faedra clasps her hands in front of her, turning once in the space, her eyes taking in small details of the room.

"It's yours to do with as you want," Jude explains. "Add anything you'd like."

Faedra nods, her gaze finding his after a moment. "I'm not sure what I'll...want," she admits.

Jude takes her hand and brushes his lips across her knuckles.

Carter's voice is low and soothing. "You don't need to have everything decided right now, Faedra. Or even this week. Once you're completely off the suppressors, what you find comforting will become more obvious. We can adjust things as needed."

She nods before a bright blush trails down her neck and across her chest.

"What about the other half, then?" she asks.

I lead her across the condo and up the other staircase. The landing is small, four doors lining it. She smiles and runs her hand along the chair nestled against the window here, her gaze catching on the cityscape Carter and Jude's rooms have for views. I open the room all the way to the left, and she turns away from the window, a small smile curving her lips.

This space, too, is simple. A standard bed with simple white linens sits against the right wall, but there isn't any other large furniture. She crosses the room and opens the door to the balcony, giggling under her breath. We follow her, moths drawn to her flame. She turns away from the mountains as we step onto the outdoor space with her.

"It's beautiful," she whispers, the fading light gilding her face, setting her skin a beautiful gold. It strikes me just how lucky we've gotten. I smile and cup her cheek, kissing her once. "And this room?" she asks, turning to Jude.

He nods. "Anything you like. Make it yours, Faedra."

Thirteen

FAEDRA

While I wait for my name to be called at the cafe, I send a few inspiration pictures to Violet without any message attached and pull up an internet search for nearby furniture stores. The movers are supposed to be here by next weekend, but there are a few pieces I know for sure I'll need. I double check that the plants from the small shop I just visited are still looking ok despite being crammed into a paper shopping bag.

"Faedra," the barista calls, a small blended frozen drink in their hands. I gather my things and take the drink from them, murmuring a thank you before starting the walk back to the condo.

The city is bustling though completely different from Los Angeles. I hum as I step into the foyer of the condo building, wondering if Jude will be back from his staff meeting. Violet calls as I'm stepping off of the elevator, and I laugh as I answer.

"Your timing is unreal, Vi," I say, hanging my bag and

tucking my shoes under the small table across from the double row of hooks.

No one comes to greet me, so I assume Jude hasn't returned.

"It's a gift, I swear," she says.

I take the bag of plants and head up the closer set of stairs to my bedroom. There's no real furniture in here yet, so I pull them out and lay them on top of the bag once I have it spread out on the wood floor up against the full length windows.

"How is it out there?" she asks after a minute.

My smile is immediate. "It's great so far. They intentionally left my room a blank slate, so I'm working on getting it personalized. I was thinking of a really soft yellow for the walls."

Violet hums.

I laugh, shaking my head. "Would you like a tour?"

"I thought you'd never ask!" Her tone is a feigned innocence, and I snort. I switch to video and flip the camera, showing the room from the perspective of the balcony. She laughs as I take her through the place, her gasp just as big as mine when she sees the view that stretches the living room. By the time I'm sitting against the windows of the room they've designated for my heats, my cheeks ache from smiling so much.

It's only been a few days, and I miss her.

Violet whistles. "Are they stacked like their finances?"

My blush is immediate, and Violet cackles. *Cackles.*

"That's a 'Faedra Yes' if I've ever seen one," she says, laughing, and I roll my eyes.

The only one I've actually seen shirtless is Jude. But he was definitely stacked. My fingers can still feel his skin under mine where I traced his tattoo. The remembered feel of his beard against my neck is just as ingrained. The memories make my thighs clench.

Violet pulls me from my daydream.

"Have they mentioned anything else about you thinking about photography?" she asks.

I smile. "We talked about it yesterday. They all took the day off to help me settle in," I say, and Violet smiles. "They're supportive of whichever avenue I take."

"Seems like you really hit the lottery with them." She says it with a laugh, but there's a layer of discontent underneath that has me wishing I could hug her.

"Has it gotten better?" I ask on a whisper.

She shrugs. "Maybe. It's hard to tell since he's never really around." She blows out a breath, and her eyes grow hard, her lips pulling down. Her voice is full of restrained anger. "Even Rylan and Jasper are getting fed up with him, but they can't separate from him since there wouldn't be the minimum number for a pack."

She blows out a long breath and sets the phone down, propping it against something so she can pull back her hair. Her eyes are glassy when she looks back at me.

"Losing Jasper a second time will break me, Fae," she whispers, and my heart clenches. I wish I could hug her.

"I'm so sorry," I say even though it's not nearly enough. "If you need me, I'll make it happen, ok?"

She offers a watery smile before blowing out a breath and shaking her head. "Fuck me, I'm not a crier. My heat must be coming soon."

"If you disappear for a few days, I'll know not to panic, then," I joke.

It works. Her laugh is thin but present, and her eyes lose the haunted look.

A door closes downstairs, and I hear Carter's baritone voice carry up the stairs. I double check the time. It's only noon.

What has him here during lunch? Is this his usual Friday routine? He didn't mention it to me when he left for work this morning, though that might have been because I had only just woken up and was still working on making coffee.

Violet notices the change, of course. "You need to go?"

I shrug. "Carter's back."

She smiles and adjusts her hair. "Definitely should go, then. Text me with what you pick. It's going to look so cute."

I smile and assure her I will. The screen flicks to black a moment later, and I take a deep breath as I unfold myself from the floor.

Carter is gathering several bags on the dining room table, rifling through each one and making notes on his phone. He glances up as I start down the stairs, and his eyebrow cocks, his hands stilling as he turns to me.

"I thought you were out with Logan," he says, leaning against the table.

I shake my head and stand next to him, looking at the group of reusable totes he has set up. "He got a call from one of the teams, I guess. I'm not totally sure. He had to leave a few hours ago."

He mutters a curse. "I would have been back sooner. Sorry you ended up here alone. We planned on being here the first few days."

I shake my head and offer a smile, not bothered by the alone time. "I went for a walk and found a cute little plant shop a few blocks down, so don't feel bad. And Violet called for a bit, too. It's been fine." I pull one of the bags towards me and peer inside.

A bottle of wine. A shirt. A hoodie. A couple notebooks. A...headlamp?

Before I can voice my confusion, Carter says, "They're completion bags for a backpacking event next weekend. Normally I have my assistant fill them, but she's had this week marked for vacation since March, and I didn't want her to have to cancel."

"Can I help?"

He smiles with a nod before pointing at a box on the island. I grab the box before he can, bringing it back to the table, opening it. There's two stacks of gift cards to various stores. Most of them are outdoorsy, but a few are what I assume to be higher end restaurants.

"We'll need to put three of those in each bag," he explains. "I try to make sure there aren't any duplicates. And then these fifteen over here will need four."

I pull the cards and start making piles, careful to keep each stack diverse.

"You're a corporate sponsor?" I ask. He pulls a cute fabric pouch from the nearest tote, tucking each card so that a corner is visible.

"For the last few years, but Jude and I have been participants for over a decade," he says, moving the finished bags to the floor. "It's actually how we met Logan."

I hum and glance at him. "It sounds like there's a story there."

He cocks an eyebrow, smirking, and I giggle, a blush making my cheeks heat. He sets the next pouch of gift cards into a tote and then pulls me into him, his hand splaying across my hip, the heat of his palm searing me through the thin tank I wear.

My breath catches, and my gaze snags on his mouth, the small laugh lines bracketing his full lips and the stubble lining his jaw.

"We picked him up like a stray, and he followed us home," Carter says, amusement making his voice dip. "We figured after the second year that he was probably going to stick around for a while."

I shake my head and roll my eyes.

"That's how Jude puts it," Carter explains, taking a step into me, the distance between us disappearing as my breasts brush his chest with each unsteady breath I take. My hands splay across his stomach, and I bite my lip.

They've been less forward than I thought they'd be once I was here with them. I'd told them I didn't want to knot until I was moved in, but I'd half-expected one of them to pursue me since landing two days ago. That small voice in the back of my mind tells me it's something I'm doing, but I shut it up the best way I've found: with action.

Carter doesn't hesitate once my lips are pressed to his, cupping my cheek and tipping my head as he deepens the kiss. A bolt of arousal shoots through me, and I clench my thighs, running my hands up his chest and wrapping them around his neck. The smell of pine envelops us, and for some reason, that makes my arousal double.

The door to the condo clicks closed, and I jump, breaking the kiss and looking over my shoulder. Carter presses his forehead against my temple, and I feel him swallow as he adjusts his hold on me, loosening his grip and dropping his hand from my face.

"Sorry that took a bit, Red," Logan says, and I offer him a smile. He doesn't even hesitate at seeing me wrapped around Carter. "Jude's on his way back from his meeting. Did you want to go out for lunch?"

Carter sighs, his breath brushing my ear and making me shiver.

My voice is breathless when I answer. "That sounds fun."

Jude guides me into a seat at the table the hostess signals as ours and then settles next to me, unbuttoning his suit jacket and draping it over the back of the chair while Logan and Carter sit across from us. The waiter comes by before I have a chance to look at the menu, so we order drinks, and Carter adds an appetizer.

"So you've narrowed down the programs, Faedra?" Jude asks, setting aside his menu and resting his arm along the back of my chair. His thumb traces shapes on my arm, and I lean into the touch.

"I think so," I say, turning towards him. "There's a few here that are in person, but the rest would be online. I'm not sure yet which would be better, so I'll apply to both styles and figure it out before the semester starts in a few months."

Logan nods. "You have everything you need for the applications?"

"I started putting together a portfolio yesterday," I say, grabbing the iced tea the waiter sets beside me and squeezing the lemon into it. "Most of the schools have specialty guidelines for Omegas that are newly matched. I need to submit the notice from the Council with the application, and they'll evaluate me even though it's past the deadline."

Jude nods. "Typically that means you'll receive an answer sooner, too. If you apply by Monday, I wouldn't be surprised if you have offers by the end of the week."

Surprise has me putting down the drink. "Really?"

When Jude nods, I sigh, a level of stress leaving my body and helping me relax. "That's way more manageable than I figured. Certainly better than after the gala."

Carter laughs. A woman walks up to their side of the table, a tablet in hand. Her dark brown hair is twisted back from her face in a claw clip, and her blue eyes seem tired.

"They didn't tell me you were here," she says, flustered. "Did they get what you needed?"

"Of course, Gina," Logan says. Her body relaxes, and she types something into the tablet.

"Everything alright?" Jude asks.

She shrugs. "Hallie is cutting her first teeth, and Ashlynn has a big project due at work now that she's back, so I've been the one up with her the last few nights."

Jude grunts. "Sounds rough. Anything we can do to help, let us know."

Gina laughs but waves away his concern. "Just a busy week. It'll even out. It did with Darius." She blows out a breath and sets the tablet on the table between Carter and Logan. "Your usuals, then? Though Fridays are not your typical," she says, giving Logan an impressive side eye.

She reminds me of Violet. A pang of homesickness twists in my chest, but I take a drink to ignore it.

"What do you want, Red?" Logan asks, and I glance at him.

The woman's gaze grows curious as she focuses on me. I give her my order, she taps it into the tablet, and then she turns to Carter.

Carter doesn't miss a beat. "Gina, this is Faedra."

Recognition lights her face, and she grins, extending a hand, and I take it in a gentle grasp with a small smile.

"I didn't realize the timeline was so condensed. I thought you still had a few weeks before everything changed." She gathers the menus and tucks them into the middle pocket of her half apron. She shakes her head, a half grin curving her lips. "That explains why I didn't see your names on the trio list for next weekend. I was worried. You'll be missed."

"You taking the kids this year?" Logan asks.

Gina shakes her head.

"That weekend is for me and Ashlynn. No kids allowed." She scoops the tablet up and steps away from the table, focusing on another group that is settling in around the bar on the other side of the restaurant. "I'll have that out for you soon."

As she turns away, I glance at Carter, messing with the

napkin still on the table in front of me. "You didn't mention you still did the competition."

He lifts an eyebrow but grasps my wrist, running his thumb over the delicate skin just under my palm. My thighs clench.

"Did you guys pull out because of me?" I ask.

Logan shrugs and runs his hands through his hair. "We weren't about to expect you to be fine with us taking a four day trip so soon after moving here. Especially with you weaning off suppressors."

Jude turns to me, twisting a piece of my hair around his finger, his gaze thoughtful.

"Is backpacking something you've done before?"

I shake my head but say, "I'm more than willing to try it, though."

If this is such an integral piece of them, I don't want to be the reason they stop. And I'm always willing to try something once. My ear piercings are proof of that. I finger the gold hoop of my orbital piercing.

"You sure? Four days in the backcountry isn't nearly as romantic as the outdoorsy influencers would have you believe," Logan says. His eyes are focused on where I mess with the piercings.

My laugh is automatic. "Neither is living in L.A.," I say, and Carter smiles. "Really, if you think I can keep up, I'd love to try it. The pictures alone will be worth it."

Logan pulls out his phone. "I'll text Doug and see if there's room in the quads."

My confusion must be obvious because Carter explains before I even have a chance to frown.

"There's a limit in each group size. They don't want too many people out on the trails at the same time."

Logan gives a nod. "We're good to go."

Gina comes back at that moment, a plate of chips in her hand along with a few dips. She glances between us and then sets the plates in the middle of the table.

"What happened?" she asks. "I haven't seen Logan this giddy since that kid made it in the MLB last year."

"You girls doing the harder trail this year?" Jude asks instead of answering. When Gina shakes her head, he chuckles. "Guess we'll see if we can keep up with you then."

A grin spreads across her face, her eyes brightening as they lose their tired look. Her gaze catches on me, and I shrug, popping a chip in my mouth.

"Oh, you're going to fit right in here, Faedra." She shakes her head and claps Jude's shoulder. "I can't remember the last time this guy laughed. Ashlynn is going to be so excited to meet you."

Fourteen

JUDE

"This one feels good to you?" I ask, adjusting the straps on the hiking pack Faedra is trying on. Logan stands next to her, double checking the height of the frame compared to her torso. She moves side to side, adjusting her weight, closing her eyes. It's her second time trying this one, but we're not about to rush her. Packs are the most important piece of gear for overnight hiking, and we want to make sure Faedra has one that won't hurt her when we're ten miles in. After a moment, she opens her eyes and nods.

"Let's have you wear it for a little bit longer," Carter says as he comes back up to us, a sleeping bag in his hand. "We can double check there aren't any pressure points, and it'll let you get more comfortable with the kind of weight you'll be carrying."

Faedra nods and pulls her hair back, twisting it on top of her head in a practiced move.

"Will my piercings be ok?" she asks. "The tragus one tends to close quickly."

Carter frowns, and I shrug.

"Let me text Ashlynn. She has a few," Logan says, pulling his phone from his back pocket.

I lace my fingers with hers, and she leans into me, resting her head against my arm.

"This feels really expensive for something I might not even be good at doing," she admits after a moment, quietly enough that only the three of us hear her. "I didn't quite realize how much equipment I would need."

Carter steps in front of her, taking her other hand in a tight grip.

"We don't mind, Faedra," he says, and she nods, her hair brushing against my Oxford. I run my thumb along the back of her hand.

"I'll pick out some cheaper furniture to offset it, at least," she says.

I shake my head, squeezing her hand.

"We said anything you like," I murmur into her hair. "Trust me when I say we have the funds for it."

She blows out a breath before giving a soft acknowledgment. Logan pulls her away from me, guiding her around the small try-on space, murmuring something that has her giggling. When they make it back to us, she stretches her neck and Logan unclips the straps of the pack, helping her out of it and pressing a soft kiss to the crown of her head. She leans into him, her mouth parting, but just as she's about to speak, Logan's phone rings, cutting her off.

He glances at it and sighs. "It's Ben. I'll find you all when I'm done."

Without a glance back, he strides out of the shop, heading toward the car. Faedra glances around, tension bleeding into her limbs, and she takes a step into Carter, seemingly unintentionally. The people are starting to get to her even if she doesn't realize it yet. Carter catches my gaze and nods towards the cafe attached to the camping supply store. It's still crowded, but the outdoor seating looks to have room.

"Why don't you go get something to drink while I take care of all of this?" Carter asks, keeping his voice low. Faedra takes a deep breath and understanding flashes across her eyes.

"That crept up. How did you notice before I did?" she asks, her lips bunching into a pout, a thin line forming between her eyes as she lowers her eyebrows.

I set my hand on the small of her back. "Instinct, remember?"

Once we're in the cafe, Faedra blows out a breath.

"This is...very different from how I normally feel," she admits, rubbing her arms.

FAEDRA

Jude nods, his expression nearly stern in what I'm beginning to think is his normal expression. I suppose if women can have RBFs, so can men—and Jude would be the prime example of one. My skin still crawls, though the feeling is less now that we stand in line in the moderately busy cafe. Crowds haven't ever been such an issue, and I struggle to reorient myself to the reality that I've nearly panicked twice now in them.

"Suppressants are known to be very effective," Jude offers as the person in front of us is called forward to order. "It'll take a bit to feel like you've reached equilibrium off of them."

The other barista calls us forward, and I order my standard: a tall iced vanilla latte with a pump of peppermint. Jude orders a simple caramel macchiato as he slips his hand around mine and laces our fingers together, paying for the drinks and moving to the side without losing the contact. For whatever reason, the extended touch calms me more than just moving away from the people.

Another moment where the realities of being Omega are more jarring than I expected. I've known Omegas need contact from Alphas, especially if they've bonded, but it's not something I've ever truly desired until being here in Denver with the guys.

Once we have our drinks, Jude leads me outside and helps me into one of the patio chairs. When he settles into the chair across from me, he unbuttons the cuffs of his shirt and rolls the sleeves to his elbows.

Which is just completely unfair. Heat rushes through me, my chest warming with an intense blush. Jude glances up at me, and he cocks an eyebrow, pausing for a heartbeat before finishing the second sleeve. I manage to take an unsteady breath as he takes a sip of his drink. My gaze catches on another small script tattoo along the base of his right wrist.

"What does that one say?" I ask.

He twists his wrist so the black lettering is more visible, but it's upside down. I shake my head and look back at him.

"Memento vivere," he murmurs, his rough voice skating over my skin, eliciting a small shiver down my spine. "It means remember to live."

I swallow. "Did you get that one after your sister, too?"

"No. Carter and I got them after we made the choice to file the paperwork with the Council to officially become a pack," he says. "It wasn't the best time, and Logan said we should have a reminder that life can be meaningful."

My heart lurches. What had happened that made registering such a painful time for both of them?

"Is it too forward to ask what happened to your sister?" I ask instead. Jude coughs, covering a laugh, and I offer a quick quirk of my lips. "I'll take that as a yes. Let's pretend I didn't ask that and start over."

He stops trying to hide his laugh, running a hand through his beard, his eyes scrunched in amusement. I bask in the sound, happy that I'm able to make him lose the stoic look.

"How long has she been gone?" I ask when his laughter quiets.

He sets his coffee down. "Eleven years this September."

"What happened?"

"A drunk driver ran through a stop sign. She was dropping a friend off after a party since she was the only one of her group that stayed sober." My stomach twists, and I mess with my orbital piercing, spinning it as I bite my lip. "Her friend somehow managed to walk away with just a broken leg, but Iris wasn't as lucky. By the time I was able to get to the hospital, she was already declared brain dead."

Jude looks out over the river.

"And no, we didn't really have any family left. Our mom was an only child and had died a couple years prior from aggressive breast cancer. And she was a single parent."

"That must have been awful for you to have to shoulder alone," I whisper, blinking away tears.

He's silent, looking across the river, his eyebrows drawn low. I reach across the table, holding my breath as I lace my fingers with his, bracing for him to brush me off. Instead, he tightens his grip and sighs.

"It was," he says. He runs a hand over his beard again before taking a drink. When he sets the cup down, he looks right at me. My breath catches. "And I think some choices I made then will have a direct impact on you."

I tilt my head, looking past him to the trolly that is getting ready to leave. Someone throws their head back and laughs, the sound startling a group of birds nearby. When I refocus on Jude, his gaze is on our joined hands, and he runs his thumb over mine in the barest touch.

It's clear he won't bring up his worry unless I ask about it.

I wouldn't be Faedra Rose if I backed away from a line.

"Why do you think that?" I ask, and he takes another long drink of his coffee, letting his eyes close.

To his credit, he doesn't look away from me as he tells me.

"I ended up dating the friend." His admission is low, gruff. He doesn't wait for my response before continuing. "People who know more about psychology would probably call it trauma bonding. She was...all I had left of Iris. It wasn't perfect, but the first year was fine. I didn't understand how it morphed until I was looking back after five years and realized who I had been was gone."

I tightened my grip on his hand but didn't say anything.

"She got her masters and an assistant professor position at the same university where I was working to secure tenure—and now have. We bought a small condo in the Highlands, which is just across the highway." He points to his left, and I glance at the mid-rise apartments lining the other edge of the interstate. "When we met Logan, Carter and I had written off the possibility of being registered as a pack. But the more we hung out as friends, the more the idea started to carry weight. Logan brought it up maybe a year after meeting him. She and I were in a rough patch anyway. The choice was simple and yet not. It's... hard to explain. I knew choosing to pursue registering was the right choice for me and my life. But she liked things as they were."

He blows out a breath and shrugs.

"You know what I ultimately decided. It was anything but an amicable ending to the relationship." His lips twist into a sardonic half smile, his eyes shadowing with a lingering wound. I tighten my grip again.

"That took a lot of bravery to realize your life wasn't what you had wanted and start over." He takes a deep breath with my words, and some tension bleeds away from his shoulders. I give myself a mental high five.

"It was actually Iris that gave me the courage to do it," he says, setting aside his coffee and reaching across the table, palm up, in silent question. I don't hesitate, placing my other hand in his and leaning forward, focusing on the way the light catches the gray in his beard, making it seem to shift colors with each small movement he makes. A pulse of heat shoots through my core.

"Really?" I ask, trying to distract myself.

He runs his thumb over my fingers, featherlight, and I clench my thighs.

What was with my body being suddenly so responsive?

"There's a small box of Iris's things that I kept. I was going through them one night while Melanie was out late with friends. I couldn't tell you why. I hadn't touched that box in years. But tucked between the pages of a notebook she'd used to write poems in, I found a list." He pauses and glances at the river, his shoulders dropping as his look turns thoughtful. "It was a bucket list of sorts. Except after each item, there was a reason why it couldn't happen. Her age. Her ability. Her lack of funding. Her designation. All these dreams, and she found a way to justify pursuing none of them under the guise of waiting for a time when she was better prepared. It was the loudest wake up call I've ever gotten."

A breeze picks up, and I tuck my hair behind my ear before tracing the bones of his wrist, the flowing script of the small Latin tattoo.

"Does she still work at the university with you?"

He gives a single nod. "In a different department, but yes. Last I heard, she was working on her doctorate so she can pursue tenure."

My chest tightens as nerves roar to the forefront, making my stomach lurch.

"I don't suppose she'll end up deciding to like me." The joke falls a bit flat, but he offers a small lift of his lips, the smile lines around his eyes showing for a brief moment. I sigh and lean across the table. "Thank you for telling me."

His lips are soft against mine, and I bask in the taste of him on my tongue.

Fifteen

CARTER

"Can you put this one up there, too?" Faedra asks from where she stands next to the ladder, a moderately sized trailing plant in her hands.

I take it from her without comment, setting it next to the two others already on the shelf above the large bed in her nest room. She hums, tilting her head, and I wait for the correction that's coming.

"Can you switch the two smaller ones?" While I work on adjusting them, she sighs and looks around, bouncing on the balls of her feet and twisting her hair into a bun at the top of her head. "Did I leave the picture boxes in my room?"

"I put them on the dresser," I say as I get off the ladder. She crosses the room, picking up one of the boxes and opening the lid. She's quick to recover it and set it on the bed, though, reaching for the other one instead.

"Were you thinking about hanging some of them in here?" I ask, coming up behind her and feathering a kiss on her shoulder.

She hums again, a tune that feels familiar but that I couldn't name. "Want me to go grab the photo lines you picked out this morning?"

She nods, but as I move away from her, she whines, the sound low in her throat and nearly silent. I pause, and she turns around, pressing her forehead into my sternum. Her body relaxes as I wrap my arms around her waist and pull her into me, pressing my lips to the crown of her head.

Today's the first day of her starting to fully wean off the suppressors, and the changes have been nearly instantaneous. I pull my phone from the back pocket of my jeans and shoot Jude a quick text. He's just outside the door, reading through a student's thesis in preparation for evaluation, but we've had the door closed to keep our distractions to a minimum.

> Can you grab the photo display hook sets for us? Pretty sure I left them on the dining table.

"You alright, Faedra?" I ask after a minute, tracing small shapes on her hip.

She takes a deep breath, her hands twisting into the waistband of my jeans even as the jasmine aroma of her scent starts to permeate the air around us. I tighten my hold on her, keeping on to my control by the skin of my teeth so I don't scent in response. The door opens, Jude stepping inside soundlessly, his eyebrow rising as he takes in her scent. His throat moves with a heavy swallow. Before she notices his presence, he sets the hangers on the dresser and closes the door, leaving us alone again.

After another quiet minute, Faedra releases her hold on me, messing with her ear piercings as she pulls out of my arms.

"Thanks," she whispers, her shoulders tighter than I would like. I don't push her, though, letting her have this moment to recalibrate while I open the packages and lay out the displays on the bed. She takes the box of photos and sits on the edge, flipping through them and arranging them on the cords without comment, and I step back, leaning against the windows, content to watch her. She bites her lip the entire time her hands move, readjusting and moving photos around until she stands and smiles.

"Can they go above the dresser?"

"Of course," I say, moving the ladder and getting her opinion on where she wants them.

While I work to get them hung up, she takes a deep breath and asks, "How often do you see Gina?"

Not the question I was expecting.

"We try to get together every couple weeks for brunch, but it depends on her schedule. We haven't managed recently with Hallie being little still and Ashlynn just returning to work." I step off the ladder and move it out of the way so that she can see the photos in their entirety. A soft smile makes her eyes brighten.

"You want children?"

If there's one thing I've learned about Faedra since she's been out here with us, it's that she doesn't beat around the bush. She never intends for it to be rude or insensitive, but she never backs away from uncomfortable or taboo topics. I offer her the truth in exchange for her bravery.

"Eventually," I say, tucking my hands into my pockets again, watching as she hops onto the dresser and rearranges a couple of the photos. She glances over her shoulder, a few strands of her hair falling out of the haphazard bun and framing her face. "I wasn't sure if I did for a long time. But seeing Gina and Ashlynn have Darius and then Hallie has changed my perspective. I'm not in any rush, though."

Her look turns contemplative, her eyes unfocusing as she taps the wall a couple times.

"You've been friends with them a long time?" she asks, and I offer a nod.

The chime of the dryer finishing has me opening the door to the ensuite, stepping inside and grabbing the new linens she picked. They're a deep navy with gold veining, reminding me of an oddly colored marble. Faedra is quiet as she watches me make the bed, tucking the comforter in at the bottom and fluffing the pillows. When I glance back up at her, she's locked on my mouth, a deep blush staining her cheeks.

Jasmine fills the room again.

"We met them the first time we did the hike," I say, helping diffuse the tense moment between us.

Her craving for touch is getting more intense, and I want to make sure it isn't influencing her desire to have sex with me. Or at least that it isn't the driving factor. She licks her lips, and my cock notices, pressing against the zipper of my jeans.

I say something before my good intentions are thrown out the window and right over the balcony's edge.

"That was twelve years ago." My voice drops, rougher than I intend.

She nods, ducking her head and taking a deep breath. Her feet land on the parquet floor a moment later.

"What do you think?" I ask her, crossing the room to stand in front of her. She gazes at the room around me for a half second before focusing on me again—on my lips. Before I can prepare, she's on her tiptoes, pressing her body into me as she kisses me.

Fuck it.

I cup her cheek and twist my fingers into her hair, guiding her head to the side until I have the perfect angle to delve into her mouth. Her hands slide up my sides, taking my shirt with them, and she whimpers into the kiss as she palms my chest. I grab her thighs and lift her back onto the dresser, pulling her legs open and stepping between them. Her hands tremble against my skin even as she presses her hips into me, the scrape of her pussy against my jeans making me groan.

She pushes my shirt up as far as it can go, and I pull it off with one hand, tossing it on the floor behind me. When I try to kiss her again, she unbuttons the front of her tank top, the sides falling open and exposing the nude colored lace of her bra. Her scent wraps around us, intoxicating me, and I finally let go of my control, letting my own pine scent mix with hers as I trace the edge of one cup with my tongue. She shudders against me, a near silent whine coasting across my ear.

The moment I run my hands up her thighs and trace the outline of her panties, she tenses and pulls away from me, her chest heaving. Her cheeks are a deep red, and her eyes are shy as she bites her lip. When I pull my hands back to her knees, tracing circles around them, she blows out a breath and ducks her head.

Yeah, that's not going to work for me.

"You alright?" I ask, tucking my finger under her chin and making her look at me.

"Um, yeah," she says, her blush deepening. "I'm just..." She groans. "I'm still on my period even though it's been forever."

I squeeze her knees, reassuring her with my touch as much as possible. Period sex doesn't bother me. It's just a little extra clean up, but it clearly worries her.

"You want to stop?"

She nods, and I cup her face, offering a soft kiss to assuage her embarrassment. I help her down from the dresser and pick up my shirt.

"Do you still want to go get the rest of the furniture for your room?" I ask, and she smiles, murmuring an affirmative. I run my hand through my hair. "Let me grab a shower, and we'll see if Jude is able to go, too."

"Sounds great," she says, opening the door before grabbing both photo boxes.

Jude doesn't make a comment as our combined scents follow us out of the room, though his eyebrow raises and his lips thin. I don't offer an explanation, hell bent on getting to the shower. Once I'm under the spray, I finally give in and rub one out, groaning her name the entire time.

Sixteen

FAEDRA

The computer screen flashes, the small dialogue box indicating the application was successfully submitted. I breathe out a sigh of relief, stretching my neck and pulling my hair down from where it's clipped. Seven applications filled out and submitted. Seven portfolios curated to each school's requirements. I glance at the small clock on the dresser across from where I lay on my bed.

Quarter to midnight. My eyes burn, and my head feels like mush, but there's an antsy energy in my limbs. Closing the laptop, I set it on the nightstand and cross the room to the bathroom, brushing my teeth and washing my face, going through my normal night routine in the hopes of it calming me down enough to actually fall asleep. I stare at the bed as I finish switching into a satin slip, my eyes aching but my limbs still full of twitchy energy. I blow out a breath, running my hand through my hair as I collect it over one shoulder.

Before I realize what I'm even doing, I'm standing in front of

Logan's room, my hand falling against the door in a soft, hesitant knock. There's a pause and the sound of some shuffling behind the door before it opens in one quick swing.

Logan's hair is disheveled, his blue eyes full of sleep, but he quickly focuses when he realizes it's me standing on the threshold.

"You alright, Red?" he asks, taking a half step into me. I tilt my head back to keep eye contact, my body relaxing at his touch. When I nod, he breathes out a sigh. "What's up?"

"I just finished all my applications and can't manage to fall asleep," I say, keeping my voice soft, unsure if the others are light sleepers. He palms my waist, his fingers brushing along my ribs and hip bone. Heat rushes through me, and my cheeks flush. His gaze darkens as he hums, a low vibration in his chest. God damn it, I swore I wouldn't be the blushing virgin. Clearing my throat, I ask, "Can I stay with you tonight?"

He pulls me into him, my chest crushing against his, and brushes his lips against mine. The kiss is soft and quick, but my heart races all the same. I swallow my groan as he pulls away and guides me into his room.

I do my best not to gawk, but my eyes catch on the simple oak dresser and large canvas hung above it, the scene a gorgeous panorama of a canyon with walls that are nearly black. In front of me, a small lamp illuminates a nightstand beside the largest bed I've ever seen fitted with white linens.

Logan settles in the bed without missing a beat, pulling the comforter back enough that I can slide in next to him. His bed smells like his cologne—sandalwood and cedar—and the faint musk of his sweat. The restless sensation in my chest calms as I breathe deeply, and Logan chuckles under his breath, his eyes bright with amusement while wrapping an arm around my waist and pulling me flush with him. The warmth of his body seeps into me, and I close my eyes. Goosebumps ghost across my skin as he rests his lips in the crook of my shoulder.

"Thank you," I murmur.

Logan laughs, the sound low and derisive. "Don't thank me, Faedra. I crave you just as much as you're craving me."

JUDE

My phone flashes with another text from Melanie, and I don't bother to hold back my sigh, frustration making my movements clipped as I close my bedroom door and head down to the kitchen.

> You've been scarce. Get lunch with me.

Jesus Christ.

Before I can close the thread, another message appears.

> Come on. You enjoyed the last one. 😉

As if I need another goddamn reminder of my poor decision after the gala. I send back a single word and then tuck my phone into the front pocket of my slacks.

> No.

The living room is still dark, the sunrise not yet illuminating enough of the sky for it to make it to this side of the building. Leaning against the island counter, I look across the mountain view, breathing deep to try and center myself. Once I'm sure the insidious self-hatred hasn't gotten any worse, I grab one of the breakfast burritos Logan batch makes every few weeks and set it to warming in the microwave.

Three sequential vibrations tell me that Melanie's not going to be deterred today. I silently curse her, myself, and that drunk driver as I go about getting the espresso machine working.

Three days and then I don't have to deal with her for a solid week.

There's a soft click of a door closing, and I glance up, my eyebrows furrowing. Who was up in the loft so early in the morning?

Faedra's copper hair catches the light as she turns away from the door to her nest room, and my confusion eases away. Her hands are closed tightly around an impressive camera and lens. Her hair is pulled back into a messy bun, a tendril of hair tracing down her neck the way I want to with my tongue. Her legs are practically bare, a navy blue satin slip hitting her mid-thigh, and I swallow a groan as I realize she's braless, her nipples peaking through the thin material. She's ethereal in the low light, her skin the alabaster of the snow capped mountains in winter, and my throat dries as the realization sweeps over me that she's *mine*.

At least until she realizes just how fucked the situation is with Melanie and requests reassignment. Disgust sours my stomach, and I turn away, opening the door to the microwave before it reaches the end of the timer. Her soft footfalls pause on the stairs.

"Oh," she says, her voice blending in with the quiet morning.

I plate the burrito and start to heat another one, turning once I hear her steps resume. Her movements are careful as she sets the camera on the island and walks around it, her hand twisting the tragus piercing in her right ear.

Sparkle catches the light as her fingers move. She's changed it, the small gold hoop replaced with a flower, each petal a different sapphire gem. Once I notice it, I realize her other one is different, too. She's added a small gold moon pendant to the hoop, the delicate chain brushing against the shell of her ear.

Fuck, but I want to follow that with my tongue, too. My cock presses against my slacks in complete agreement.

"I didn't realize you would be up this early," she says, biting her lip.

"Department meeting." I explain on a rasp.

She nods as I grab the caramel syrup and milk and go about recreating my preferred coffee house drink in a to-go cup. By the time I turn back to her, my cock has decided to play nice, and I can look her in the eye without imagining the way she would look on her knees in front of me.

I hand her the plated burrito before grabbing the second one.

"What were you photographing?" I ask, leaning against the counter. My phone vibrates again, and I hold back a sigh.

"The sunrise," she says, finishing her burrito and putting the plate in the sink. "The balcony on that side has a small section that looks over the city instead of the mountains. I was playing around with silhouetting the buildings."

She grabs the camera and flips through a couple photos. "It's always hard to tell on the small screen, but I think I finally managed to get the settings right for the last half dozen or so." I move to stand beside her, running my hand down her spine before palming her hip and pulling her into me enough that I can see the camera screen, too. "I was going to add a couple of them to the groups of photos I have in my, um, nest room."

Her cheeks bloom with a dark red blush, and her fingers twitch, her eyes dropping to her outfit before flicking to me. Setting the camera on the counter, she clears her throat and ducks her head.

"Let me go grab a sweater."

I grab her hand before she takes more than a couple steps away from me, running my thumb over her knuckles.

"Are you cold?" I ask, playing naive. I know damn well she's going because she thinks it's improper for her to be in this slip around me.

She shakes her head. I squeeze her hand, trying to tell her with my touch that it's fine for her to dress however she wants in her own goddamn home. Her throat moves with a swallow, and a thread of her jasmine scent surrounds me. The moment stretches between us, her arousal permeating the space around us, until she finally nods and steps into me, tilting her head and pressing her lips to mine.

My control snaps as easily as a twig beneath my foot on the trail.

I have her on the counter and her knees bracketing my hips before she can pull away, her slip bunched to her hips and the matching panties covering her cunt on full display.

She whispers, "Why didn't I smell your cologne before?"

I trail my hands up her legs, smirking when she shivers in my hold.

"It's not cologne," I say, sucking on her bottom lip and nipping it.

Her scent increases, and I pull her towards me, stopping myself from grinding into her only when I see the light reflecting off the slick already drenching her thighs. Her eyebrows furrow for a heartbeat before understanding flashes across her face.

"Oh," she murmurs, kissing me again, digging her nails into the back of my neck and using the leverage to pull herself closer to me. A soft whine falls from her lips as her nipples brush across my suit jacket.

Fuck, but her scent is so strong I'm practically choking on it.

I feather a touch along the edge of her panties, and she whines again, pressing into my hand. The invitation is enough for me. Pulling her panties to the side, I flick my gaze down, soaking in the sight of the short red curls nestled between her thighs, her pussy bare and soft, opening for me the moment my hand strokes across it.

"Fuck," I mutter, circling her clit. Her hips jerk, a surprised gasp making her chest brush across me again. "You good?" I manage to finally check in with her.

She nods, dropping her forehead to my shoulder, her hands skating down my chest and to the belt around my hips. I shake my head, pressing a kiss into her hair before grabbing her wrist, stopping her movements.

"No?" She double checks, and I nod, increasing the pressure of my touch on her clit. She rolls her lips together and sets them against my throat, her breath hot on my skin and making my cock ache even more.

If she so much as undoes my belt, I'll have her laid out and coming around my cock hard enough that she won't notice my knot locking us until it's too late. And I really, really can't call out of this department meeting. She presses her palms against my stomach, her hips rising to my touch, trying to entice me into moving faster. She breathes a moan when I press a finger into her pussy, her walls clamping down around me tighter than I've ever felt before.

Fuck, is she a virgin?

The question sits at the back of my mind the entire time I press into her, the wet heat of her cunt making my cock so hard it practically weeps. Before I can voice the question, though, she grinds against me, another desperate moan coasting between us, her nails digging into my skin. Her entire body tightens when I curl my finger, a strangled cry echoing around the kitchen as she squirms on the counter, clamping her thighs around my wrist. She grows impossibly tighter as her orgasm builds, and I swallow a groan. I press my thumb into her clit again, drawing small circles around it as I suck on the pulse point below her ear.

"Oh god," she gasps just as her body locks. Her knees press

into my hips, pulling me toward her, a subtle invitation that I don't even think she knows she's making. A second later, a rush of wet heat drenches my hand as her body responds with slick despite my knot being uninvolved with her orgasm. "Oh *god*."

All I want is to stay right here, her body pressed against me, her cunt open and inviting, her scent enveloping us so completely that I can't even smell my coffee on the counter next to her. Kissing her hair, I slow my hand. She turns her head, pressing her lips into my shoulder as she whimpers, her thighs trembling with my softening touch against her clit.

My phone rings with my warning alarm, and I sigh. I trace my nose down her throat, pressing a kiss into the sensitive spot where her shoulder and neck meet.

"I have to go," I murmur into her skin. Her nails dig into me again as she fists her hands, but she takes a deep breath and drops them to her sides, grabbing the edge of the counter. "Fuck, Faedra, I don't want to."

I kiss her again, distracting her from my pulling away from her cunt, and she shivers, her knees tightening for a heartbeat again. My cock aches, the desire to knot with her slamming into me so overwhelmingly that it's all I can manage to think about.

I push away from the counter, feathering two soft kisses across her temple, a sense of pride making me grin as I take in her disheveled appearance, her hair mostly fallen from the bun and cascading around her shoulders. Grabbing the coffee in my still wet hand, I cup her face and kiss her thoroughly.

"I'll miss you," she admits against my mouth, the words quiet but sure.

I groan. "I'll miss you, too, Omega."

Before my cock can derail me any more this morning, I turn from her and head across the condo, closing the door as quietly as I can manage. Pulling my phone, I accidentally tap on the unread messages from Melanie.

> Is it because there's someone new?

> Harper hasn't mentioned you guys going anywhere. Aside from that weekend trip you just took.

> I miss you. Don't you miss me?

The last is just another picture of her in a racy set of lingerie, posing for the camera. Bile makes my throat burn, and I curse before deleting it.

I text her again.

> Don't miss you.

The only woman I miss anymore is the one I just left on the counter of my condo.

Seventeen

FAEDRA

"Oh shit," I mutter, dropping the hexagons I'm working on and pressing my thumb against my lips. The salty taste of my blood makes me grimace, but I don't risk moving and getting blood on the fabric. Part of me wants to toss the whole project off the balcony, but I manage to breathe through the urge. It's not the quilt's fault my attention is nearly as shot now as it was when I was trying to fumble through my finals a month ago.

My phone vibrates, and I grab it, my thumb temporarily forgotten as my heart lodges in my throat. The notification sticks out against my wallpaper, the calm notice that the package from the university has been delivered. I wipe my thumb on my skirt, twisting it into the hem until the last of the bleeding stops, and then collect the flowers I was working on, tucking them into the project bag and stashing it on the end table beside the sofa. I catch my reflection in the mirror above the entry table, and I adjust my hair, pulling back the top half and securing it with a small clip, a few pieces falling and framing my face. The elevator seems to take forever, and my heart rate picks up with each minute that passes until my head is light and I have to close my eyes in the mail room to keep from passing out.

My hands tremble as I open the mailbox, and my anxiety triples when I realize there's more than one information packet waiting for me. Nerves double in my belly as I flip through them, all three of my top choices in the pile. My hands shake, and I lean against the mailboxes, letting the cool metal calm me enough so that I can think.

My first instinct is to call Logan, but when I grab my phone, I realize he's in the middle of one of his weekly training sessions with an athlete. I pull up the addresses of both of the other guys' offices. Jude's is across the city, nestled between the event center and the amusement park. But Carter's is just down the street in a building that borders the river and the highway—a manageable walk.

I put the rest of the mail back in the box with the promise that I'll take it up to the condo when I get back before shoving the college packets into my bag and slinging it over my shoulder. My phone is a bit confused about my location as I leave the condo through the lobby instead of the garage, so it takes a couple minutes to figure out which direction I need to go. The sun is bright, reflecting off the nearly all-glass buildings I walk towards, and I cover my eyes until I can get my sunglasses on to cut down the worst of it.

The city is bustling around me, people walking in every direction. Several pass me as I cross one of the main public transport stations, heading across the tracks in the opposite direction of where the train goes. The cloudless sky helps clear my head, my nerves easing, and I manage to smile as I take in the architecture of this part of the city, the high rises giving way to much smaller buildings and then a large greenway that runs the length of the river.

My phone guides me across a small pedestrian bridge and then down a much quieter street, the trees here taller and the buildings only a couple stories high. The building it stops me in front of is all glass and wedged right up against the highway. Its lobby is open and modern in the extreme, low profile, metal desks situated in front of a few large glass doors and groups of black leather chairs situated across the main space of the floor. The suite number on the address Carter gave me indicates the sixth floor—which I'm almost positive is the uppermost. The elevator confirms it only a moment later as I step inside it and select the proper floor. My skin grows tight in the small space, and I breathe through my nose to help alleviate it.

The elevator opens into a single wide foyer, a woman sitting behind a sleek black desk about ten feet away, her voice carrying across the room despite the unobtrusive placement of sound dampeners along the walls. I glance around, taking in the warm tones of the space before walking up to the woman.

"How can I help you, ma'am?" the woman asks, turning from her computer and smiling at me.

"I'm here to see Carter Bennett," I say, keeping my posture relaxed and my voice light.

She raises an eyebrow but points to the hallway to my left.

"All the way at the end. His assistant will be able to get you checked in."

I murmur a thanks and walk down the hall, noting the amount of offices between the receptionist and his office in the corner. Aren't start-ups typically small ventures?

The door at the end of the hallway is open, so I step inside, adjusting my bag and dropping my phone into the side pocket. A woman about Aiden's age sits behind a desk made nearly entirely of glass. Her dark hair is pulled back into a no-nonsense chignon, and she is wearing a deep plum pencil skirt that contrasts with her pale pink sleeveless blouse. I pause just inside the door, watching as her hands fly over the keyboard as she responds to something, muttering under her breath. A small nameplate rests on the edge of the desk just in front of her computer monitor, announcing her as Amanda.

"May I help you?" she asks, clicking through something before glancing up. Her apology is immediate as she gets up and rounds the desk. "Sorry, I didn't realize. Faedra, right?"

I smile, trying to allay her worries without speaking too much. My skin still feels tight, and my attention is fried, the calming walk already giving way to the fuzzy feeling I felt when I was quilting.

"Is Carter available?" I manage to ask, my voice only a bit breathless. "I didn't give him any warning I was on my way."

Amanda smiles and glances back at the computer, clicking on something before nodding.

"He typically works with the door closed even when he doesn't have an appointment," she explains, tucking her bangs behind her ear. "Feel free to walk on in. I've blocked out his schedule and phone until his meeting this afternoon so you don't get interrupted."

My cheeks heat, but I ignore them, offering a smile. "Thank you, Amanda."

She waves me off, a quiet "No problem" following me as I head towards the door behind her desk.

The restlessness in my body seems to double, which is both impressive and infuriating. It feels as if all I've done the last several days since nearly weaning off the suppressors is get more hot and bothered than any other time of my life combined. Memories of Jude fingering me on the kitchen counter pass through my mind, and my body flushes, a shock of lightning shooting down my spine. Sharing Logan's bed nearly every night certainly hasn't helped, either, but I refuse to regret it. The way these men make me feel, the sensations they've pulled from my body without even knotting with me, is worth every moment away from them feeling like this.

Blowing out a breath, I adjust my bag, switching it to my other shoulder, and then gently push the door open.

Carter's office sits on the side of the building overlooking the highway. I take a careful step into the space, my breath catching when I take in the view. The mountains stand tall behind the row of mid-rise apartments, the highest peaks still covered in snow despite it practically being the middle of June. The windows must be top tier because I can't hear any of the cars racing by on the road below.

"Faedra? Is everything alright? I thought you and Logan were working on your room again today."

Despite Carter's voice being full of worry, his cadence dropping into a low, soothing baritone, the restless energy roiling through me settles a bit. Finally able to pull in a full breath, I let his voice pull my attention away from the full height window. He stands from where he's perched behind his large walnut desk, a series of files spread across its surface nearest me and an Apple monitor and keyboard nestled into the middle of the other portion, the screen black.

He's dressed in navy today, his grey tie held with a minimalist tie tack that matches his cuff links. He pulls off a small set of readers and sets them behind the keyboard. When I don't say anything, he rounds the desk and crosses the room, extending a hand to me.

"Are you reacting to coming off the suppressors?" he asks.

"I'm fine," I assure him, taking his hand and lacing our fingers together.

He runs his thumbs over my knuckles, and my thighs fucking clench. I amend the thought. Turned on and flustered as hell, but *technically* fine. He pulls me into his chest, arms wrapping around my waist as he kisses the crown of my head.

"I got packets from three of the schools and didn't want to open them alone," I explain, my lips brushing the buttons running down his chest. "Logan got a call a while ago, and now he's meeting with one of his regular athletes."

He kisses my temple as he steps away, leading me around the desk. "Come sit," he says.

I'm content to follow him.

Once he's settled in the chair, he extends his other hand to me, keeping me steady while I arrange myself sideways in his lap. I lean my head against his shoulder just as I drop my bag to the floor at his feet. His scent surrounds me, and I turn until my nose is buried in his neck. His hand rakes through my hair, and I can't help but shiver as goosebumps echo the path his fingers take along my shin. His chest vibrates with a content hum.

With each second that passes, my stomach settles and the insidious restless, anxious feeling that's been with me since Logan left finally starts to subside. Another deep breath full of his pine scent, and I manage to sit up and grab the packets from my bag. The hand that's in my hair drops to my waist, coasting down my spine, and I clench my thighs again. Another hum rumbles through him, lower than I've ever heard before.

I grab all three packets, resting them in my lap, tapping my thumb on them as I look at Carter, my lip between my teeth as I try to decide in what order to open them. Eyes intent on me, he grabs a small letter opener from the top drawer of the desk, his arms creating a strong cage around me. I settle deeper into the safety of his touch, his body, *him*. He makes quick work of all three seals before wedging the packets between our bodies and putting the letter opener back. I blow out a breath and grab the first one, pulling the first page from the envelope.

"Accepted," I breathe, and Carter squeezes my shin. He

hands me the next packet, and my nerves tick higher. This one doesn't have a succinct letter outside of the information, so I pull the entire packet out and fish through the papers until I find the one I'm looking for. I laugh, nerves falling away. "This one, too."

Carter smiles, pulling me into him and kissing my temple. Blowing out a breath, I grab the last one.

"This is the one I really want," I say, turning the envelope over in my hands. "It's nearby and offers both an in person and a hybrid option. And it seems to be one of the more progressive schools in terms of accommodations for Omegas during their heats."

I can't manage to open the envelope, the words printed on the small, impersonal labels feeling larger than life at the moment. Carter gently pulls it from my hands, and my breath catches. He hooks a finger under my chin, guiding me to look at him. I go willingly, locking my gaze with his a moment before he's pressing a gentle, intimate kiss to my lips. My eyes flutter shut, and he deepens the kiss, tongue tracing over mine. His hands brush mine as he pulls a single piece of paper from the envelope and sets it in my lap. I kiss him harder, eliciting a soft groan from between his lips.

Eventually, he pulls away, that finger under my chin becoming his entire hand cupping my jaw.

"Look, Faedra," he whispers. "I want you to look before I see what it says."

A lump settles in my throat, and I swallow, trying to get it unstuck. Why is this one so much harder than the paperwork the Council sent about my match?

Probably because I could actually fail this one. And I *really* don't want to fail this one.

My eyes flick to the paper resting against my thighs, and my breath catches. I look up at Carter, a grin on my face, at the same moment he looks at the acceptance letter. He smiles just as I slam my lips into his, dropping the paper and twisting my hands into his wavy hair. His arm bands around me, fingers spreading across my hip, and pulls me closer into him.

"Good job, Faedra," he whispers against my lips before kissing me again. "I'm so proud of you."

His words touch a place in me I didn't know existed, a deep well that absorbs them and desires more. A shot of heat races through me, pooling in my core, and I clench my thighs again, trying to find enough friction to ease the ache blooming between them. Carter's hand tightens, fingers digging into my hip bone, but it only causes my skin to grow hotter, tighter. My tongue moves more insistently against his, communicating everything I can't manage to put into words at the moment.

My scent floods the space in the next heartbeat, overwhelming us both before I can hope to stop it. He pulls away with a groan.

"Faedra, love, you're hell on my control."

His own scent strengthens, cocooning me in the smell of pine and smoke. I hum, pushing into him again, chasing his lips, following the instinctual drive of my body, the feelings more intense in the sudden absence of the suppressors.

Carter groans again, chest rumbling, and then I'm in his arms as he stands, the information from the universities crashing to the floor at his feet. He reaches out, pushing the open files to one side of the desk, making some of them fall off the edge. His urgency sets me aflame, and I whine into his mouth as he perches me on the desk. He steps between my legs, forcing them wide even as I squirm, my clit hyper sensitive.

I don't even think as he crowds into me—I just grab my shirt and pull it over my head, dropping it at his feet. Carter's response is instant, his hands cupping my breasts, his thumbs pushing aside the cups of my bra. His lips trace down my throat, his tongue flicking across my collar bones. A quick flick, and he has my bra falling to the ground beside my shirt.

He wrings a gasp out of me as he sets his mouth against me, pulling my nipple past his teeth and sucking gently. Goosebumps ghost across my skin, and I shiver. He moves to the other breast, giving it the same attention, his teeth lightly scraping as he pulls his mouth away. I can't help but moan, squirming again, my clit so sensitive I can feel my heartbeat. Slipping beneath my skirt, his hands skate to the tops of my thighs, his fingers brushing the creases of my hips, and his eyes are hot as he takes in my green lace panties. He traces my pussy, and he groans, his finger coming away wet from my slick.

Slick I didn't even realize my body could create until Jude wrung an orgasm from me a few days ago.

"Are you really going to let your Alpha eat you out on this desk, Faedra?" Carter's voice lowers until it vibrates through my bones.

Rolling my hips, trying to ease the tension lacing my body, I nod. My chest shudders with my desperate breaths.

"You'll have to be quiet," he says, running a palm up my sternum to rest at the base of my throat. I can't help but arch into his touch. "I don't want anyone else hearing what my Omega sounds like when she comes. I'm horribly jealous."

I hum, running my hands up his stomach, letting my nails bite into his skin through the fabric of his shirt.

"I'll try, Carter," I manage to gasp.

He hums and grabs my hips, pulling me closer to the edge of the desk. A moment later, he's on his knees, ripping my panties at the seams and dropping them to the ground. His eyes rake over me, and I squirm, suddenly nervous.

Should I tell him this is my first time? That Jude fingering me on the counter is the farthest I've ever gotten with a partner? Does he even know about what Jude and I did?

His hands tighten on my hips, forcing me to stillness.

"Perfect," he whispers, and I gasp at the feel of his breath against me, the sensation foreign.

He smirks, running his thumbs along my center, and I feel my slick running onto my thighs—and his fingers. My blush is as fierce as it is fast, but my thoughts drift away in the next moment because his tongue is on me, flicking across my clit.

Oh. My. God.

I twist my hands into his hair and hold him to me, any thought of embarrassment lost to the moment. When my fingers start to tingle, my toes curling as that wave begins to crest inside me, I pull on his hair.

"Let me knot with you," I whisper, just shy of begging.

Eighteen

FAEDRA

"Please, Carter." I am definitely begging now. I pull on his hair, keeping his tongue from sending me over the edge. "I need you."

He stands in one smooth motion, his lips and chin glistening with my slick. He swipes his forearm across his mouth, the sleeve coming away soaked, and I blush. A flash of a smile, and then he kisses me, hands cupping my face, thumbs tracing my cheekbones as he twists his tongue into my mouth. The taste of myself on his lips makes me even more needy, a groan spilling out of me as I trace the buckle of his belt.

"Faedra," he groans. "Please tell me you've been on top of your pill."

I nod.

"Thank fuck," he murmurs. "I don't have condoms here."

I want to make a joke, but my body is strung too tight, the arousal quickly bleeding over into something painful.

"It aches," I whisper when he pulls away, my fingers still tracing his belt. "It's never felt like this."

His eyes narrow, his hands running down my throat before he closes the space between us, the weight of his erection nestling against me. My breath catches. He feels enormous, and when his hands drop to manage the belt and zipper keeping him from me, I start panicking over how this will work.

I should tell him, shouldn't I? But what if he feels like we should stop and wait for a more romantic moment? My body rebels at the thought, my pulse pounding through my clit, making me hyperaware of it. I swallow, trying to soothe my suddenly dry throat as I grasp the edge of the desk with one hand and mess with my piercings with the other.

"What is it, Faedra?" Carter asks, gaze focusing on my fidgeting.

He leans forward and catches my bottom lip between his teeth, biting until I gasp and licking the mark the moment he releases me. He places his hands next to my hips, easing me forward until I'm perching on the very edge of the desk, the head of his cock rubbing against my clit. I suck in a breath and let my eyes flutter closed.

"Faedra," he murmurs against my lips. "You alright?"

I swallow again, stealing a kiss before opening my eyes and whispering, "Promise you won't panic."

I will quite possibly die if he stops when I tell him the truth.

His eyes narrow, but he nods, pulling away from me and cupping my knees. I roll my hips, whimpering at the feel of him against me, against my clit. He groans but doesn't move to do anything more.

I run my tongue over my lips, twisting the gold hoop once before admitting the truth.

"I've never done this before."

The confession falls from my lips, breathed in the scant space between us a second before his lips are against me, his tongue twisting with mine again.

"Good," he grunts as he pulls away. "I'm glad I'm the first one to fuck you on a desk." His voice is practically a purr, so low it vibrates through his chest.

My body responds in a heartbeat—a rush of wet heat pulses through me, my scent grows suffocatingly strong, and my hips push forward, notching the head of his cock at my entrance. He laces his fingers with mine, cupping my face and tracing my piercings as he teases me, pressing in just enough that I feel the intense stretch.

"Carter," I whimper.

His voice is a rasp against my skin, his brown eyes intent on me, and I shiver. "Little Omega."

He presses in again, the sensation even more overwhelming, and it elicits a throaty noise as my thighs tremble.

I squeeze his hand.

"I meant I've never had sex," I whisper.

Carter drops his forehead to mine, eyes closing, an almost mournful groan rumbling through him.

"Fuck," he mutters.

I squirm against him, wedging his cock deeper. Need consumes me so thoroughly, I know it's something only my Alpha can satisfy. I need his knot, and I need it now, however impractical taking my virginity in the middle of his office might be. He hisses as I manage to get him to sink a bit deeper, taking the tip entirely. He grabs my hips, forcing me to stillness, his hold tight enough that I'm pretty sure there'll be bruises when we're done. I squeeze his hand again, my heart in my throat at his continued hesitation.

A whine builds as he forces me to stay still, and another rush of slick drenches me—and now him. It pulls a low, wounded sound from him, rumbling through his chest.

"Please, Carter," I whisper again, desperate. "I need you."

His eyes flick open.

"Give me a minute," he rasps, kissing me once.

My breath catches, and I wiggle as much as his grip will allow, trying to take him deeper, ignoring the burning stretch of it all. I clutch at his neck, my nails digging into his skin.

"Carter...Alpha, please," I beg, and he shudders.

"Jude is going to kill me," he admits, letting go of my hand and twisting my hair around his palm, pulling lightly.

My head falls back, my neck arching, and he kisses the hollow of my throat. My nipples brush across his shirt with every breath, and I shiver at the sensation. I roll my hips into him. He pulls harder on my hair, and I moan.

"Fuck it. It'll be worth it," he says against my skin, biting my collar bone before cupping my face and kissing me, his mouth devouring me in a matter of moments. My heart races, my breath coming in choppy pants. I cry out as he pulls away from me, his cock suddenly gone, a feeling of emptiness overtaking me.

"Carter," I whisper, my voice breaking.

He brushes a thumb across my cheek, his gaze intent on me. "I'll fuck you, Omega. But you're going to let me make sure I don't hurt you. Understand?"

"I don't mind if it does, though. I know..." I chase his lips, but he evades me, cupping my chin to keep me in place, focused on his gaze. "I know knotting can be uncomfortable. I'm fine with it."

Carter shakes his head. "I'm not talking about knotting, Faedra."

My eyes flutter shut, and I swallow the protest forming in my throat, focusing on the feel of his body against mine. He runs a hand down my arm, threading his fingers with mine and kissing the back of my hand before kneeling in front of me again, his eyes locked on mine as he runs his lips across my inner thighs. I bite my cheek, keeping my whimper behind my lips as he sets his lips against me again, his tongue moving across my clit as thoroughly as before. My thighs shake, my hand tightening around his.

He smiles, a content hum making his lips vibrate, and I gasp. Before I can recalibrate, he's running a finger through my pussy, spreading my slick across every inch of my skin and then pressing into my entrance, the stretch just as consuming as when Jude did it in the kitchen.

"Fuck," he mutters, the breath against my clit making me tremble.

His movements are careful but not slow, his finger plunging into me and then out in the time it takes me to fist my hand in his hair. I drop my head back, my eyes unfocusing as I look at the ceiling, and he adds a second finger, curling them and brushing a spot inside me that has me biting my cheek again, my thighs tensing. My body rushes for the edge of that precipice, dangling me over the edge, but I fight to keep from falling, my nails digging into his skin as he adds a third finger and wrings a startled gasp from me.

"Let go, Faedra," he murmurs, squeezing my hand. I shake my head, and he hums, curling his fingers again as he speeds up, the stretch fading with each confident movement of his. "Let me taste it."

"I want to come with you," I whisper, keeping my orgasm at bay by the skin of my teeth.

He laughs. "You will," he says and then nips at my clit, his teeth scraping across it.

I'm gone, my body flinging itself over the edge, a wave of sensation rushing through me, stealing my breath. Before I can recalibrate or catch my breath, he's standing, forcing my knees wider, his undone belt brushing the sensitive skin of my inner thighs as he nestles the head of his cock into me, pressing forward just until I whimper. He lets go of my hand, palming my neck and tracing the hollow of my throat with his thumb while he places his other hand on the table, his arm caging me in.

His eyes are dark, and another rush of slick pulses through me at the sight. I drop my eyes and whimper at the sight of us together, his cock wedged partially inside, the buckle of his pants scraping along my skin with each small movement from either of us.

He tilts my chin up with his thumb, the pressure enough that I don't try to fight it.

"Eyes on me, Faedra," he orders, voice dropping, growing ragged.

"Is your cock not considered you?" I ask, managing a half decent smirk, and he laughs, pushing himself deeper into me.

"It's most people's favorite part, actually," he says, nipping my lip.

A flash of jealousy has me tightening my hold on his hair. He hums as he pulls away from me, his gaze intent as he forces himself deeper.

"I want to watch you as I take you, Omega. I want it burned into my brain this moment when I took you in my office instead of building out a more appropriate romantic occasion."

His words scrape over me, a caress that has me shaking with desperation. He adjusts his hold on me, twisting his fingers into my hair, his palm pressing flat to the nape of my neck as his thumb traces over the moon pendant I have attached to my orbital piercing right now. His cock presses into me, and I can feel myself stretching around him. Sweat coats my chest despite him doing all the work. A feeling of fullness overwhelms me, and he groans, his hips settling fully into the cradle of mine, his eyes still locked on me.

"You're beautiful," he whispers.

A mewl climbs up my throat when he doesn't immediately move again, and I roll my lips to keep it from falling into the space between us. He traces the shell of my ear, pressing gently into the sensitive pulse point just below it as he pulls out. The same agonizingly slow push back into me makes me writhe, my body urging him into something faster, more substantial, as it pushes me towards the precipice again already.

He smirks, and I press my lips together, pouting. His laugh is a warm balm to my sensitized skin.

I bask in the feel of his lips along my jaw as he whispers, "Such an impatient little Omega. Trying to show she knows more than her Alpha." He nips at the pulse point under my other ear hard enough that I clench around him, gasping. "Trust me, Faedra, I'll give you what you need."

His hips pull away from mine again, the stretch easing for a moment, before he snaps forward, burying his cock completely with one swift thrust. I can't contain the loud, keening moan that fills the room around us as I squeeze my eyes shut. My hands clench, and I feel his skin break under my nails.

"Shit, Faedra," he groans, kissing me, his lips tender against my own.

The cool metal of his belt buckle brushes along my thighs, making them tremble as he moves his hand from the table and around my hip, pressing his thumb into my clit and making me arch against him. It's an overwhelming mix of sensations. He's so deep I can practically feel him in my throat, but it doesn't feel like enough. I roll my hips, needing more. Needing everything.

"Such a beautiful Omega, taking my cock so well," he whispers, and I fucking *preen*. "You're stretched around me, Faedra, and it's so fucking hot. Feel us. Feel how well you take your Alpha's cock."

He grabs my hand from his neck and guides it to where we're connected, urging me to touch where he moves leisurely inside of me. His hips pull away from mine, his cock dragging against a spot inside of me that has me whimpering when he slides back in.

I drop my head to his shoulder, resting my forehead against his shirt as I press my hand into his stomach, but it doesn't feel quite right.

I whine, shaking my head, and Carter hums.

"Does my Omega need to taste me?" He murmurs the question against my temple. "Does she need to be able to feel my skin?"

Yes.

That's what's wrong. I nod, reaching for the buttons of his shirt, pulling at his tie. A whimper builds in my chest at its staying put.

Carter disentangles both hands from me before making quick work of the tie and buttons, all the while moving his hips in an agonizingly, torturously slow pace, his cock dragging against that spot inside of me with each thrust. The moment I can see his skin, chest dusted with dark hair, I wrap my arms around him, palms flattening against the smooth expanse of his back, and set my lips on the hollow of his throat, tracing his collar bones with my tongue. A groan vibrates under my mouth, and I smile.

My body races towards the edge again, his movements coaxing sensation from me despite my already coming once. I clench around him, and his pace picks up. Whimpering into his skin, I cling to him, adjusting until my face is buried in his shoulder. His lips skate over my ear, a rush of goosebumps ghosting across my skin from the featherlight contact.

"Such a good little Omega," he whispers, and I shiver, clenching around him again, pulling a moan from between his lips. "You're being so quiet, just like I asked of you. Good girl."

His thumb circles my clit as he sucks on the sensitive pulse point under my ear.

I fucking *shatter*. Lightning floods me, my limbs tingling as I arch against him, pressing my mouth into his neck as a trembling moan spills from me. My body shakes, and Carter growls, his hips snapping once, twice.

"Holy fuck, Faedra," he murmurs, his hips stuttering for a heartbeat as he comes. He licks the sore spot on my neck, tangling his hand in my hair again as he grabs my hip, pulling me into him as he buries himself to the hilt a moment before a sudden pressure fills me.

Holy hell, his knot.

I cry out, trying to keep the sound pressed into his skin as his knot locking us together triggers a third, all-consuming orgasm that strips me of all thought. My fingers tingle and my mind empties, a rush of blistering sensation cascading through my body. I can't help but wiggle, the pressure nearly overwhelming, stealing my breath.

Carter presses his lips to my ear. "Such a good Omega," he whispers.

A mewl rises in my throat, and I push my lips harder against his skin in an attempt to hide the sound, a forgotten part of me screaming that anyone could find us if I'm too loud. His hand tightens on my hip as I try to squirm again, and he hums, flicking his thumb over my clit once. I collapse against him with a groan, my body over sensitized. He brushes his lips across my jaw.

"So good, little Omega. Ride it out with me," he says, and I tighten my arms around him, pulling him to me until we're completely flush. His voice is a rough mumble. "You take it so well. You make me so proud, little Omega."

My thoughts drift away, swept up in the consuming sensation of Carter knotting with me, the minutes passing as I relax into him, his hand gentling on my hip and tracing up my spine. My eyes snap open as I hear the distinct click of his office door opening, worry replacing the weightless contentment. I rock my hips, testing his knot, and panic tightens my throat when I realize it's nowhere close to releasing us.

Carter tangles his fingers into my hair and pulls me tighter against him, pressing my cheek into his chest and my nose into the hollow of his throat. His hand moves from my hip and plants firmly on the desk next to me as he twists us, adjusting us just enough that I can see the door out of the corner of my eye, his arm serving as a small block between me and whoever is about to ruin this moment between us.

"Carter?" I whisper, tears flooding my eyes and spilling down my cheeks. His hand tightens as he shakes his head.

Amanda's harried voice filters through the small opening of the cracked door. "Ma'am, I told you that he's currently unavailable."

Nineteen

CARTER

"Carter's never made me wait before, Amanda." A woman's voice carries across the room as the door opens wider, her voice cutting like a knife as she says my assistant's name like it's a disease. "I doubt he'll start now."

You have got to be *fucking* kidding me. I lean over Faedra, resting my chin on the crown of her head, using my body to cover her as much as possible. The door swings wide in the next second, Harper pushing past Amanda, shoving her into the door frame as she storms into my office, her dissatisfaction at having been slowed down evident in the cruel twist of her lips.

Amanda pales as she takes in how I'm wrapped around Faedra, her eyes wide as she covers her mouth. She flicks her gaze to me, and I give a subtle shake of my head.

Harper stumbles as she realizes I'm not alone, her gaze catching on Faedra's hair before coasting across the rest of her body that I wasn't able to hide, her lips twisting into a grimace as she takes in Faedra's lean leg wrapped around my hip.

"What the *hell*?" she sputters, taking another step forward, crossing her arms. I growl, low in my throat, and she hesitates, pausing just inside the door. It only takes her a minute to recover, her surprise fading behind her cold exterior. "Get her the hell out of here. We have things to discuss."

Faedra tips her face enough that she catches my gaze, her confusion evident. I adjust my hold in her hair so that Harper can't see her before pressing my lips into a thin line, shaking my head once. She blows out a breath, her hands shaking where she has them pressed against my back.

"Get out, Harper," I snarl, my gaze locked on Faedra, keeping her grounded as my knot still urges her into a state of bliss. "We have no appointment today."

Harper, predictably, scoffs and waves the truth off, turning to Amanda, trying to push her out of the doorway so she can close the door. Amanda, thankfully, stands her ground.

"*Harper*," I bark, my voice cutting across the room. She spins on her heel, her eyes wide at my unusual force. "The next time you barge past Amanda is the last time you get to see me at all. Am I clear?"

Now she hesitates, the first flash of her being unsure of the situation crossing her face. She runs a hand through her hair, shaking out her bangs before tucking the brunette pieces behind her ears, her eyes running over Faedra again.

"The rumors are true, then?" she asks, undeterred by my threat.

She takes a confident step forward, and Faedra presses harder into me, twisting so that her body is a barrier between me and the others, her nails digging into my back as she clenches her hands. A low growl builds in her throat, though she keeps her lips pressed to my sternum. She takes a deep breath before rubbing her face against me.

Fuck.

The last thing she should need to do right now is self-soothe. I need to get Harper out of here before Faedra does something that has her moving my knot and hurting herself.

"For fuck's sake, Harper," I snarl, curling over Faedra more, "get *out*."

She stops, confusion breaking through the cruel mask she wears around anyone she thinks is close to me. Faedra presses harder into me, and I adjust my stance so I'm not knocked back on my heels. I mutter a curse as my knot presses deeper into her. Faedra's whimper breaks through whatever bullshit is keeping Harper standing in front of me, and she gasps as she takes a half step back.

"You're fucking an *Omega*?" Her voice raises, growing shrill, and the last bit of patience I still had snaps under the sound.

"I swear to God, Harper, if you don't get out of my office right now, I will bury you and your company, the contract be damned," I threaten, lowering my voice and threading it with a promise of violence that I know she'll recognize. Goosebumps race up Faedra's arms, and I tighten my hold on her in silent comfort.

Harper's self-preservation finally kicks in, and she scurries from the office, ducking her head. Amanda keeps her eyes on the ground as she offers a quick apology before closing the door and turning the lock. I blow out a hard breath.

"Fuck, Faedra," I murmur into her hair, guiding her to look at me. "I'm so sorry."

Tears well all at once, falling over her lashes and down her cheeks before I can wipe them away. My hand tightens in her hair, tracing the shell of her ear as I run my other hand up her spine and across her shoulder. She squirms against me, testing my knot, and then collapses against me when it doesn't release. Her fingers twist into the loops on my slacks, and my heart clenches.

Why the hell didn't I think to lock the door?

Anybody else would have listened to Amanda, would have waited until I was officially available for a conversation. Fury settles heavy in my chest, burning up my throat as I swallow back bile.

I trail my hand down Faedra's spine, brushing my lips along her neck, trying to distract her from the absolute cluster that our knotting has become. This isn't how we were supposed to enjoy knotting for the first time. The anger burns hotter in my gut the longer I let myself think about it, so I focus on my Omega instead, feeding that innate piece of me the softness of her skin and the fluttering of her cunt still stretched around my knot. It settles as the minutes pass. Faedra whimpers as my knot releases, and she collapses against me even as I pull out.

"Faedra, I'm so sorry," I murmur against her throat. No amount of apologies will fix what Harper ruined, but I'm giving them anyway. Faedra takes a stuttering breath, and I wipe away the tears on her cheeks, cupping her face but not making her look at me. I press a soft kiss under her ear, sighing. "Let me clean you up."

She tightens her hold on my hips, nodding once. I waste no time picking her up, wrapping her legs more completely around my hips, locking my arms around her waist. She presses into my sternum harder while I carry her into the private bathroom in my office. I set her on the counter before returning to my desk to grab her shirt and bra. Her eyes are glassy and unfocused when I return to her.

"Faedra?" I ask, keeping my voice a soothing murmur. She focuses on me after a long minute. Forgoing her bra, I guide her shirt over her head and then set about prepping a washcloth, careful to keep an arm around her. She shudders, whimpering, and her vacant reaction makes me worry that she might be dropping into her heat. Today's her final day weaning off the suppressant, so it would be early, but the way she's holding herself right now combined with how she described her arousal feeling earlier has me concerned it's going to happen sooner rather than later.

She sucks in a breath when I run the washcloth over her core with as soft of a hand as I can manage. She's trimmed short, but it takes a few extra passes to get her cleaned well enough I don't worry about her getting an infection. Not that I mind. Her short curls hold my scent infinitely better than if she were completely bare, and it makes my intrinsic Alpha nature puff up in pride. She wiggles a bit on the counter, and it reminds me to put my dick away before it gets any more ridiculous ideas.

There's a flicker of guilt as I look down and see the streaks of blood on my dick. I run the clean portion of the washcloth across the base of it to get the worst of the blood off before redoing my zipper and belt.

"You were perfect," I whisper, dropping the cloth into the sink to deal with later. She looks up at me, her eyebrows furrowed, but her lips tip up in a smile after a moment. I cup her chin and pull her lips to mine, setting a gentle kiss to them. "What does my Omega need now?"

Her eyes flutter shut.

"I'm tired," she whispers. Her eyes squeeze tighter. "But there's this panic I don't understand. Like if you leave, everything will fall apart."

Fuck, but those suppressants really work, don't they?

"It's normal, Faedra," I tell her, keeping my voice low and soothing.

She shakes her head once, a whine rising in her throat, and I wrap my arms around her, my fingers threading through her hair again.

"I've never felt this. I don't understand," she says, growing hysterical. I tighten my grip on her, guiding her nose into my throat. "Y-you need to work. I can't keep you from doing your job. But—" She chokes off a sob, pulling me closer to her. Her tears soak the shoulder of my unbuttoned shirt.

I run my hand up her spine, pressing my lips under her ear. Wrapping her legs around my waist again, I walk us back into the office and straight to the wardrobe tucked into the far corner. I intentionally added items to it when the Council informed us of matching with Faedra, figuring there would come a point when she would be with me here.

Her tears are still falling onto my shoulder, her arms locked around my neck as I adjust my hold in order to grab one of the fluffy blankets from the bottom shelf and drape it across her shoulders. Grabbing the other blanket, I walk back to my chair and carefully set her in it. She presses her thighs into her chest, grabbing her shins and resting her cheek on her knees, glassy eyes locked on me. I set a small kiss to her hand before wrapping the other blanket around her legs and crossing back to the wardrobe.

"Carter?" Her voice is a bare whisper, shaky enough that my chest clenches.

"Yes, love?" I ask, doing my best to keep my voice soft.

"Do you know why I feel like this?"

I grab the pillow stashed in the bottom drawer. When I turn around, Faedra's eyes are locked on me, her eyebrows furrowed, a faint tremor in her arms. I nod as I walk back to her and arrange the pillow on the ground next to the chair, tucked away from any wandering eyes that might be looking in from the door. I have a meeting today with the administrator from Hawkins Corp that can't be rescheduled for anything less than her dropping into her heat. While I prefer these types of meetings happening in my own office, I'll have Amanda prep the conference room for me.

She takes in my actions without comment. When I reach for the second blanket, she gives it easily, her hands tucking between her shins. I lay it out, moving the acceptance packets she received, carefully arranging the papers and setting them next to my keyboard.

"I don't have a mattress," I say with regret, looking up at her. "I'm sorry. I'll be sure to get one tomorrow."

She gives a shy smile. "I liked the desk just fine. You don't have to go out of your way."

Smirking, I shake my head. "It's not for sex, love."

Her cheeks darken, but her words are confident. "Still. A mattress wouldn't fit under there. I'm fine without it."

Nodding, I hold out my hand.

"Come here," I order, putting just enough bite into my tone that she inherently wants to follow the direction.

She unfolds herself from the chair, settling onto the blanket in front of me, grabbing the pillow and clutching it to her stomach. I strip out of my Oxford and hold it out to her. It takes her a moment to decide she wants it, her eyebrows furrowing as she picks at the pillow. Humming, she sets the pillow aside and brings the shirt to her chest, dropping her face into the collar. She breathes deeply, and her shoulders relax a fraction.

"I don't understand," she whispers into the fabric.

I cup her chin, guiding her to look at me again.

"This is part of being Omega, Faedra. The fact that you've never felt the need to nest is testament to how effective your suppression was."

A spark of recognition brightens her eyes. "This is nesting?" When I nod, she blows out a breath, her eyebrows lowering. She presses her forehead into my lips, eyes fluttering shut. "I didn't expect it to be so...overwhelming."

The distinct vibration of my phone against the desk has me breathing out a sigh.

"Rest. I'll be here. If there's something you want, tell me, no matter how odd." I instruct her, guiding her to lay on the blanket. "I want you to be comfortable."

A small nod, and she follows my guidance without protest, curling up on her side. She takes a moment to adjust until she's comfortable, clutching the shirt tightly, keeping it pressed just under her nose. As I spread the other blanket over top of her, she gives a soft smile, and then her eyes close, her breathing extending into the cadence of sleep.

My phone vibrates on my desk again, and I swipe it with an angry growl. I open the message from Logan as I get to my feet.

> Hey, have you heard from Faedra?
>
> She didn't text me about where she was headed, and Jude is in a faculty meeting.

> She's with me. She got decisions from a couple of the schools and didn't want to open them alone.

> Good news?

> Of course.

> I'll text Jude about meeting up with you both. We'll take her out somewhere tonight to celebrate.

> Can you bring the bag she packed in case of her heat starting? It hasn't, but she needs a new outfit.

> Jude's gonna be pissed, dude. Your office? Seriously?

I ignore his text.

Who honestly expects me to have control when my Omega

scents and then asks me so nicely? I was a goner the moment she said please.

I put on a new shirt and tie with quick movements, fixing my belt while stepping into the bathroom to make sure my hair isn't too wild. A new sort of pride spreads through me at the wrinkles in my slacks, the nail marks along my neck.

Knotting with Faedra was everything I'd hoped it would be and more. I was already committed, beyond happy with the Council's matching us. Knotting just solidified it for me. She was perfect. The moment was perfect for us. I had always been too much of a rebel to cement a relationship somewhere as traditional as a proper bed. Feeling her surrender to her Omega designation had been everything I didn't realize I needed.

And then Harper had to be a selfish bitch and ruin it.

I scrape my hands down my face, trying to get Faedra's stricken look out of my mind. The small comfort is that at least Harper hadn't seen anything of Faedra's body. Between her hair and my own body, I made sure of it.

But, fuck, this is going to end up being a cluster.

My eyes coast over her as I walk back into my office, my chest clenching at the soft, vulnerable look on her face. I wipe down my desk, the smell of bleach cutting through our mingled scents. Pulling my phone out of silent mode, I send a quick text to Jude to warn him of Melanie and then step out of my office to chat with Amanda.

Her eyes are wide, her hands shaking, as I cross the room and stop beside her desk.

"I'm so sor—" She starts, her chin wavering.

I shake my head, waving off the apology.

"Not your fault. I should have locked the door." I assuage her, and she takes a deep breath.

"Is she alright?" she asks after a moment of quiet, her gaze dropping to her keyboard. "It seemed like she was in pain."

"She's fine," I assure her. When she doesn't immediately say anything, her eyebrows pinched, I offer, "I have no intention of firing you, Amanda. If there's something you want to know, you can ask me."

She glances up at me, eyes wide again, fingers picking at the edge of her desk.

"Were you, um, knotted?" Amanda's voice is barely a whisper, but I manage to hear her fine. Her cheeks darken before I can respond. "Sorry, I shouldn't be so intrusive. I've just never worked with an Alpha before."

I give a half smile as I run a hand through my hair. "Yeah, we were. Otherwise I would have moved us so that Harper couldn't see."

She nods, eyes darting to her monitor, her hands flying over the keys as she responds to something. My phone pings with a text.

"Can you prep everything for me to be out of the office for a week or so?" I ask her, grabbing my phone.

> I swear to God if it was your idea, I will kill you and make it look like an accident.

Surprise to absolutely none: surly ass Jude is pissed.

"Aside from this weekend?" Amanda asks, her voice filling with confusion. "When else will you be gone?"

She clicks some more before turning her monitor to face me. Harper's name on the schedule for late next week makes me scowl.

"Contact her office and demand the proper manager come this time. I don't want her in here anymore," I order, pointing at the calendar event. Amanda nods, marking the slot and inserting a note.

"And I'm not quite sure when I'll be out. How much are you aware of pack life?"

Amanda shakes her head. "Not really anything. Everyone in my family is a Beta."

"Omegas go through heats," I tell her.

A spark of recognition in her eyes as she nods.

"Is that what's happening?" She glances at my office door. "Shouldn't you be with her?"

I shake my head. "It's not started yet, but it will soon. Once it does, I'll be unavailable for the duration. I just need you to prep everything so that it's an easy transition. Heats tend to come on suddenly. I can't guarantee that I'll be able to give much more than a few hours warning. It'll probably be even less than that."

She nods again, her hands flying across the keys after she repositions her monitor. "I can get everything prepped."

I smile. "Thanks, Amanda."

She blushes, ducking her head. "Your afternoon appointment is here, by the way. I have him waiting in the lobby with Rachel," she says, nodding her head to the closed frosted door behind me.

"Can you set him up in the smaller conference room?" Amanda raises an eyebrow but doesn't ask, nodding once. "I'll need about five minutes or so before I'm able to meet him in there, if you'll temper his expectation a bit." I head back for my closed office door. Five minutes probably wasn't enough to put the files back in order, but I wasn't about to regret what had caused them to be messed up in the first place. "And Jude and Logan will be here at some point, too. I don't imagine this appointment will overlap with them, but if it does, just let them into my office. Faedra will be here the rest of the afternoon."

A soft agreement follows me into my office.

Twenty

CARTER

"Not only did you knot her when we'd all agreed to wait until after backpacking, but you also took her *virginity* in your goddamn office?" Jude growls at me, arms crossed over his chest, his suit jacket thrown over my desk. Logan raises an eyebrow behind him, tucking his hands into the pockets of his slacks as he shuts the door, Faedra's bag slung over his shoulder.

"Let's say it louder, Jude," he says with a dry tone, his look devoid of any of its usual carefree humor. "Pretty sure Rachel didn't quite hear you down the hall."

Jude turns around, scowling, a growl rumbling low in his throat.

"I know you're not about to put emphasis on that when it's the most patriarchal bullshit around, Jude," I mutter.

Logan grunts an agreement.

"I don't care that you were the first," he snarls, stepping

closer to the desk. I cock an eyebrow. "I care that it was in such a vulnerable place and that she wasn't even given proper aftercare."

"Fuck you for thinking I wouldn't make sure she was cleaned up afterwards," I say, anger making my voice drop.

Logan barks a sardonic half-laugh. "Yeah, that's fucking rich coming from you, Jude, since *I'm* the one who had to help clean her up after you left her newly post-orgasm on the island the other day."

Now I scowl, setting my elbows on the cleared portion of my desk, perching my chin on my knuckles. "You did *what?*"

"It was either that or knot her, and since we had *agreed*," Jude seethes, "and I had a mandatory department meeting, I chose the former." His jaw clenches, a muscle in his neck twitching with the force of it. "She was safe and completely down from the orgasm before I left."

Logan scoffs but doesn't say anything else.

Jude opens his mouth, but I cut him off, my patience worn thin from the entire afternoon's bullshit. "If you had taken even a minute to survey my office before rampaging," I say, the words particularly biting, "you would have noticed that she's cleaned up and comfortable enough that she fell asleep." I shake my head and undo the cuffs of my shirt, quickly rolling the sleeves to my elbows. "I'm not an asshole, Jude. Of course I made sure she had what she needed."

Logan nods once, stepping up next to Jude, his eyes immediately finding Faedra where she's still resting at my feet under the other portion of my L-shaped desk.

"Does this mean I can start taking naps here, too?" Logan asks, chuckling, dropping her bag onto the desk, and I smile, shaking my head.

"Hell no, man. You fucking snore," I joke back.

Logan laughs harder, shrugging. "She doesn't seem to mind."

Jude scowls again but collects his jacket and settles into a seat across from me. The mood of the room sours, and I sigh, rubbing my hand over my eyes.

"I'm grabbing some whiskey," Logan announces.

He doesn't ask us if we want any, but I know he'll pour us each a knuckle's worth. While he rummages in the bar tucked next to the wardrobe, I stare at Jude, an eyebrow cocked.

He grunts before blowing out a breath. "Fine. My bad for coming in here guns blazing. It's clear she's alright."

I nod once but don't say anything, waiting until Logan's returned. "Oh, don't drop the anger yet. I'm just making sure you have it aimed at the right part of this whole situation."

Jude raises an eyebrow, taking a large gulp of whiskey, waving me on as he does so.

I sigh, running my hand through my hair. Keeping my eyes on him, I say, "Harper walked in while we were still knotted."

Logan flinches, and Jude curses viciously before slamming the rest of his whiskey.

"Please tell me she didn't see Faedra," he groans as he sets the empty tumbler on my desk harder than necessary.

I shake my head. "I made sure she couldn't see anything more than her hair." I drop my hand, tapping the desk lightly. "Pretty sure she thought I was just fucking some random hook-up, but Faedra made a noise when I moved a bit, and she realized we were knotted."

"That's why you warned me Melanie might lose her shit," Jude says. He glances out the windows, running his hand over his beard, lips tipped down.

Logan leans forward, perching his elbows on his knees. "We need to explain who they are. If Harper was persistent enough to barge past Amanda—who is downright terrifying when she wants to be—then I imagine Melanie is going to make a move soon, too. And the last thing Faedra deserves is being blindsided by your crazy ass exes."

Jude sighs at the same moment I groan. Who the hell wants to explain to their Omega that a Beta they dated over five years ago is still refusing to let them go and goes out of their way to get attention from them—to the point of intentionally getting hired by a company contracted with their own?

Fuck.

"That's on Carter," Jude says, breaking me out of my thoughts. "I've already explained Melanie—at least who she is and that she works at the university."

Logan relaxes marginally, his shoulders dropping, though he taps his finger on the desk.

"Alright, yeah. I'll make sure to explain it all to her. But not tonight," I say after a few minutes. Both men frown. I explain, leaning back in my chair and taking a sip of the whiskey. "She got into her top choices for the photography degree. Tonight we celebrate her, yeah? If she brings Harper up, then I'll be honest. Otherwise I want to wait a day or two so that it doesn't overshadow the good things that happened today."

It's clear that Logan doesn't love that answer—but he's always the one to charge into something head-on with no tact. It works well for his chosen career, but not so well with relationships. It surprises me when Jude agrees quietly with Logan, though he doesn't push me on it at the moment. Faedra hums a bit, turning over until I can see her beautiful green eyes when I look over at her. The smile is second-nature as I go to her, crouching and running my hand through her hair.

"Hello, little Omega. Did you rest enough?" I ask, keeping my voice low.

She smiles, and my heart soars. "I did." Her voice is soft and a bit raspy, and it has my dick hardening in an instant. I run my thumb across her cheek, and she turns into my touch. "I thought I heard Jude."

"They're both here. We wanted to take you out tonight to

celebrate you getting accepted," I tell her. She sits up after a moment, and I move my hand to the back of her head, keeping her from hitting the edge of the desk. She glances down at the state of her clothes, her lack of bra obvious, and her cheeks darken with a blush.

"I'm not really put together well enough for a dinner out," she whispers, frowning.

Logan clears his throat. "I brought the bag you had packed in case of your heat."

She smiles, looking up towards him, and I see him smile back, just as soft as hers. "Thank you," she says, slowly moving to stand, her hands still clutching my shirt to her belly. As she steps around me, I reach up and adjust her skirt, eliciting a low groan from Jude. Standing, I grab her bag, keeping one hand on her back, and guide her to the bathroom.

Logan chuckles. "I see you over there, man. You act all high and mighty, but you're struggling the most, aren't you?"

"Shut the fuck up, Logan," Jude mutters.

"If you don't feel up to it, we can go home instead," I murmur in Faedra's ear. She shivers, whimpering, and turns into me, resting her head on my shoulder. She takes a deep breath before saying anything, her hands digging into my stomach.

"I'm fine," she says against my shoulder. I set her bag on the vanity. "Just...just figuring out my new normal."

I nod, setting a finger under her chin and guiding her lips to mine. The kiss I give is gentle, but she whimpers again all the same.

Fuck, I'm hard.

Offering a smile, I pull away, tucking a piece of her hair behind her ear, and then back out of the space, closing the door gently behind me.

Jude's staring at the closed door. "She's been like that all afternoon?"

I grunt an affirmative. "It got worse after we knotted. I thought she was going into her heat at first with the way she was talking about her body feeling, but her temperature wasn't any higher than normal."

Logan whistles. "We're going to be lucky if she doesn't drop into her heat in the next couple days, aren't we?"

Jude nods but voices a disagreement. "I think it's a reaction to weaning off the suppressors. She'll probably even out over the next few days now that's she's finished the step-down dosing. Coming into heat so soon after getting off of them is rare."

I lean against my desk and throw back the rest of my whiskey. If anyone would know, it's Jude. That man is a walking encyclopedia.

"I hope you're right," I say, setting the tumbler next to the keyboard. "Her going into heat while we're on the trail would be rough at best."

Twenty-One

FAEDRA

Dinner passes in a blur of laughs and soft, near constant touches from the men. My cheeks ache from how much I've been smiling as Jude opens the door to the condo. He catches my hand, squeezing it as he feathers a kiss against my temple, and then walks deeper into the space, stretching his neck and pulling out his phone.

Carter grunts as I frown. "It's probably one of his graduate students looking for guidance before we're gone for the next several days."

Right.

He runs his hand down my spine. "You've got everything prepped for tomorrow? It'll be an early day so we can get up there on time."

"I packed everything the way you showed me," I confirm.

He nods, kisses the pulse point under my ear, and then heads to his room, his footfalls silent on the stairs. Blowing out a breath, I grab the information packets from my bag before stowing it on one of the hooks. Logan walks with me into the great room, his grasp on my hand gentle. He tightens his grip as I set the packets on the island and then turn towards the living room, pulling my hand to his lips and brushing a gentle kiss across the back of my palm.

"You need anything?" he asks, and I shake my head. He nods, crossing the space and opening the door to his office, leaving the door ajar as he settles into his chair and pulls a binder from the drawers behind his desk. I pull the clip from my hair, massaging my scalp, and grab the small bag that has my quilting pieces in it.

I only manage to sit and look out the windows for a few minutes before I'm too antsy, and I close my eyes, trying to figure out what has changed to make me feel so off kilter since getting back from dinner. After several deep breaths don't seem to help, I put away the quilting supplies, not trusting myself to keep from bleeding on the project again. The restlessness gets worse, so I head to my room, leaving my phone and the packets on the kitchen counter. My skin absolutely crawls by the time I close the door to my bedroom and lean back against it, closing my eyes and breathing deeply. A soft knock on my door a few minutes later has me freezing.

"You good, Red?" Logan's voice is muffled, but the concern layering the question is clear enough.

I twist the doorknob and open the door as I adjust to stand in the small gap. Logan's normally carefree smile is gone, replaced with a deep frown. His shoulders are held tight, his hand clutching the doorframe tight enough to whiten his knuckles. Biting my lip, I shrug. Logan cocks an eyebrow, crossing his arms and leaning against the threshold. The faint scent of sandalwood reaches me, and I inexplicably relax.

He takes a half step into me. "Was dinner too much?" he asks.

I swallow. "I don't think so. I just..." I blow out a breath, trying to put into words the bone deep craving I have for being enveloped in his scent. And Jude's. And Carter's. "Carter called it nesting earlier, but I'm not sure that's totally accurate. I feel like my skin is too tight right now unless I can, um, smell you guys."

My cheeks burn with a deep blush, but Logan doesn't laugh. In fact, his gaze sharpens.

"Why didn't you say anything while we were out?" he asks, crowding the doorway until there's a hairsbreadth of distance between us.

"Because I could smell Jude during dinner," I say, trying to be subtle in my breathing in his unique smell. That aftershave is fucking divine. "It wasn't a problem until we got back here."

Logan blows out a breath and cups my cheek. "Give me just a second, alright?"

I steal a kiss before whispering my agreement against his lips. He pulls away, disappearing into his own room. My skin grows tight again, the antsy feeling creeping back in, and I rub my arms, humming under my breath. Logan is back a minute later, one of his workout hoodies in his hands.

"Here," he says, holding it out for me.

I reach for it, but he shakes his head, helping me into it instead, smoothing it down my belly and wrapping his arm around my waist in the same fluid motion. Sandalwood overwhelms my senses, and I relax into him.

That must be his scent and not just an aftershave.

He twists his hand into my hair, kissing along my jaw.

"Thank you," I whisper, and he tightens his hold around me, pulling me against him until we're flush. My scent weaves in with his, and he groans, pulling away from my throat. His eyes are bright, his touch gentle.

"I have to work on some administrative things before we

leave tomorrow or my accountant is going to lose his shit," he says. "You alright?"

I hum, pressing into his hand where he still cups my face, giving him a half smile. "Much better. Thank you."

I watch him disappear down the stairs and then glance across the landing. Carter's door is open, but I can't see him. Tucking my hands into the pockets of Logan's hoodie, I cross the space and lean against the door jamb, my gaze locking on where he's prepping a set of clothes on the monstrosity that he calls a bed. It's easily as big as Logan's, outfitted with a cream comforter and a brown throw draped over one corner.

He disappears into what I assume is a closet, returning a moment later with a backpack similar to the one they got for me —though mine is a happy teal where his is a simple dark gray. I clear my throat as he works on getting everything packed, and he glances up, his eyebrows drawn in.

"So..." I start, uncharacteristically nervous.

It hadn't felt right to bring up what had happened with the woman in his office while we were out for dinner. But where I typically don't mind facing down a problem head on, I find myself hesitating in his doorway, nerves a tight bundle sitting heavily in my stomach. He finishes packing the clothes and sets aside the pack, stretching his neck as he crosses the room, holding out a hand in invitation.

"Do you want a bath?" he asks when I set my hand in his, lacing our fingers together.

My cheeks heat as I'm reminded of the soreness between my legs that's gotten more pronounced over the last couple hours.

"Maybe in a bit," I say. Tightening my hold on his hand, I ask what's been bothering me since we knotted, keeping my eyes locked on his. "Who is she?"

His frown is instantaneous, but he doesn't move away from me, his thumb tracing patterns along the back of my hand.

"She's the Vice President of Operations for one of the companies contracted with mine," he offers after a minute. I step into him until I can feel his heat like a wall in front of me, the sensation bringing nearly as much comfort as Logan's oversized hoodie. He sighs. "And she's also my ex."

Shit.

He doesn't wait for me to ask for more. Drawing me into his arms, he lifts me bridal-style and then carries me to the small lounge chair positioned in the far corner of the room that's angled to look out over the city. He keeps me from being jostled as he situates himself in the seat and then guides my legs over the arm. When I glance up at him, he cups my cheek, running his thumb over my lips.

"We started dating about a year after Jude and Melanie made everything official between them. They've been best friends as long as I've known them—they met Iris during Rush week in undergrad and the three of them were inseparable." His jaw clenches, and I take his hand in mine, resting it in my lap. He continues, his voice low, "It was a slow change in our dynamic. We spent a lot of time together, both being the awkward extra wheel to Jude and Melanie. It didn't take me long to realize that she had become so interested only after she found out that I had money. It's not something I broadcast—and I certainly didn't back then. Part of me hoped that I was wrong about her motivation."

I lean into his hand on my cheek. "What did you do?"

"Made sure she couldn't access any of it," he says. I raise an eyebrow, and he curves his lip into a half smile. "But for what you're wanting to know, I did...nothing. Breaking it off would have meant I lost Jude, and I wasn't willing to have that happen. She had a wandering eye, and I let her because it kept her from questioning why I wouldn't put her name on anything."

My heart clenches. What must it have been like to be in that situation? To know your partner was unfaithful but turn a blind eye in the name of keeping your closest friend?

"Did Jude know?" I ask.

Carter shakes his head. "He still doesn't. It's not something I want the world to know."

"Is that why you never saw yourself having kids?" I ask, and he nods. I run my thumb over his hand, humming.

"When we met Logan during backpacking, it was like something clicked. There had always been a piece missing with just Jude and me, and Logan filled it so seamlessly, it was like he'd been part of our lives for years. He breathed new life into us, helped us realize that dreams we'd long since buried might still be possible." He runs his thumb over my lips, and I nip at him. The smell of pine threads around us, and I smile. "When he brought up the idea to me of requesting to be recognized as a pack before the Council, I was all in. It was a no-brainer for me. But Jude was resistant. It was...a very stressful six months on our friendship."

Six months.

It took six months for Jude to find that list in her belongings and realize that he really did want to become a pack.

"The worst part, honestly, is that she's the one that won't let go. She spent four years fucking anyone who so much as gave her the time of day, and yet five years later, she still finds ways to force me to notice her. She got the job at the company after I won the contract. She always demands to meet instead of sending the manager actually in charge of the account—and she always requires that I handle everything personally. It's a large enough contract that I haven't fought her."

"Is she always so..." I search for the right word. "Forceful?"

Carter nods. "Always. It's even worse if there's someone she knows is important to me involved."

I'm not really sure what to say in response to that. Most of me just wants to punch her for being so intentionally cruel. And maybe because I'm a bit smug, too, thinking about the black Amex he'd given me while I was still in L.A.

Carter blows out a breath.

"I had Amanda submit paperwork through the proper channels so that the team members who are supposed to handle the account actually do so from now on. I've given my team explicit instructions that she is not to be entertained if she shows up again."

Happiness blooms in my belly, dissolving the worry and making me smile. Gratitude quickly follows, borne of my surprise that he would know something like that would be important to me.

"For what it's worth," I say, "if there were any previous partners, I would expect you to demand I cut off all ties with them, too."

He nods, smirking. "I know. Removing her as much as I can is the least that you deserve."

"Thank you," I tell him. He kisses me, long and deep, and my core heats, my body awakening under his touch. "I'd like that bath now," I murmur against his lips.

He grins as he carries me into his ensuite.

Twenty-Two

FAEDRA

"Everything still feel alright?" Logan asks, adjusting the straps I've learned are called load lifters. He's been fussing with the fit of my pack since I got it pulled from his Jeep and put on twenty minutes ago.

It's heavy, but not more than I think I can reasonably manage. When he doesn't stop messing with everything after I give him a soft affirmative, I grab his hands and place them on my waist, kissing him before he can protest. He huffs a laugh, twisting his tongue with mine, exploring my mouth with a thoroughness that has me clenching my thighs, holding desperately onto my control and being moderately successful. Only a bare trace of my scent threads around us.

The hard crunching of footsteps on gravel has me pulling away from him, breathless and flushed. Carter has an eyebrow raised but is smiling when I look at him. He's dressed in dark wash jeans and a flannel layered over a thin black tee, and the sight has me wishing I'd taken up his offer of knotting early this morning while the others were still asleep.

Jude walks by me, his hand outstretched towards the man with Carter. "Doug, it's been a minute."

The man shakes Jude's hand, grinning. "You've made yourself scarce the last few weeks. Normally you guys are already showing off the newest pin from Black Canyon." He glances at me. "Though I can understand. It was a whirlwind when we matched with Brianna, too."

Jude nods.

"She joining this year?" Logan asks, his hand still splayed on my waist.

Doug shakes his head. "She didn't want to leave Blake alone for so long. Hopefully we can bring him with us next year." He extends a hand to me, and I shake it, giving him a smile. "I'm Doug. I'm the main coordinator of the event these days. My partner, Willa, did most of the work for the last decade, though."

"It's nice to meet you," I say. I glance at Carter. "I thought we would see Gina and Ashlynn."

He shakes his head, stepping around me and putting on his own gear.

Logan says, "We'll probably run into them on the trail. Quads start first since they tend to move slowest. Trios will be allowed to start in another hour or so, and then duos and singles start about midday."

Doug stands next to me while the guys get everything from the Jeep and finish situating their packs. When they're finished, Jude hands me a strange looking straw with a murmured instruction to tuck it in the pocket on my waistband and then presses a kiss to the crown of my head.

"Alright, let's get that before picture!" Doug says, moving to be in front of us, leaning against the back door of the Jeep. Logan and Carter wrap an arm around my waist, and Jude stands behind me. The feel of them so near to me has me smiling before Doug even asks, and he chuckles as he looks at his phone.

"This is going to be perfect for all the social media things Willa has me doing." He glances up and then frowns. "Are you alright with that, Faedra?"

"Totally fine," I say, adjusting my own camera so it lays across my body now that both of the guys have stepped away from me.

Logan laces his fingers with mine and waves to Doug even as Carter chuckles and says, "See you in 40 miles, Doug."

"Don't crash the car," Logan instructs, suddenly serious.

Doug looks affronted. "What do you take me for? Irresponsible?"

Jude's response is dry. "Yes, Doug."

The man laughs, throwing his head back, the sun catching on a thin silver chain around his neck. Dog tags. My curiosity peaks, but Logan has me turning from the man, squeezing my hand as I take a deep breath.

"See you in a few days," Doug says, and I smile over my shoulder.

And then we're starting on the trailhead, heading into the forest, crossing the mountain on our way to Estes Park.

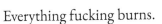

Everything fucking burns.

My legs burn. My lungs burn. My eyes burn. I'm pretty sure I will fall down if I stop. I don't pay any attention to the forest around us, and I put my camera away at our last break. My hands are shaking too much to get a steady photo. My footing stumbles for a heartbeat, and my breath catches. Logan comes up beside me and laces his fingers with mine.

"Just a bit farther today, Red," he says.

Jealousy rushes through me at his easy grin and boundless

energy. I offer what I hope is a reassuring smile. If I say anything right now, it'll be a complaint, and I really don't want to do that, especially on the first day. I'm not unfit, but this is a whole different level. And Logan said this was the *easier* trail.

Fuck. Me.

I'd honestly thought I'd be up to convincing Carter to knot tonight, but I'm not sure I'll be able to stay awake for it.

"How's your water, Faedra?" Jude asks, looking over his shoulder.

I don't manage to smother the groan. If I have to drink any more, I might just vomit. Carter chuckles.

Jude ignores him. "You get through the second one?"

I pull the bottle from the side pocket, showing him that it's empty. His lips twitch, and I mentally do a happy dance. No way am I managing to do one physically.

"Good. We'll go about another half mile and then see about camp options," he says, turning back around, his feet never faltering.

Carter drops back, walking opposite Logan, his hand grasping mine, and kisses my temple. "You good?"

The question is a whisper, so soft I can barely hear him. If Logan can, he doesn't let on.

I shrug, and Carter squeezes my hand, brushing his lips against my temple. Despite my exhaustion, I scent strongly enough that Carter's breath catches.

"Jude, let's see what's nearby," he says, louder.

Logan leans forward, looking at Carter with an eyebrow cocked, and I blush. Jude doesn't argue, pulling out his phone and double checking the map he'd downloaded before we lost phone signal.

"Looks like there's something promising just past this turn. It's about nine miles in total, so someone might have already gotten there, but it's worth checking."

The men agree, and Logan speeds up, walking next to Jude.

Carter leans into me, his breath caressing my neck, making a shiver run down my spine. My scent grows stronger. "Once we get there, you can rest. Just a bit farther, alright?"

I nod, still not trusting myself to say anything remotely positive.

By the time we reach the spot Jude mentioned, even my shoulders are burning, my hand still held tightly in Carter's, his body so near to mine that I can feel his heat. Logan and Jude already have their packs off, expertly unpacking everything without forming a giant collective pile between them. While they start setting up the tent, Carter helps me out of my own pack, massaging my shoulders and kissing the spot under my ear.

I can't contain my grateful moan at the loss of weight, and all three of them laugh.

"I'll be back," I say, and Carter releases me. I give myself a mental high when I manage to not blush this time while I grab the needed supply bag from the side pocket of my pack.

The third time is, in fact, *not* the charm thanks to my aching legs, and I curse as I wipe off my hands and then douse them in hand sanitizer. I'm nearly back to the campsite when my foot catches on a root, and I'm tired enough that I don't manage to catch myself before stumbling, dropping down the small embankment with a gasped curse.

There's a rush of movement above me as I crash into a tree before finally hitting the bottom of the small hill, the hit knocking the wind from me on a hard wheeze. Logan's above me before I can manage to take another deep breath, his face grim as he touches each of my arms and then legs. Jude's next to him a minute later, shaking his arm for a moment, and I see Carter standing at the edge of the embankment I just decided to explore against my will.

"Anything hurt, Red?" Logan asks, offering a hand. My own shakes as I take his, and his fingers tighten.

"Just my pride," I mutter, and his lips lift in a small smile, though he's quick to hide it. My body protests as I sit up, and I groan, closing my eyes and tilting my head back. There's shuffling around me, and then a new set of hands is picking stuff out of my braids, carefully avoiding the pins that keep them out of my face and off my neck.

"You got her?" Logan asks, and Carter murmurs an agreement, his hands moving to brush off my back and arms. When I manage to open my eyes again, Jude and Logan are gone, and I see their backs as they head back to the campsite to keep prepping everything for the night. Carter tucks his finger under my chin and guides my mouth to his, pressing a soft kiss against my lips.

"You're doing a really good job, Faedra," he murmurs before backing away and helping me stand. When I scoff, he doubles down. "You are. Most people do a single night to start. The first day is the hardest. Let's get you some dinner and you can relax for the rest of the night, alright?"

His voice is low and soothing, washing over me so thoroughly that I open my eyes and take a deep breath, smiling as I lean into him. He kisses me again, lacing our fingers together, and then helps me up the embankment. To my extreme embarrassment, it's only about five feet. My back feels like it was double that. I rest my head against Carter's arm once we're back on the main ground, humming a bit as we get back to the campsite.

Pausing, I frown, and Carter squeezes my hand. Instead of one large tent, there's two smaller ones, arranged across from each other, two of the single burner backpacking stoves set up between them along with the camping chairs. Blowing out a breath, I grab my camera from my pack and then drop into one of the chairs, flipping through the photos while I try to decide how to ask who I'm sleeping with.

Crap, that sounds dirty.

I glance over at Jude where he pauses a moderate distance from the edge of camp, knotting a rope before dropping it on the ground and pulling out his water bottle. The sun hits his face as he takes a drink, his eyes closing, and I turn my camera to the last preset I used, hoping it doesn't underexpose the photos.

"Alright, Red," Logan says, taking the seat next to me. "Do you want tacos or Alfredo pasta tonight?" He holds up two opaque reusable bags filled with different ingredients that I've been carrying in my pack.

"Pasta," I say, taking the right bag, and he smiles as he puts the other one back into my pack. A moment later, he carries the entire thing over to Jude and sets it against their own packs.

Carter sits across from me, messing with the burners until they light, setting a pair of bowls on them filled with water. Once it's boiling, he reaches for the bag, and I'm happy enough to give it to him, my stomach twisting into knots from both hunger and nerves.

"What's bothering you?" Carter's voice is a whisper, ghosting between us but going no farther, and I bite my lip. He mixes the food together, not needing a recipe, and then looks up at me, his brows pinched and his lips unsmiling.

Guess it's best to just say it.

"I expected one tent," I explain, blushing before I even get to the awkward question. "How are we deciding who I sleep with?" I stumble over the words, and my face grows hotter, the blush tracking down my neck. I adjust one of the pins in my hair to help distract me. "That sounds just as dirty as it did in my head."

He smirks, and oh my *God* the bolt of heat that rushes through me is hot and fast. Maybe I'm not tired? I adjust in my seat, and my thighs scream at me.

Never mind.

"We figured we'd draw straws if you didn't have any strong preference," he explains, not put off by the question at all. He raises an eyebrow. "Were you feeling like you needed one of us particularly close?"

Damn it all, my blush gets even more intense, and I close my eyes and mess with the small studs I replaced my earrings with before leaving this morning.

"About three miles ago I was pretty set on convincing you to knot me tonight," I admit on a sigh. His laugh is loud and immediate, and it has me smiling despite my embarrassment.

He's still chuckling when he says, "I imagine right now that isn't the most pressing thing on your mind."

I pout as I open my eyes, and he laughs again.

"Want to play a card game?" Logan asks as he and Jude join us around the stove, a deck of cards in his hand.

Rubbing my face, I turn to Logan. "The same as the one before graduation? That one was fun and easy to follow."

The men agree, and I go back to flipping through photos, deleting some of the most obvious duplicates to help clear up some of the memory.

"Faedra?" Jude asks. "You alright?"

I glance up at him, putting the camera in my lap with a shrug.

"Tired," I say, and he nods.

Logan hums, running his hand down my arm and kissing my shoulder. "Let's skip the card game tonight then."

Carter reaches across the bowls, squeezing my fingers and running his thumb across my knuckles. My scent permeates around us all, though not as strongly as it has been the last few days. Carter glances at the others, an unspoken conversation happening in the span of seconds, and then lets go of my hand, returning to the dinner, mixing in the last couple ingredients. Logan pulls two forks from his pocket and hands one to Carter.

"Eat," Jude murmurs, handing me one of the bowls and a fork before taking a bite himself. "And then you can sleep with Carter."

Twenty-Three

CARTER

Jude brushes the worst of the dried mud off his pants before switching into the pair of sweats laid out on the camp chair. Logan pulls Faedra's toiletry bags from her pack and tosses them to me before putting her pack over his shoulder.

Glancing at Jude, he asks, "Your arm doing ok?"

I raise an eyebrow, looking at Jude more closely. He twists his arm, showing a nasty set of scratches along his left forearm. They're scabbed at this point and relatively clean, clearly taken care of at some point.

"Yeah, they're fine," he says, waving Logan on. "I don't need anything from the kit."

Logan nods and then walks out past camp, his headlamp illuminating a narrow patch of land in from of him. While he works to tie out Faedra's pack with ours, I get ready for bed, rolling my jeans to stick in the bottom of my sleeping bag along with the rest of my clothes for tomorrow.

"You hear back from the jeweler?" Jude asks when I'm finished, stretching his neck and then his shoulders.

"He's on retainer for once we decide what we want," I say, following his lead and stretching.

Logan laughs as he comes back to camp. "I've trained you so well," he jokes, laughing. "It only took, what, six years?"

Jude rolls his eyes, but the corner of his mouth twitches, giving him away, and Logan laughs harder.

"What were you saying about the jeweler?" Logan asks, dropping into one of the chairs and pulling his Kindle. Jude doesn't say a word as he does the same, the tension slowly bleeding out from him as the moments pass. I sit and look up at the sky, letting myself feel small under the mass of stars, the complexity of it all soothing me. After a few minutes, I give Logan the same answer I gave Jude.

He hums, running a hand through his hair. "Still like the idea of giving her a stacking ring for each of us. They're the traditional choice." He pauses and runs his hand through his hair. "They can be thin so there's not as much bulk. Or she could wear them on a necklace."

Jude grunts. "Her family is all Betas. I think it's a good idea to offer her a traditional engagement ring, too, even if it doesn't signify an engagement for us," he says without glancing up. Logan frowns, tilting his Kindle down.

I clear my throat. "We could do both. There's no rulebook saying it has to be one or the other. And it's not like funds are a concern."

Jude nods, tapping his knee. "If we do stackers, let's make them those ones with the gems laid all the way around. She loves color."

"Sounds good," I say.

The silence between us is comfortable, and I slowly sink into our normal routine, the time passing amicably. When I'm about to head to bed, Logan says, "Let's do the engagement ring. There'll be lots of time to give her pieces from each of us if we want."

I nod and then stand up, turning for the tent. "Once we're back, I'll have him come up with a few ideas based on some of the pieces she already has. Hopefully it'll be ready before we have to submit the paperwork with the Council."

JUDE

The stillness just before dawn is my favorite part of these backpacking trips. The air bites at my face as I pull the packs down from where we tied them out overnight and walk them back to the camp. I'm careful to keep Faedra's things organized as I grab the instant coffee from her pack. I set about filtering the last batch of water Logan had grabbed before going to bed and then set a bowl of it to boil over a camp stove. I tilt my head back, looking at the lightening sky, and sigh.

Ten years.

Iris would have loved Faedra. She has that same tenacity, that spark in her eyes when someone offers up a challenge.

A rustling behind me has me checking the water and then adding the packet before grabbing drinkware from Logan's pack. I'm returning with all four mugs when Faedra's bright red hair pops out of the entrance of her tent. She glances around a minute, her eyebrows drawn low, and then she smiles, grabbing her shoes from where Carter moved them just to the side of the tent's entrance. She steps out of the tent, closing the entrance and pressing her toiletry bags to her belly while I pour out enough of the coffee into my own mug and take a drink.

She freezes as she spots me, her cheeks flaring a deep red before either of us say anything.

"Good morning," she says, and her voice has heat racing through me.

Holy fuck, this is ridiculous. The backwoods is absolutely not where we'll be knotting.

"Good morning," I murmur. Her blush gets even darker, and my cock takes notice.

"I'll be right back," she says after a moment, and I nod, taking another drink, grateful for the chance to calm my body down, adjusting my half hard dick so it's not as obvious.

It's not been so long that I knotted with someone that this reaction is really warranted. But fuck if my body doesn't care in the least, the faint trace of her scent wrapping around me and making my skin ache.

Her heat is definitely close.

The crunch of her footfalls has me grabbing her mug.

"Do you want tea this morning instead of coffee?" I ask.

She murmurs a negative, and I pour the coffee into the mug and hand it to her, letting my fingers brush along hers as I pull away. Her breath hitching is its own reward.

"What's Black Canyon?" Her question is breathless, her movements halting as she moves one of the chairs to be closer to me. Our knees brush when she sits, and she hums, leaning closer into me.

Not the question I was expecting.

"Black Canyon of the Gunnison," I say, palming her knee, running my thumb along the edge of her thigh. "It's a national park on the other side of the mountains here. It's one of our favorites to hike."

She tilts her head. "Is that the one in the photos at the condo? In Logan's office and above his dresser?"

The twinge of jealousy is fleeting. We're not robots. Her

dynamic with each of us will be different, and I know that she's been staying with Logan most nights the last week. I offer a nod, and she smiles.

"Carter said you guys have been doing this for over a decade," she says, taking a drink of the coffee. She grimaces as she sets it down and walks to the packs, grabbing a packet of sugar from one of the bags. It's clear it doesn't quite fix the coffee for her, but she puts on a brave face anyway, finishing it in three large gulps before I can answer.

When she sets the mug beside her feet, I palm her knee again and say, "This particular event, yes. This is our 12th year, actually. But we've been hiking since we were sophomores in college."

She cocks an eyebrow, her lips pursing. "So, like, twenty years now?"

I scrunch my nose. "That reminds me that we're old ass men when you say it like that," I say with a laugh, and she smirks.

"If the shoe fits," she says, her tone rising at the end as she twists a finger into her hair, the comment clearly a joke. I laugh again before finishing my own coffee and setting the mug next to hers.

Her look grows thoughtful. "Was this something Iris ever did with you?"

My stomach twists, and I tighten my hold on her knee as I nod. "She loved it. She did this one with us the first two years, too. We did it as a trio."

She bites her lip and laces her fingers with mine.

I clear my throat. "It was one of the things I found on her list, actually. She wanted to hike Denali." Faedra squeezes my fingers.

"What did she have written for that one?" she asks after a minute.

"Not enough time," I grunt. "It's a dangerous hike that takes months of preparation and has a narrow window to actually attempt. She'd written that she didn't have the time to commit for the trip." I shake my head and rub my beard. "Carter and I would have happily dropped the cash to get out there with her. But she never asked."

Faedra hums, tracing shapes along the back of my hand. "What about you?" she asks, looking over at me, her touch gentle. "Do you have a list? Dreams you still have?"

"I'd like to do the thru-hiking Triple Crown," I say without hesitation. She frowns, and I clarify. "It's a set of three thru-hikes, like what we're doing now. You end up in a different place than you started. There's one that spans the west coast, one that spans Appalachia, and one that goes up the heart of the Rockies."

"Those must be long," she says, and I laugh.

"The Continental Divide Trail is over 3,000 miles." Her eyes widen, and her jaw drops. I lean over and kiss her. "At best it takes about six months to finish."

"Wow," she whispers. I run my hand down her shin, leaning into her, and she bridges the gap, kissing me until we're both breathless.

"Bonding is another one," I admit when we pull apart. She combs through her hair as she frowns, her tongue tracing her bottom lip.

Shit.

I probably should have come up with a better way to bring up the idea of bonding. She's young, and we've only really been around each other for a couple weeks. It's one thing to be matched. It's another thing entirely to bond.

I shrug, squeezing her hand before pulling away. "Obviously that isn't one I can decide to do on my own," I say. She takes a careful breath. "And I don't expect it, either."

After a moment, she nods, licks her lips, and starts to say something.

There's rustling across from us a second before Logan gets

out of the tent, his back towards us as he heads into the forest without looking back. Carter unzips his own tent before Faedra recalibrates. She turns, and he offers an intimate smile that creases the corners of his eyes.

"Good morning," she says, keeping a firm grip on my hand. He kisses her just as thoroughly as I did.

"Good morning, little Omega," he murmurs as his hand drags down her neck before stepping away in the same direction as Logan.

"We should get breakfast ready," she says after a minute, the easy feeling between us now tense.

I blow out a breath.

She glances at me. "I'll think about it."

Better than her cursing me, at least.

Twenty-Four

FAEDRA

"Red."

Logan's voice is warm and soft, brushing over me, and I nuzzle harder into him, pressing my lips to the hollow of his throat. His laugh vibrates through his chest, and I smile. His hands are gentle where they comb through my hair, though at this point I feel like I should encourage him to not touch me at all until we're back at the condo and freshly showered.

"Red, we have to get up," he says, tracing his thumb down my throat and across my collar bone. "If we don't, Carter will eat what's left of the decent food and leave us with the shit he hates."

My mind flicks back to Carter pretending to gag on one of the granola bars.

That has me rolling off of him and crawling out of the sleeping bag that was absolutely not large enough for us both but that he insisted we could make work when I cried in the middle of the night from not being able to smell his skin. I'm pinning that one completely on being off the suppressors.

What in the weird ass Omega shit even is that?

I couldn't smell his *skin*. The skin that has been only wiped down since Friday and smelled so strongly of his sweat that he didn't even need to perfume for me to smell the sandalwood. (Spoiler alert: it's now Monday.) Not that he'd been even remotely weirded out by it—or at least if he had been, he'd been a phenomenal actor. He simply slid to the far side of the bag and helped me sidle in, pulling me into his chest before falling back asleep like this was perfectly rational behavior.

"I'm not sure there's decent food left," I tell him, pulling on my hoodie and braiding back my hair. "If you make me eat another dehydrated banana I might just decide to file a complaint with the Council."

Logan throws his head back, his laugh filling the tent, and I smile.

We're just getting out of the tent and tying our shoes when there's voices from nearby and Jude starts laughing as he works to get the tent he shared with Carter torn down and repacked.

"It took you long enough," Carter jokes, walking to the edge of the camp, looking back towards where we came from yesterday. A couple hundred feet away, two women hike towards us. Their packs are a happy purple, and they hold hands, swinging them as they traverse the area separating us. "Honestly thought you'd forgotten to show up this year."

One of the women mutters an impressive curse, and I smile. Logan brushes his lips against my temple as he hands me one of the packs of dehydrated fruits and peanut butter.

"Apple," he murmurs. "No complaint required."

I purse my lips. "Don't suppose Jude left any of the cashew butter," I say in my best grumpy voice.

Logan grins, grabbing a single packet of it from the back

pocket of his jeans. My laugh is breathless as I collapse into his arms, kissing him before he can recalibrate. His arms tighten around me after a moment, his hand burying into the base of my braid, his thumb tracing the nape of my neck.

"Cashew butter *and* no bananas. I am truly blessed," I say, giggling against his lips, and he shakes his head, laughing.

"Forgive us for thinking you'd take it easy on Faedra since she hasn't ever done this," Gina says, her voice much closer than before. "You've been running her ragged, no doubt."

I pull away from Logan, ripping open the packet of cashew butter and spreading it over one of the dried apple slices. I'm on my third by the time the women reach us. Jude's gotten the tent completely packed away, and Logan walks over to help him with the other one, rolling our sleeping bags and rearranging everything in the packs.

"No rest for the wicked and all that, of course," the other woman says, laughing.

"You make it sound like we're monsters, Ashlynn," Carter muses, his hands not stopping where he pulls down the chairs and gets them worked into the packs as well. In fact, I'm the only one *not* working on getting the camp put away. I start to walk towards Carter, but he shakes his head. "You eat, little Omega. We've got this."

Jude glances up. "You have enough, Fae? I can grab a packet of something else if you need more."

I shake my head, holding up the rest of the apple pieces. I tuck the empty packet of cashew butter into the pocket of my hoodie and then rip into the peanut butter. It's not my favorite, but I've learned the last few days that enough protein is more important than if I really enjoy the taste or texture.

"Damn, they don't even have you packing out. I need to figure out how to get me a pack, Ashlynn," Gina muses, stopping beside me. I glance at her, my cheeks flushed, and she winks. The woman next to her rolls her eyes. Gina offers a quick introduction. "Ashlynn, this is Faedra. Faedra, this is my wife, Ashlynn."

I wave, and the woman smiles before taking a drink from the water bottle strapped to the side of her pack.

"How many miles have you been averaging then?" Ashlynn asks once she's put it back away. "We thought we were doing decent with ten."

Jude shrugs. "Right about twelve. We did nine the first day to ease her into it."

I never thought nine miles would be considered easing into *anything*, but here we are.

"Shit, when did you pass us then? Did you go the higher route?" Gina asks. Logan nods. "Good grief, you really did run her ragged."

By the time I've finished the small breakfast, the guys have the camp torn down and the packs rearranged. Carter helps me into mine, adjusting the load lifters until my shoulders don't ache quite as much, his hands lingering on my waist. I don't try to hold back my scent, and he steps closer into me, twisting us so that his body blocks the others.

"Seven miles and a shower, and then I'm knotting you, little Omega," he murmurs, his voice low and rich, dragging across my skin. I grin, grabbing his belt loops and pulling him closer into me. "I've done nothing but drown in jasmine the last four days."

"I'll hold you to it," I say, trying to keep my face serious.

His grin is resplendent, and I bask in it.

"Good," he says, and I clench my thighs.

These seven miles can't happen fast enough.

Ashlynn flips her long black hair, shaking it out before pulling it back into a high ponytail. She smiles as she grabs the baseball cap from my hand and situates it on her head again.

"Thanks," she says, grabbing her water and taking a long drink. "Sweat on my neck is one of those things I can't stand."

"Mine is when it makes my thighs chafe," I say, shoving the reusable bag that's been designated for trash into my pack before closing it. "It's probably my own fault since I prefer skirts, but it was windy enough on the coast to not be a deal breaker. Denver is very different, though."

Ashlynn nods. "Best solution for it is baby powder. Get the stuff that's talc free so it doesn't irritate your lungs. Or switch to wearing dance shorts. The super short inseams function almost like boxer briefs."

"Why didn't I think of dance shorts?" I ask. "That's brilliant."

She helps me reposition my pack, letting me adjust everything until it feels decent.

"You guys coming?" Gina asks from up ahead where the others are already hiking. Ashlynn gives her a thumbs up and then we start following them.

"Carter mentioned you have two kids?" I phrase it as a question since he only mentioned them in passing.

Ashlynn nods, smiling. "Darius just turned three. Hallie is four months." She looks over at me, pursing her lips. "Naturally, since I'm the one who did all the work, they look just like Gina."

"Of course," I say. "Isn't there a rule somewhere about that? My brother and I look just like our father. Especially my brother. People have mistaken them for brothers before."

Her nose crinkles when she laughs, and the sun catches on a small silver stud in her ear.

"Do you normally wear a hoop in your daith piercing?" I ask, twisting the back of the stud I put in my orbital piercing.

She nods. "Studs work best out here I've found. They're less likely to catch on anything, especially if you're having to navigate pretty heavy underbrush."

We walk in comfortable silence for a while, helping each other scramble down a particularly steep section of the mountain. Ahead of us, Carter says something just quiet enough I can't understand him, and both Logan and Jude start laughing. Gina pushes Jude half-heartedly a moment later even as she smiles.

Ashlynn leans closer to me. "This is the most I've seen Jude laugh in a long time."

I swallow around the sudden lump in my throat.

"They were beside themselves when they got the announcement from the Council," she continues before I can decide what to say. "They called us because they were scared to open it alone."

She smiles and pulls the water bottle from her side pocket without missing a step.

"I was scared to open mine, too," I say, twisting my braid around my hand to keep from fidgeting with my pack. "I opened mine with my best friend. She didn't have any problems looking at hers alone, though. Violet's always been like that."

"Gina is, too," Ashlynn says, shaking her head. My lip burns with how hard I'm biting it as I suck in as deep of a breath as I can manage on the side of a mountain.

Before I can chicken out, I ask, "Were they happy?"

Ashlynn's smile is radiant, lighting up her entire countenance as she bumps my shoulder with her own. "Ecstatic. Carter cried. They've been going to those galas for the last four years. After the first few times they were shortlisted but not matched, everything just stopped. They'd go and then not hear anything at all." She frowns, her eyebrows pinching. "They were talking in January about this being the last year. It was really demoralizing for them."

Logan had mentioned at the gala that they'd been to a lot of them. My heart hurt then, but it aches even more acutely now that I've gotten the chance to really get to know them. It must have been awful to have so many years pass with nothing to show for it. Did Jude wonder if he had made the right decision?

"Anyway, it's been fantastic seeing them adjust over the last month." Ashlynn gives me another bump of her shoulder. "I know you probably have better things to do, but we'd love to take you out for a girls day if you're interested. Logan mentioned that your best friend was matched, too, and that the distance has been hard on you."

How in the *world* did he even notice that?

I stare at the back of Logan's pack, his blond hair messy but bright in the midday sun.

"Of course," I say, pulling my phone from my pocket and turning it on.

She enters her information and then Gina's before handing it back. I bite my lip as I hesitate, and Ashlynn is quick to notice, her eyebrow quirking. I blow out my breath and just say it. That's the "Faedra Way" according to my mother.

"I'm not sure we should schedule anything for a bit. My heat is probably going to start soon, and I don't want to have to reschedule with you since babysitters need lead-in time."

Ashlynn nods. "Whenever you're wanting some estrogen, just let us know."

Twenty-Five

CARTER

Faedra knocks on the frame of my door, her hair still pulled up into the single braid she wore while hiking this morning, her teeth biting her bottom lip. I set aside my hiking gear, leaning it against the window to deal with later, and then cross the room, pulling her into my arms the moment I'm able. Her shoulders move with her heavy sigh, and she twists her hands into my belt loops, tightening her hold around my waist.

"You feeling alright?" I ask.

She nods, humming a bit. "The nap back from Estes Park was perfect. Thank you."

My lips are featherlight as I press a kiss to her temple.

"Good," I murmur.

"I'm ready for that shower," she whispers. A rush of heat licks down my spine and straight to my dick. Faedra notices, my sweats hiding nothing, and she laughs under her breath. "I'm ready for *that*, too."

A soft chime sounds before I can decide what to say. She pulls away from me, her eyebrows furrowed. I step away from her, running my thumb over her cheekbone.

"I'll go get the water started," I say. She grabs my hand before I can turn around, and I cock an eyebrow.

"It's Violet," she says, flashing me the screen of her phone, a notification obscuring the picture Doug took of the four of us before we started the thru-hike. I squeeze her hand as she glances at her phone and sighs. "Actually, it's Jasper. She's in heat apparently."

She tosses her phone onto the foot of my bed and then strips out of her shirt. I have her in my arms before she can manage a gasp.

∼

JUDE

"Can I join you?"

Faedra's voice is quiet, blending into the darkness of the library I've made of the loft. I glance at the time.

Is she always up so late? I haven't heard her, but I know she's been sleeping with Logan most nights, and he tends to have the earliest night routine of all of us. I save the document I'm working on and close my laptop, setting it on the table beside me so that I can hold out my hand to where she stands at the landing of the stairs. She clenches a dark blue tablet case to her chest. Her hair falls in a sleek sheet over her shoulders, and she's opted for a loose fitting knit dress in a deep green that compliments her hair and makes her freckles more pronounced.

"Of course," I say, keeping my voice the same volume. She flushes, her chest darkening, and then she crosses the loft and takes my hand, letting me guide her onto my lap without a word of protest.

"What were you working on?" she asks after a minute.

"My department chair assigned me another intro class, and I didn't have an updated course syllabus." I run a hand down her spine as she fidgets a bit on my lap, finding a better position and then pulling out her tablet. She opens an editing software, selects several menu options, and then hums as a dialogue box appears stating that the import is in progress.

"How many photos did you take?" I ask, and she blushes.

"About a thousand," she says. I cock an eyebrow, and her blush intensifies as she glances at me. "But this batch is about two thirds of that. The other set I won't be editing for potentially printing them. At least not as large. I'll probably print a few and put them up in my room."

"Why won't you be printing them larger?"

She ducks her head.

That's enough of that.

I tuck my finger under her chin and turn her towards me, her green eyes fluttering open as she blows out a breath. She pulls her phone from a pocket of her dress.

I hadn't even noticed her dress has pockets. The action rucks the hem a few inches up her thighs, and my cock is immediately interested, pressing against the soft fabric of my sweats. She taps a few times on her phone and then turns it to me.

It's a picture of me on the hike, my flannel shirt tied around my waist, my jeans marked with the mud from her tumble and the scratches on my arm mostly scabbed. I'm at the edge of our camp, my pack no where to be seen as I take a drink of water. The positioning of the sun has it looking like someone added a filter.

It's stunning.

"Faedra," I murmur, shifting my gaze from the photo to her.

She's biting her lip, her eyes shy and her cheeks a deep red. "You haven't edited that?"

She shakes her head.

I blow out a breath, rubbing a hand over my jaw, the prickling of my beard a small comfort.

"That's phenomenal. You could sell that to a magazine. National Geographic would be foaming at the mouth if the others are half as good as that one."

Her smile is resplendent, and I bask in it, moving to cup her cheek, tracing some of the freckles along her nose and lips. They've gotten darker the last several days we were out in the wilderness, and I crave being able to trace them with my tongue. My body goes tight at the thought, my cock twitching.

"I don't want the whole world to see it," she admits, breaking me out of the fantasy. She sets the phone in her lap and props her hands against my stomach. A race of heat flashes down my spine, and I hold back a groan. "That side of you is something we get and no one else, and I'm content to keep it that way."

When I nod, she goes back to the tablet, checking on the program and then pulling up a photo. It's mesmerizing. Watching her edit the photos is soothing in a way that I've only really experienced when lost in my own research. My laptop stays closed, the half finished syllabus pushed aside until tomorrow as I allow myself to focus on her, a feeling of contentment making me smile.

When she yawns, relaxing farther into me, I feather a kiss to her temple and cup her knee. "It's after midnight," I murmur. "And we just got back from the trip this afternoon. You should sleep."

She hums, tapping on the tablet a few times before turning off the screen and putting it back in the cloth carrying case. "Can I sleep with you?"

My cock jolts, but I ignore it. No way am I going to suggest knotting when she's barely awake.

"Of course," I say, not able to stop my voice from lowering. She shivers, her eyes dilating and her scent surrounding us, and I groan. I coax the tablet from her hands and set it atop my laptop, kissing her to distract her, and then stand up, my arms wrapped tightly around her back and knees. She giggles into my mouth as I start across the condo, her cheeks flushing the longer I hold her tight to me.

Her gaze is curious as I step into the bedroom and ease her back onto her feet. I leave the light off, closing the door and brushing past her to my ensuite, prepping for bed while she decides what she's most comfortable doing. When I walk back out, she's curled up on the far side of the bed, her head perched on her arm as she twists the quilt between her fingers. Her gaze is locked on the city beyond the windows, but there's a tightness to her expression, a slight frown that has my heart lurching.

"You alright?" I ask, leaning against the bathroom door, crossing my arms.

She glances at me, her cheeks pink.

"I...think so," she says after a long hesitation, her throat rippling as she swallows. "I'm not used to feeling so out of control. It's...difficult to adjust to."

My gut clenches. "We should have had you opt for a slower step-down," I say, but she's quick to shake her head. She pulls her hand away from the quilt and holds it out to me, a thread of vulnerability in the way she holds her shoulders. I don't hesitate to take the offer, crossing the space and settling in behind her, pulling her against me as I wrap my arm around her waist. She hums, and I trace her throat and shoulder with my lips, a featherlight touch that calms her more than anything else up to this point.

"I don't like the idea of me slowly feeling this way over a long period of time. I would have thought I was developing an anxiety disorder," she murmurs after a while. "This way I know it's my designation. It's just..." She blows out a breath, grasping my arm with both of her hands. "I don't think I ever realized just how visceral all of it is. It was always just something I knew in my head, like how I have green eyes and freckles."

I kiss the sensitive spot just under her ear that I found while on the hike. She leans her head back, giving me more space, and I take it, kissing and sucking her throat until she's pushing back against me and her scent drowns the room. I stop her hand as she reaches back for me, and she whines.

"Sleep, Faedra," I whisper in her ear.

She protests, but she doesn't push for more, and after another few minutes, she's limp in my hold, her breathing slow and even.

It takes me another ten minutes to remember how to sleep.

Twenty-Six

FAEDRA

The sun is bright through the windows, blinding me as I wake all at once. Jude's arms are still around me, but we've rolled so that I'm laying across his chest, my nose pressed into the crook of his shoulder. I'm careful as I roll off of him, not wanting to wake him before his alarm goes off. His face is peaceful in sleep, none of the wariness he carries present, and it makes my gut clench.

Bonding is another one. Obviously that isn't one I can decide to do on my own.

Bonding still feels too intimate, too unnerving. But the idea of seeing him like this all the time, of knowing what goes on in his mind when his eyes are distant and his face stoic is almost tempting enough to have me entertaining the idea. As if spurred by my thoughts, Jude's eyes flicker open, focusing nearly immediately on me.

"Good morning," he says, his voice rumbling through the room, sending a lick of arousal through me.

My scent surrounds us before I can control my reaction, and he groans, grabbing my knee and pulling it over his hip. He lays hard and heavy against me, and I grab his shoulders, using them as leverage to roll over and straddle him, the feel of him urging me on.

"I like this kind of greeting," he murmurs, grabbing my hips and pushing up into me. "Every time I manage to be the first one awake, I get these little extra bonuses. Almost makes me a morning person."

The corner of my mouth tips up before I pull off my shirt and toss it on the ground. Jude doesn't hesitate, sitting up enough to take my nipple between his teeth and pull gently. I whine and press down on him, arching my hips, trying to find the right pressure against my clit.

"So impatient," he murmurs, blowing against my wet nipple, making me gasp before turning his attention to the other, pulling more forcefully than before.

"Don't make me beg," I moan, scrabbling at the waistband of his sweats and pushing them down just enough that his cock springs free. He grunts when I take him in hand, stroking him with a tight hold, flicking my thumb across the head and smearing the bead of pre-cum.

"I like hearing it, though, Fae," he whispers, flicking his tongue over my nipple again. My breath catches, and he pushes aside my panties, running his thumb through my pussy before circling my clit. "All your little whimpers and mewls and gasps. It's nearly as intoxicating as your scent."

"You like it? My scent?" I ask, stroking him with a tighter hand, smiling as he grunts and thrusts up into me, holding my hips still as he rubs the head of his cock against my clit.

"Fuck yes," he mutters.

I smile and stroke him faster. The musk of his own scent envelops me, blending with my jasmine until they overpower the room, and I moan, massaging my breast and tensing my thighs to relieve the building ache. His lips curve into a sly grin.

All at once, his hands tighten on my hips, lowering me until my pussy rubs against his cock, forcing my stroking to stop.

"Ride me," he mutters, looking up at me, his eyes burning.

Desire consumes me, a rush of heat spearing my core, making slick drip down my thighs. Even still, nerves get the better of me.

"I've never been on top," I whisper.

He blows against my nipple, and I arch with a gasp.

"Do what feels good, Fae. It'll all feel phenomenal for me."

His words are husky, vibrating through my breast and making goosebumps rise along my collar bones. I don't hesitate, grasping the base of his cock and guiding myself over him, lowering myself inch by torturous inch.

The stretch has me moaning, my breath coming in short pants, and his jaw clenches as I sink to the root, my toes curling into the sheets.

Oh my God. *Oh my God*.

He's huge, the stretch of him nearly burning, and I whimper, scratching his chest where I rest my hands to stabilize myself. His fingers dig into my hips, small pinpricks of pain that just inflame me more.

"Goddamn, Faedra," Jude mutters.

He encourages my hips forward, rocking them while he's still seated so deep it makes my breath catch. The added sensation has me scrabbling at his chest, my head falling back on a moan. When I lift myself off him and then lower back down, he moves his hands, running them up my sternum and down my thigh, the soft trailing of his fingers adding to the cacophony of sensation.

I bite back a moan, but Jude makes a low sound in his throat. "Let me hear it, Faedra. Just how much do you like my cock?"

I lower myself again, whining when he brushes a spot that makes my toes curl.

"There you go," he murmurs with a chuckle. "Just wait until I knot you, Fae. I'll be so deep you won't be able to walk straight."

Sweat already forms a light sheen across my chest and belly, my thighs trembling despite us just starting.

How the hell do guys do this?

Jude palms my throat, his thumb and finger settling just under my ears, and I flush, a flash of heat spearing through me, making more slick drip down his cock as I manage to speed up, taking him deep with each downward slide.

"You like being choked, Omega?" Jude asks, his voice nothing more than a rumble that vibrates through my body.

I moan and let my eyes flutter closed. The pressure around my throat increases, his thumb and finger pushing in until my head starts to go fuzzy. When I dig my fingers into his chest and speed up again, lost to the need building inside me, he chuckles and snaps his hips up into me, forcing himself deeper.

"Oh fuck," I gasp, breathless, and he does it again, his timing terrifyingly perfect, his erection brushing a new spot so deep inside that I feel like he's going to end up being the death of me. I whimper, goosebumps erupting across my hips.

My orgasm builds in my belly, sparks of lightning racing down my limbs and tightening my nipples. He seems keyed in to me on a different level because he trails his fingers up my leg, his thumb and finger still tight around my throat, and then circles my clit with a practiced touch that has me trembling with need. My moans are loud, falling from me with each snap of his hips as my own movements falter with the overwhelming sensory overload.

The moment the climax roars through me, Jude releases his hand on my throat, the sudden oxygen making the sensations unbelievably stronger. My arms give out on a sharp cry, and I collapse on top of him, my nose pressed into the crook of his shoulder. He chuckles, his hips still snapping up into me, his cock wedged so deep I press another strangled cry into his skin.

He turns his lips to my ear as he freezes, pulling my hips down into his with a rough groan. "Faedra," he whispers, his voice low and rough, his breath skating across my neck and making me shiver.

The all-consuming pressure of his knot fills me the next moment, and I scream, my toes curling and my nipples tightening to the point of near pain. His arms wrap around me, warm, immovable bands across my back, but his lips are soft where he trails them along my neck and shoulder.

"Such a good Omega," he murmurs against my skin as I begin to tremble.

"Oh *fuck*," I whimper, pressing my forehead into his sternum, my palms flat against the bed and bracketing his ears. He chuckles and nips at my wrist, the bite of his teeth making me clench around him and pulling another desperate mewl from between my lips. The trembling in my limbs grows until I'm a shaking mess above him, my lips pressed against his chest to muffle the frantic, high pitched whines I can't help but make while his knot continues to lock us together.

He feathers soft kisses across my wrist, draws small circles on my hip, and breathes calming words against my skin, soothing me even as my body begins to rebel against his knot, my core burning from the stretch. Just when it feels like it's too much, it suddenly releases and Jude rolls us as he pulls out, covering me with his body but not giving me any of his weight.

"Faedra," he whispers, his lips brushing mine. It takes me a moment to remember how to move, how to make my body respond, but when I manage to flicker my eyes open, his bright green eyes are intent on me, his lips are pulled into an unsmiling line. "You alright?" he asks.

Instead of immediately offering an agreement, I check in

with my body, swallowing as the soreness becomes more apparent with just the small adjustment I make under him. It hadn't been this sensitive with Carter—not so soon, at least.

"Sore," I whisper, and he frowns. "Which honestly sucks because I'm interested in round two."

The corner of his mouth quirks up, and I grin at the small victory. He sets small kisses down my sternum and belly, his beard scratching at my skin and making me squirm.

If he's interested in this being round two, then I'm not going to stop him. I dig my hand into his short hair, scratching my nails against his scalp when he runs his cheek across my inner thigh, the scrape of his beard making me jump.

But the moment his tongue presses against my clit, I whine and pull him away, my body still so sensitized that it borders on pain, sending a shiver down my spine as I arch away from his touch.

He presses his forehead into my belly, muttering something I can't understand.

"What did you say?" I ask.

He glances up, his lips pulled into a wry grin. "Just admitting out loud I've never had a better knotting in my life."

My smile is bright, satisfaction making me preen, and he laughs.

"Come to work with me?" he asks, tracing circles along my hip. "I don't have any appointments."

Biting my lip, I adjust under him, rolling my hips, and he groans, low in his throat.

"Sounds fun," I say, and he kisses my navel. My body clenches.

Maybe there'll be time for an interesting lunch, too.

Twenty-Seven

JUDE

Three knocks on my door have me looking up from the syllabus I'm proofreading, my frown deep. It grows even more pronounced when I see who's standing in the threshold to my office.

"What do you need?" I ask, not bothering to be polite.

Melanie purses her lips and takes a step inside, adjusting the door so that it's halfway closed, blocking her body from the hallway. Unease has me standing and rounding the desk, closing the drawer that has Faedra's bag in it. Scowling, I cross my arms and lean against the front of my desk, crossing my ankles.

"Was your hiking trip decent this year?" Her voice is nearly sickly sweet, her eyes large as she scans my office with a keen eye she hasn't bothered with in several months—a year, probably. My skin crawls under the scrutiny. I adjust where I lean, making sure I can see out the door. "Seemed like an interesting time."

I narrow my eyes, trying to remember if Doug posted our group to the organization's social medias. Melanie raises an eyebrow, flipping her hair over her shoulder, and I force a swallow.

"It was good," I tell her, trying to distract her as she takes another step into my office, her hands resting on the back of one of the chairs, her fingers tapping on the fabric. "Backpacking is always enjoyable."

Simple, easy information that anyone would be welcome to know. Melanie hums, flipping her hair again, leaning over the back of the chair enough that it pulls the neckline of her blouse taught.

Bile rises to the back of my throat, and I clench my fists, the bite of my nails in my skin keeping me from completely losing my shit.

"What do you need, Melanie?" I ask, my voice dropping in irritation. "I have work to finish."

"Do you?" she asks, rounding the chair, standing directly in front of me. "From what Harper tells me, there's some pretty interesting *work* happening at Carter's office. I wonder if you've decided to share his little whore, too, like you've shared everything else?"

Anger rises, swift and fierce, and I pull back my lip, snarling, "Call her a whore again, and you'll regret it."

Melanie reels back like I've struck her. Her eyes narrow as she recovers a moment later, and she runs her fingers down my arm, wrapping them around my wrist, trying to encourage my touching her. I resist, keeping my arms locked around my chest, and she pouts when I don't concede to her.

"Maybe I should remind you of last month? You were more than willing to entertain me then. Maybe you've just forgotten how good we are," she says, and then she's stepping into my own space, running her hand up my arm and grasping my neck, her thumb digging into the pulse point below my ear. She's crashing her lips to mine before I can push her away, her body pressed against mine, her eyes fluttering shut as she moans. It takes a moment for the shock to break through, and then I'm glancing at the doorway.

Faedra stands just outside the door, paler than I've ever seen her, her hands pressed against her belly, her green eyes wide and glassy with tears. The anger burns through me hotter, and I push Melanie away, not attempting to help her as she stumbles back into one of the chairs and trips over it. She grabs onto the back at the last moment, sputtering, but I don't look at her, keeping my eyes locked on Faedra.

"Get the fuck out, Melanie," I growl. Faedra steps to the side as Melanie continues sputtering, but I hold out my hand in silent invitation. Her throat ripples with a delicate swallow, and she blinks several times, the tears disappearing as she takes a deep breath. Another long moment, and she opens the door wider and walks to me, taking an exaggerated path that avoids Melanie completely.

My chest tightens when she sets her hand on mine and I feel the trembling in her fingers. I close my hand around hers, squeezing tightly, and don't look at Melanie where she stands awkwardly just behind the chair.

"Get out," I tell her.

She flips her hair, her gaze narrowing on Faedra, her lips screwed up into a grimace. "So desperate you had to scalp the arts department? Just wait, girl, he'll get bored of you, too. He *never* commits, especially to such desperate whores like you."

She turns on her heel and storms from my office as Faedra twists to see her, eyes wide again, her mouth open in shock. When she doesn't say anything after a few minutes, I run my thumb across her knuckles and murmur her name. She flinches, glancing back at me, and I palm her cheek, moving slow enough that she can pull away if she prefers. Her eyes flood with tears again, and I curse, stepping into her.

"Faedra," I say, but she talks over me.

"That's her?" Her voice trembles just like her hand, and it makes my skin crawl. When I nod, she makes a disparaging noise in her throat and pulls away from me, running her hands down her skirt. "And you slept with her last month? Was that before or after we matched?"

A stone settles in my stomach. "Before."

She nods, turning her face so I can't see what she's thinking. Her shoulders are tight, her hands still smoothing her skirt. "Would you have done it again if we hadn't matched?"

"No." My answer is immediate. "It was a horrible decision that I shouldn't have made."

"And the testing Carter said you all did? Was it long enough after to account for her?" She won't look at me, her voice growing more unsteady, and that insidious self-hatred rears its head, making me want to vomit. "Do I..." She blows out a breath and shakes her head. "Am I ok?"

"Absolutely," I tell her, my voice dropping. She shivers, her scent filling my office, and she closes her eyes. "I would never risk you for my own gain, Faedra. Never."

There's a horrible stretch of silence, the soft chime of my phone notifications the only ambient sound. Faedra takes a deep breath, her throat moving with a swallow.

"Has this..." She trails off, shaking her head. "I shouldn't ask. It was before me, anyway," she mutters.

It's easy enough to guess what she wants to know.

"Twice before last month," I offer, tucking my hands into my pockets, switching my phone to silent without looking at it. "All three of them have been when I was drinking and should never have happened."

"Why? If it had been so horrible, why would..." She hesitates, and I don't make her finish the question.

"There's been a couple times across the years where I've been at some really low points. And she has this horrible way of reaching out to me when I'm feeling the worst." I blow out a breath. "Why does an addict return to his vice when he's been sober—and desperately wants to stay sober?"

"I'm going to call Logan," she whispers, rounding the desk and pulling her bag from the drawer. "I...I don't think I can be here anymore."

My stomach drops.

"Alright," I say, but I step in front of her as she stands and turns for the door. She keeps her gaze on my chest, her eyes tracing the pattern of my tie. My touch is hesitant as I circle her wrist, guiding her to sit in my chair, and she chokes back a sob as she falls into it.

"Faedra," I murmur, and she swallows another sound.

She shakes her head. "Why did you—"

"I didn't kiss her," I say, and she freezes, her gaze finally meeting mine. I swallow at the blatant distrust in it. "On the Council itself, I didn't. I pushed her away the moment the shock faded."

She takes a deep breath, biting her lip.

"Does she know that we're matched?"

I shake my head. "I have no contact with her outside of her pursuing me." Her unspoken question sits heavily between us. I take her hands in mine, crouching in front of her. "All of my colleagues know, though. I'm not hiding you."

She nods. The moment stretches between us, her body still held tightly, her hands limp in my grasp.

Not even tenure is worth seeing my Omega hurt like this. The decision is simpler than I ever expected it to be.

"Let me talk to my department chair, alright? I'll make sure she can't bother us anymore. Promise."

She finally squeezes my hands and leans into me, her forehead pressing into my sternum.

"Thank you," she murmurs, and I comb through her hair until her body loses its tension and she moves into my lap.

I feather a kiss against her temple. "Let me update my office hours, and we'll go home. We can do whatever you want."

She's quiet as I scoop her back into my chair. It takes a few minutes to get everything updated in both systems, and then I send an email to Chris requesting a meeting first thing tomorrow. She accepts the calendar request before I've put my phone in my pocket. Faedra stands and adjusts her bag, wiping her hands on her shirt before blowing out a breath.

Her smile is more confident when she looks up at me as I take her hand.

"She really doesn't—"

I cut her off with my lips on hers. "Nothing, Faedra. She hasn't for a very long time."

Faedra glances at me as I come down the stairs, adjusting my suit jacket and making sure my tie is tucked into my vest. She sets her tablet down on the counter, her throat moving with a swallow, and it cuts me to see her so unsure around me. I set the folder and my phone on the counter and step around her to the espresso machine, trailing my fingers along her waist as I go. Her breath catches, but a thread of her scent hits my nose.

"I shouldn't be gone more than an hour," I say once the machine is running. I turn to her, grabbing the edge of the counter as I lean against it. "Would you like to go for an early lunch? You wanted to see if the music place had that record delivered, right?"

We'd gone to a local music shop yesterday, and she'd picked out a vinyl record player. State of the art but designed to look vintage, with a white case and painted florals on it, I helped her set it up in her room. Her guarded look had faded over the course of the afternoon until I could manage a half decent breath again around the tightness in my chest.

She bites her lip. "Are you sure?"

"Absolutely," I say. "Just like yesterday. Whatever you want to do, alright?"

After a long moment, she nods. "You have a meeting?"

"With my department chair. It shouldn't take long."

Resignations rarely take more than a few minutes in reality. The longest part is fielding the follow-up questions.

"Alright," she says after a while. Her hesitation fades as the minutes pass by, and I palm her neck. "There's a shop a bit north that I'd like to visit. Maybe we could eat in one of the parks?"

She hums when I nod, pressing a soft kiss to my lips. The vise around my chest releases, and I take a deep breath, basking in her scent as she responds to my soft touches.

"I'm sorry," I whisper against her lips. She shakes her head, twisting her fingers into the belt loops of my slacks, pulling me closer to her. Her kiss deepens, grows more insistent, and I let her, communicating what I can't manage to put into words. She relaxes against me with a soft hum as I pull away, and relief rushes through me.

"I'll be back soon," I murmur, and she presses her hands into my stomach as she nods. Her eyes are bright, her cheeks flushed, and it's so goddamn alluring that I almost ask Chris to postpone the meeting.

The stricken look Faedra had in the hallway flashes behind my eyes and resolve settles heavily in my stomach. The feel of her hands on me lingers as I step away, grab my things, and head to my car.

I spend the drive rehearsing, swallowing down the nerves that crowd my throat at the thought of losing everything I've worked for over the last decade. The nerves double once I'm actually standing in front of Chris's office, the folder held loosely at my side. I triple check my phone and grimace when a text from Melanie flashes on the screen.

Blocking her number will be next.

Chris glances up from her computer when I knock on the door jamb, her gaze coasting over me and catching on the folder. Her mouth tightens, and her shoulders drop.

"Come in," she says, standing and rounding the desk. "I'm assuming it's important since it was such short notice."

When I nod, she sighs and closes the door. I lean against the back of a chair when she stays standing in front of the door, her arms crossed.

Before I can hand her the letter, she asks, "Why? And don't give me the normal general bullshit people say. We've worked together too long for that."

I purse my lips, debating if I should be honest.

"You're tenured and newly matched," Chris says, stepping up to me. She's even smaller than Faedra, barely coming to my chest, but the anger in her eyes has me taking a deep breath. "Something happened, and I want to know what it was."

Honesty it is, then.

"You know of my history with Melanie Williams."

When Chris nods, I offer the full story of yesterday.

"What else has happened? For how long?" Chris asks, rounding her desk and pulling a form from a drawer. "Would you be willing to submit a statement?"

Sighing, I lay out the last few years, detailing the dynamic. When she asks for more details, I offer them, pulling out my phone and scrolling through the messages, capturing screenshots and sending them to her when she asks. By the time I'm finished, I feel wrung out, bile sitting at the back of my throat. Chris goes through everything again before turning the paper to me so I can sign it.

The look on her face would make most people cower, but I find it comforting. I go to hand her the folder, and she shakes her head.

"I'm not accepting that yet. Give me a week to fix this. If you still want to give it to me then, I won't stop you." When I nod, she blows out a breath. "And I'd love to finally meet her, Jude."

I offer a half smile. "I'll let you know."

∼

FAEDRA

Jude's hands are soft, his touch light, as he combs through my hair, letting the pieces fan out across his legs. The large trees of the park help shade us from the sun, and I take another moment to look up at him. He's taken off the suit jacket and rolled his sleeves to his elbows, the script of his tattoo catching in the light. The sun highlights his beard, catching on the gray speckles throughout, reminding me of the backpacking trip, and I have the sudden urge to kiss him like I had that morning, long and slow and deep until my body pulsed with heat.

My scent responds to the thought, and he glances down at me, a smirk lifting the corner of his lips.

"I thought you wanted to wait for the others," he says, his voice low enough that it rumbles through me.

My cheeks heat, and I turn, pressing my forehead into his thigh. "I can't help it," I whisper. He palms my waist, his thumb brushing my ribs, and my scent grows stronger. His laugh is just a bit breathless, and it eases my embarrassment. "Literally anything right now makes me scent. It's frustrating."

Another hand cups my knee, and my scent doubles again.

Carter groans, and I flush, pressing my face harder into Jude's leg.

"It means your heat is getting close," Jude says, fingers trailing through my hair again. Nerves crawl up my throat, and I swallow twice to try and alleviate the heavy lump settled in the back of it.

Logan's sandalwood scent hits me, and I glance up, finding him sitting next to Jude, his gaze locked on me, his hair damp from a recent shower. His workout shorts and shirt are a deep blue that offsets his eyes, and for all that is good in this world, I can't help but groan at the sight.

"Really close," Carter murmurs, his hand tightening on my knee. "You mentioned you wanted to be in control of when it starts. Is that still what you want?"

I twist so I can see him, slowly rising from Jude's lap and adjusting my hair so it isn't quite so unkempt. "Yes. The idea of not knowing when it'll start is...not my favorite," I say, scrunching my nose. "My doctor gave me a referral for someone out here. I can call and see what it would take to have that happen."

Carter nods. "Whatever you decide, we support you."

Jude kisses my temple while Logan pulls a bag from beside him, sifting through it.

"Now," he says, grinning as he pulls out a cheesesteak sandwich and hands it to me, "let us feed you, Red."

Twenty-Eight

LOGAN

Faedra's laughing as I walk back towards her, her sunglasses pushed up onto her head. It's the real laugh, the one that's soft without being too delicate, the one I first got to hear at the gala and knew she was different. She smiles as I come up beside her and hand her the drink, wrapping my arm around her waist and kissing the sensitive spot under her ear.

"Oh my gosh, Violet," she says, leaning into me with a quiet hum. "I'll chat with the guys and let you know, alright? And send me pictures of his make-up present!"

She laughs again and then tucks her phone into the small bag sitting across her chest.

"Did you figure out where he is?" she asks, twisting in my hold until she's pressed against my front.

When I nod, she smiles, the faint scent of jasmine drifting around us. She laces her hand in mine as she pulls away, murmuring a quiet instruction for us to go find him. I guide her through the stadium, the people around us bustling despite it being squarely in the warmup timeframe of the game.

"What were you going to chat with us about?" I ask as we weave through people.

She pulls her hair over her shoulder. "Violet's birthday is next month, and she's wanting to fly out here and celebrate it with me. Is that ok?"

Faedra's always quick to double check with us, and we're just as quick to remind her that we're not her owners. I do it again, and she scoffs.

"It would be all of them. That's a lot of people to commit to, Logan," she says, and I shrug.

"They'll probably prefer finding a different place to stay, but I assure you that we're happy to adjust as needed if you want her to fly out."

Even as she nods, she bites her lip, and I pull us out of the flow of people, tucking us against the wall, palming her cheek.

"What is it, Red?" I ask, and she flushes, her freckles becoming more apparent.

Fuck, those freckles are my weakness.

I kiss her before she can answer, and she collapses into me. The jasmine gets stronger, and I groan as I pull away, desperately reminding myself that we have a baseball game to watch.

Faedra licks her lips, and I scent, the sandalwood blending with her jasmine. She tangles her fingers with mine even as I continue to cup her face.

"If they're going to fly out in a couple weeks, then I should really go through my heat before that," she says. I take a step into her, groaning when her eyes dilate and her chest flushes. "The doctor warned me that the stimulant tends to make them more extreme. And that my suppressing three of them makes it almost certain it'll be significantly more intense than a normal one."

"What would you like to do?" I ask, stepping away from her before my dick decides to skip the game. She bites her lip.

"I think I want to wait until after the weekend. Maybe it'll happen on its own? I don't feel ready for it yet."

I nod and cut back through the crowd, heading towards the first base line, guiding her down the stairs of the section on the far side of the dugout, my hand on the small of her back. A couple of the players glance up as we head down, handing back a baseball to a young girl. Once Tyler realizes it's us, he grins and waves, heading down the line and opening the window in the netting before we make it all way down the stairs.

"You made it!" he says as we step up to him, taking my hand and clapping my shoulder.

"I wasn't going to miss your first start, Ty. Who do you think I am?" I joke, and he laughs. As he steps back, his eyes catch on Faedra.

"Shit, man. I'm not put together enough to meet your Omega," he says, and I roll my eyes.

"This is Faedra," I say, and he holds out his hand. "Faedra, this is Tyler. He's been my project for the last four years."

Tyler throws his head back and laughs. "I finally figured it out, though!"

Faedra laughs and leans into me, and I press a kiss to the crown of her hair. Jasmine snakes around us, but Tyler doesn't react, so it must not be as strong as it was before.

Or maybe I'm just keyed into her on a different level.

"I'll see you on Wednesday, yeah?" Tyler asks, and I nod. Another player comes up to him, handing him a ball, and Faedra gasps. He grins, touching his cap before heading back to the dugout. Tyler groans. "He always has to show me up, doesn't he?"

He hands the ball signed by the team's star player to Faedra, and she giggles, tucking it into her bag. "Tell him thank you," she says, and I pull her tighter into me, running my hand up her side.

Tyler nods before closing the net and stepping back. "Enjoy the game," he says before turning and heading onto the field for final stretches.

Faedra hums happily under her breath as we work our way to our own seats, stopping to grab a couple things to eat on the way.

"Really? No salt on your pretzels?" I ask her, injecting my voice with mock incredulity. She rolls her eyes and dips a piece in the cheese, turning a bit as she bites into it, her focus falling back on the field where they're prepping for the first pitch. My attention, though, is stuck on the way her lips stretch around the piece of pretzel. I uncross my ankles, spreading my knees to take the pressure off my hardening dick.

After a few minutes, she turns to me, her brows dropped, her lips tilted like she's deep in thought.

"What's up?" I ask.

"How do you feel about having kids?"

The question isn't surprising. I shrug.

"It's on my 'eventually' list. I'm not in any hurry." She hums. "I know that Jude and Carter are ready. But I don't feel like I am."

She nods, murmuring an agreement. "Me, too. There's a lot I think I'd like to do first. I never really let myself think past matching. But I'd like to explore a bit before everything changes."

I press a kiss into the crook of her shoulder, and she smiles, her scent surrounding us so quickly it's overwhelming. Someone scoffs behind us, and then a woman makes a snide comment. Faedra freezes for a heartbeat, but I just feather another kiss, trying to distract her.

Just as the teams take the field and the game starts, the woman jeers behind us.

"Get a room. No one wants to see you fuck around with an Omega in public. Disgusting."

A few people laugh, and Faedra ducks her head, the last bit of her pretzel forgotten. I run my hand through her hair, encouraging her to lean back into me. When she does, I whisper against her ear. "Do you have scent blockers?"

She pales, twisting to look at me, her eyes wide as she bites her lip.

Her look is answer enough, though she shakes her head a second later. The woman makes another comment, and I turn to her, scowling. The man next to her has an arm swung around her, but his attention is on Faedra, his eyebrow raised.

"God, they already get preferential treatment by pretty much everyone. Can't they just leave us be with the Alphas that don't want to bond? Honestly."

The man murmurs something into her ear, and she scoffs. I growl, but Faedra grabs my wrist, her face still pale. Breathing through my nose, I take a minute to regroup before I lose my shit on an insecure Beta. I'm up and guiding Faedra into the aisle the moment the inning ends, my focus locked on her.

"Let's go, Red," I whisper, and she sucks in a breath.

"I'm sorry." Her apology is faint, her shoulders rolled in a rare display of nerves, and that rage boils in me again.

"It's alright. You don't deserve hearing that the whole game."

"I'm sorry I forgot scent blockers," Faedra says. Again. She sets her shoes under the table, gathering her hair over one shoulder before glancing back at me, her eyebrows pinched. "I know you were so excited to see your client play. I'm sorry I—"

I can't take it anymore. I set a finger against her lips, stopping her mid-sentence, and step into her. She doesn't shy away, her eyes growing bright as I close the distance between us, her jasmine scent intensifying.

"There will be plenty more times to go see him," I say, dragging my finger down her lips and to her chin, tilting her face so I can kiss her. "Do you want something to eat?"

She nods and turns to walk into the kitchen, but I grab her hips and pull her against me, letting my own scent mix with hers. She hums, tilting her head back against my shoulder.

"You smell like sandalwood," she murmurs, her eyes half closed, her cheeks flushed.

She's on the cusp of her heat. There's probably only a matter of days until she drops into it even if she doesn't take the stimulant. The idea excites me more than it probably should. I've never gotten an Omega through a heat before. I could royally fuck it up, especially when she hasn't even taken my knot. She presses her nose into my throat, humming against my skin before tilting her head enough to catch my gaze.

I swear she reads my mind because she whispers, "I don't want our first time to be my heat."

"It won't," I assure her.

"I've been here for two weeks," she murmurs, and I run my thumb up her throat, swallowing a groan when her scent manages to double in intensity again. "Part of me thinks you don't want to knot me at all."

I make a derisive noise in the back of my throat.

"Trust me, Red. I spend most days dreaming about different ways to fuck you. You eating that pretzel was damn near torture."

Honestly, I'm going to be lucky to get food in her before *I'm in her*. With a soft touch on her back, I guide her through the condo and to the kitchen. She hops onto the counter, adjusting her skirt as she sits cross-legged, her eyes intent on me.

Fuck, I'm hard.

Raking my hand through my hair, I open the fridge and start pulling options. Faedra sings under her breath as I work, a Taylor Swift song that she has playing nearly everyday from the small speaker we keep in the living room that I still don't know the words to.

"What's that one called?" I ask as I bring over a bowl of fruit and the container of yogurt.

She blushes, the dark red obscuring her freckles and making her eyes even brighter. Her tongue darts out and traces her bottom lip, and I stifle a groan.

Have I mentioned that I'm hard?

Because holy hell.

I pull a strawberry from the bowl and dip it into the yogurt, raising an eyebrow as she hesitates to respond.

"I always forget that one. Remind me," I say, holding the strawberry out for her.

"This Love."

She takes a bite as I nod. "Do you have the vinyl?"

She's been collecting her favorites all week since Jude got her the record player. It surprises me when she shakes her head. "I didn't have a record player at school, and it only came out last year."

"I'll get it for you," I tell her. She swallows, her throat moving with it, and my gaze catches on the hollow of her throat.

"Taylor's Version," she says. I grab another strawberry and hold it out for her. "It has to be Taylor's Version. We don't support assholes."

The juice from the strawberry drips down her chin as she takes another bite, and I wipe it away before it can fall onto her clothes.

"You support Jude," I say with a smirk.

She pouts, and I laugh.

"It's not the same. Jude never tried to trap someone in a

shitty ass contract nor launched an elaborate PR campaign to run someone through the mud just because he was upset about their success."

She pauses, and I offer a blueberry. Her look turns thoughtful as she chews, and I can't help but lean closer, tracing the inside of her knee with a feather light touch. Her scent grows stronger even as she grabs another piece of fruit from the bowl.

"And I like when Jude is an asshole with me.Under the right conditions, at least." She blushes again, and I laugh, taking a half step into her.

"He does have a way of making his behavior palatable," I admit, and she giggles.

I offer another berry, but she shakes her head, leaning into me and grabbing my shirt a moment before she slams her lips on mine. I don't hesitate, dropping the fruit and cupping her face, tilting her to a better angle as she deepens the kiss, her tongue seeking mine.

Her scent overwhelms the space in a matter of seconds, and I breathe it in, relishing it even as she scrabbles at my shirt, pushing it up my chest until it's high enough that she can undo the buckle and zipper of my shorts. Her movements are as confident as they are frantic, and I respond the same, dragging her towards me and wrapping her knees around my waist before pulling her top down far enough to reveal her breasts.

She's fucking braless.

I groan, pressing my cock into her, rubbing it across her panties. She hisses when I flick her nipples, arching into the touch.

"Fuck me, you spent the entire time we were at that game braless, and I just now find out?" I groan, thrusting against her again, pushing her skirt back until her thighs are completely bare.

"The shirt has one built in," she says.

I don't have a good response that won't sound horribly sex-crazed, so I lean down and pull one of her nipples into my mouth instead, letting my teeth graze the taught peak. She shudders, her scent doubling, wrapping around me like a cocoon. I'm all too happy to luxuriate in it.

Her touch is feather light as she traces the lines of my stomach and chest, her mouth parting around a near silent whimper when I switch to her other breast and give it the same attention.

"Logan," she whispers, and I'm fucking *gone*.

I grab her blue satin panties, my knuckles brushing her clit and making her jerk. I'm two seconds from tearing them when she shakes her head.

"Not these ones," she says without further explanation.

Fair enough.

I push them to the side, baring her pussy, and I mutter a curse as my cock wedges into her entrance, guided by her own movements. She pushes into me, but I manage to stop her as I pop off her nipple.

"Do you want me to grab a condom?" I ask.

It's something I should have asked long before my cock got anywhere near this close to her, but best laid plans and all that. At least I got food into her. She shakes her head, whimpering as I press an inch into her wet heat.

Holy hell.

She grips me like a vise, and I lose hold of what little patience I was managing. I pull back, ignoring her desperate whine, and then shove forward in one hard thrust, relishing her surprised groan that bleeds into a gasp as I grab the counter under her legs, propping her knees higher to get myself deeper.

"Logan," she gasps, and it's the sweetest thing I've heard all day.

She clings to me, her nails digging into my back as she holds me, her moans pressed against my ear, shooting goosebumps down my neck. Any thought of taking it slow is gone when she widens her legs, using the leverage I have to move closer to the edge of the counter, driving me deeper. The sounds of our skin slapping echo around the room, and I grunt as she tightens around me, her body growing tense. I move her leg to sit over my shoulder, making the angle more intense, and then circle her clit, increasing the pressure with each swipe.

Her broken shout has me grinning, and I snap my hips into her once, twice, before my legs lock and a bolt of lightning races down my spine and through my cock, making it jerk.

"Shit," I mutter, pulling her more thoroughly into me as my knot locks us in place. She cries out again, a keening moan against my throat, and I drop her leg, moving slow enough to not move where we're locked together.

Fuck, she's beautiful.

Her face is flushed, her lips swollen, her breasts pressed against me, begging for more attention. How have I managed to have her in my bed nearly every night and *not* fuck her? It's certainly never happening again.

"Shit, Red," I grunt, and she clenches around me, making me groan. "Tell me I get you tonight, too. I'm selfish to start with, and this is the best fucking knotting of my life."

She manages a breathless giggle, tracing shapes along my shoulders.

"I promised Carter," she whispers, and I curse. Her hand twists into my hair as my knot releases, my cum and her slick dripping down her thighs and onto the counter. She blushes, fierce and fast, and I kiss her.

"At least let me clean you up in the shower," I say against her lips.

Her smile is bright, and she tightens her knees around my hips.

"Sounds like a plan," she says.

I have her up the stairs and pressed against the wall of my shower before she can protest, the water fogging up the room as I sink into her again.

"Red," I groan against her lips. "I think I'm addicted."

Her laugh is music to my ears.

Twenty-Nine

FAEDRA

"Shit, Fae. It all just stopped?" Violet asks, and I hum an affirmative.

"We were all pretty sure it was going to happen this last weekend. But here we are on Wednesday, and honestly I feel kind of normal. Like, new normal. Not suppressed normal." The train stops in front of the campus, and I get off with a large group of people, stepping over to one of the benches so I'm out of the way while I get my bearings.

Violet clicks her tongue. "That's strange. I don't think I've heard of that happening."

My laugh is more brittle than I'd like as I spot the sign I need and adjust my bag.

"Let me know if we need to adjust us going out there," she says after a minute.

I shake my head even though she can't see me, making a low noise in the back of my throat. "I don't want you to have to adjust everything. I'm sure it'll work out."

She sighs. "You could always get a stimulant if you're worried."

I don't mention the one I have in my bag already. It feels like one of those things I should discuss with the guys instead of my best friend even though just thinking about it has me biting my lip. I've always told Violet everything, and it feels strange to have this distance between us. It's normal, I know. But I still feel emotional about it.

We end the call a moment later, and I tuck my phone into my bag before following the signs across campus. The building is incredibly modern, and the receptionist at the main desk is all smiles as he directs me to the right floor and section.

The door to Jude's office is closed. A flash of uncertainty runs through me, but I breathe through it, reminding myself that he promised his encounter with Melanie didn't mean anything and that it wouldn't happen again. My knock is light, and there's shuffling behind the door almost immediately. Jude's scowl drops the moment he sees me, a small smile replacing it as he kisses my temple.

"Hi," I breathe, and he chuckles, taking my hand and guiding me into his office.

It's messier than last time I was here, the bookcases lining every open piece of wall crammed full of books, several sitting in front of others, waiting to be put back in their proper place. He has two large textbooks open on his desk, sticky notes littering the pages, a printed essay laid next to them, red pen in the margins in his messy, heavy scrawl.

A woman about his age sits in one of the chairs in front of his desk, a small bag resting in her lap. Her chin length blonde hair leans silver, but I'm pretty sure it's her natural gray and not from a salon. Her gray eyes assess me so thoroughly I have the odd sensation of being stripped bare. She stands before I can offer a greeting, smoothing her charcoal pant suit and extending a hand to me.

"I'm Chris," she says when I shake her hand. "I'm Jude's boss."

Tension bleeds from my body—though I'm a bit ashamed I was anxious at all over there being a woman in his office. I'm not one to be jealous. But being back here has me just nervous enough for small seeds of it to bite at me.

"Nice to meet you," I say. She gives a half smile.

"I'll let you get to lunch," she says. "I just wanted to give him an update about what happened last week."

I chance a look at Jude, and he nods.

"Thank you," I say.

She doesn't offer anything else as she walks out of the room, leaving the door open as she heads deeper into the building. Jude takes my bag and stashes it in the bottom drawer like last time before lacing his fingers with mine and guiding me around the desk. I perch in the center of it, careful to avoid his work materials, and he doesn't hesitate to stand between my legs, his hands on my throat, his thumbs guiding my face to his, his lips insistent against my own.

"You feeling alright?" he asks me when he pulls away. When I nod, he kisses me again, his tongue moving slower against mine, and I relax into him, pressing my hands against his stomach.

By the time I pull away from him, I'm willing to bring up my worry.

"Violet thinks it's odd that I didn't go into heat, too," I say, and his eyebrows draw low, his lips turning down at the corners. "I should really take the stimulant."

He nods, and I blow out a breath.

"I'm scared to, though." I whisper the admission, and he drops his hands to my waist, pulling me closer to him. He doesn't offer any words, just his touch as he runs his lips down my throat and across my shoulder, his beard scratching at my skin enough that it warms my belly. My scent encircles us, and his hold tightens.

"We'll make sure you're safe," he murmurs against my collar bone. "Carter and I have both been part of heats. You won't scare us away."

A swift stab of jealousy has me digging my nails into his shirt, and he grunts.

"They were before...everything," he says, tracing his lips back up my throat, "when we were still wild and in our early twenties."

I relax into him, letting him kiss along my jaw and then my lips.

"Alright," I whisper against him. "It's in my bag."

He pulls the small pouch I keep my birth control pills in and hands it to me.

"Let me clean up, and we'll grab a quick lunch on our way home." His words are soft and soothing, and I bask in them, letting them coast over me until the worry isn't quite so big. I take the pill with a sip of water, and he starts cleaning up his desk, organizing everything in succinct piles beside his computer before setting my bag on his chair.

He's offering me his hand to help me down from the desk when there's the distinct sound of crying from farther down the hallway. I look over my shoulder as Jude hesitates, his eyebrows lowering, his frown deepening into a scowl as someone stops in front of his doorway.

Melanie's hair is disheveled, her blonde hair falling from its updo. Her mascara runs down her cheeks, pulled there by large tears, and her hands are shaking. Her lips curl into a snarl when she sees me.

"What did you tell him, little girl?" she hisses, fisting her hands as she takes a step into the room. "That you'd spread your legs for him if he got me fired?"

Surprise races through me, freezing me to the desk, my hand held limply in Jude's grasp.

"What the hell are you talking about, Melanie?" His words are sharp.

"Your little side piece went and told my department chair that I've been harassing you in the workplace!" she says, hurling the words at me with so much venom that I flinch. "You have to tell him that she's lying. My entire career is at stake."

Jude drops my hand in favor of palming my knee, his thumb stroking my thigh. Her eyes catch on the movement, and she grimaces.

"Iris would have hated you for this," she says.

Jude freezes, and I break my gaze away from her to double check that he's alright. His Adam's apple moves with a swallow before he tightens his grip on my knee. The action sends a bolt of lightning down my spine, and I clench my thighs, keeping my moan behind my closed lips.

"If your department chair has fired you, I can't do anything about it," Jude says after a long moment. His voice scrapes over my skin, and I hold back a whimper. His voice turns hard. "I'm positive Iris would have been angrier over my dating you than my choosing to advocate for my relationship with my matched Omega."

Melanie gasps. "You *wouldn't*."

Jude tilts his head, assessing her with a critical eye that makes even me wither a bit.

"I thought I made it clear five years ago that I would."

Her eyes widen, her body locking as she sucks in a hard breath.

Jude continues. "You of all people should understand my unwavering loyalty. Why would I not offer that to the person the

Council chose for me? The person I have endured five years of disappointment and your bullshit to be able to meet?"

My chest warms, and I cover his hand on my knee, lacing my fingers with his. She focuses in on the small movement, the moment of intimacy.

"You're nothing but a gold digging whore," she snarls.

She's storming down the hallway before the shock from her words can even register.

JUDE

"Now that's just rude. You're way more resourceful than just brute digging," I joke halfheartedly, rubbing my beard and wrapping my arm around Faedra's waist. "You flirted with Carter before he gave you his Centurion card."

She gives a breathless chuckle, shaking her head, and I can't help but smile. "I kissed him, too."

I laugh, running my hand up her leg. "I'll need a few minutes to clean up whatever mess she's making with Chris right now."

She doesn't say anything, turning into me, rubbing her forehead against my side. I run my fingers through her hair.

"Then I should probably call Logan."

Her voice drops to a scant whisper, and it has my instincts roaring. Her hands trail up my leg, fingers hooking into my belt loops and pulling me closer to her, sealing our bodies together.

"Faedra?" I ask, keeping my voice low.

Her answering whine has me pulling out my phone. She presses her face harder into me, hands digging into my hip until I can feel the bite of her nails through my slacks. I send a quick text to the others with one hand, keeping my palm pressed flat against the nape of her neck.

> Need one of you to get us ASAP.

Logan responds first.

> I'm at the gym meeting with Tyler.

There's a pause, and I'm trying to figure out a way to convince him to ditch whatever meeting he's entangled in when Carter responds.

> I can be there in fifteen. What happened?

Faedra whines again, nails scraping down my leg as she squirms in her seat.

> She took the stimulant.

> Damn it, Jude. Some warning would have been nice.

Logan's anger is understandable, but I don't have time for it right now. Faedra sets her teeth against the waistband of my slacks, and it takes all my control to not scent in response.

> Was trying to but then Melanie happened.

Carter's quick to double check.

> Everything ok?

> Yeah. She just finally learned there are consequences for her actions.

"Alpha."

Faedra's soft moan has me dropping my phone to my desk after one last quick message to Carter.

> We're in my office. I'll need help getting her out.

"Faedra, sweetheart, look at me."

I use my stern voice, the one I use to command a freshman lecture. A shiver runs down her spine before she tilts her head, running her lips along my shirt the whole time. My fingers tangle into her hair, my palm pressing against the nape of her neck. Her skin is warm to the touch, almost feverish. I run my thumb along her cheekbone, watching her eyes glaze over. She breathes deeply —and then I smell jasmine.

She scents so strongly in a split second that I can't help but groan.

"Alpha, please," she whispers, barely more than a breath. Her hands tighten even further, to the point I'm sure she's about to break skin. "It *hurts*, Alpha."

The complete shift from her using my name to using my designation is both jarring and undeniably arousing. I never thought I'd be one to desire being called Alpha, but here we are.

"Alright, Omega," I say, tightening my fingers in her hair. She whimpers and wiggles against me. "I can't knot with you here, though, sweetheart."

Her eyes flood with tears in the space of a heartbeat, and her lower lip quivers.

"Please," she whines. She rubs her legs together, and her scent increases, pulling a low moan from me.

Bending down, I press my lips to hers, tangling my hands in her hair. She leans into me, a whine catching in her throat, and I bite at her lip, urging her to open for me. She does with a happy hum, and I'm quick to take her mouth, chasing her tongue with my own. Her scent increases in the space, becoming overwhelming, driving away my sensibilities until I'm left with just the primitive need to knot with my Omega.

I push her back, lowering her to the desktop, letting her hair fan out above her and over the other edge. Her chest is flushed, her breaths coming faster as I run my hands up her thighs and encourage her knees farther apart. In the distance, I hear someone laugh, and it's just enough to snap the haze.

Ignoring her whine, I step away from her, shutting the door but leaving it unlocked for Carter. When I turn back to her, I find her slipping her hand under her skirt, pushing it up to her hips as she runs a finger over her clit. She squirms, the sensation clearly not enough to appease her heat even this early on—and it should.

Fuck.

This is going to be rough.

Faedra squirms on the desk, a whine building in her throat. I palm her thigh, pushing it open against the wood before running my tongue along her soft skin to the edge of her panties. She pushes her hips into me, grabbing my hair as she whines again. Slick runs down her thighs, and her cunt is drenched when I push her panties to the side, baring her to me. Her hands tighten, scraping along my scalp, and I don't hesitate, sucking her clit into my mouth, smirking when her hips lift off the desk.

All thoughts of being quiet are gone, her moans filling the room nearly as thoroughly as her scent, her body jerking with each change of my touch, each thorough swipe of my tongue along her. The orgasm rushes over her in a matter of moments, her body already strung tight from the force of her heat.

"Alpha," she cries, her voice breaking, and I push two fingers into her, curling them as I suck her clit again. Her back bows as she gasps, her legs tightening around my head, her feet pressing into my back as a second orgasm rips through her.

The door clicks open, and I glance up, not pausing my movements when I see Carter quickly stepping into the office and leaning against the door. She relaxes against the desk, and I release her, wiping my hand on her skirt. Carter's frowning as I help her sit up, her eyes still glazed over, her cheeks and neck flushed a gorgeous deep red.

"Already?" he asks, and I nod. He mutters a curse, and Faedra turns to look at him, her scent doubling over again, and he grunts like he's been punched. "Let's get you to your nest, little Omega. You'll have as much of me as you want there, alright?"

Faedra purses her lips, pouting, and I lift her into my arms bridal style, chuckling when she looks away from Carter in favor of burying her face in my shoulder, her teeth biting at the pulse point at the base of my neck.

Carter guides us to the staff lot, and I cock an eyebrow.

"I had Amanda drop me so we don't have to figure out getting two cars back. Get her in the back," he instructs, opening the door for me. Once I have her situated, her eyes roving over both of us, her teeth biting into her lip, Carter leans in and whispers, "If she's like this, she'll need to knot before we get her home. You want to be the one she pounces?"

"Yes, but I'll drive since it's my car," I say, walking around the back of the crossover and getting into behind the wheel while Carter arranges himself next to her.

Thirty

FAEDRA

My body is on fire. Every inch of my skin burns, and my clit is so sensitive I can feel my heartbeat in it, the added throbbing making me rub my thighs together, a desperate whine escaping from between my lips while my Alphas talk outside of the car.

Why are they outside? Why aren't they with me? Can't they tell I *need* them?

My hand creeps down my belly, intent on relieving the ache already building between my legs again, when the doors open and my Alphas get in the car.

Except only one of them sits next to me, the other one turning on the car and focusing on driving. I pout, whining, and Carter tucks my hair behind my ear, his touch gentle but making my nipples harden anyway. I twist into him, straddling him before he can tell me no, holding my skirt up enough that it doesn't get caught between us. He doesn't stop me as I work at his belly and slacks, my movements growing more frantic as the seconds pass, that haze from before starting to settle over me again.

The moment his cock is free, I'm adjusting so that I can lower myself, moving fast enough that he hisses, his hands squeezing my hips. My hips nestle against his, and I sigh, tilting my head back. I'm lost to the sensations, driven by a primitive need that I don't understand, but Carter doesn't seem to mind. His lips run over my throat, and his tongue traces my collar bones. He grunts when I lower myself onto his cock again, harder then before, whining when it doesn't relieve the ache.

"You need more, little Omega," he says, a statement rather than a question, but I whine in answer anyway. He snaps his hips up into me as he forces my hips down, the head of his cock hitting a spot that makes me scream. And he doesn't stop, his movements unrelenting, my toes curling as my orgasm inches closer.

"Please," I beg, my eyes fluttering shut. "Oh, god, *please.*"

He doesn't circle my clit. He doesn't play with my nipples. He simply tightens his hold on my hips and forces me faster, the wet sounds of us joining drowning out the sounds of the car. He grunts as he comes, his lips pressed just under my ear. I'm confused as I feel his cock twitch, my body strung so tight I'm sure I'm going to be pulled apart at the seams.

Why didn't he get me off first?

The question is barely formed when his knot swells and locks us together. The force of it sends me face first over the edge, my body locking as I scream, my voice breaking. The haze clears, and I'm filled with satisfaction at having my Alpha locked with me, his knot so intense that my core starts to burn with it. He gathers my hair, twisting it around his palm, and I push harder into him, driving his knot deeper, the ache of it shooting goosebumps across my body. He takes my hand and guides me to where we're joined.

"Feel it, little Omega," he says, his voice rough, making me shiver. He moves my fingers until they circle his cock. "This is what you needed, isn't it? You needed to be reminded that I'm yours."

His words scrape over my skin, and my thoughts go hazy again, though it's not quite the same as before. My eyes flutter shut as I slump against him, wiggling my hips just to feel his knot more acutely, the sting of it making my nipples tighten and my breath catch.

Carter hums, running his lips along the shell of my ear. "Such a good Omega," he whispers. "You're mine, Faedra. Just like I'm yours."

My body relaxes more heavily into him, the aching burn of my heat fading under the throbbing stretch of his knot. My thoughts drift away, my hands loose where they hold my Alpha's hips.

Carter's voice is a warm caress as he talks to Jude. "You hear from Logan?"

There's a terse sound from the front of the car.

Carter sighs. "He must have been in the middle of something big," he says, his voice rumbling through his chest. I brush my forehead against his sternum, the crush of his chest hair making my thighs clench. He presses a kiss to the crown of my head. "You ok, little Omega?"

I squirm on his lap, the ache of his knot turning painful, and he grabs my hip, forcing me to stillness.

"There he is," Jude mutters.

The back door opens at the same time Carter's knot releases, and I gasp as he adjusts me, guiding me to sit back on my knees, my head still pressed against him. My legs are sticky with his cum, and I can feel it dripping onto his pants, but he doesn't seem to mind.

"Red?" Logan's quiet, his voice no more than a whisper between us, and I hum, not opening my eyes. "How long?"

"Minutes," Carter said.

"Think she'll sleep first?"

I move side to side on Carter's lap, the ache returning to my clit with each minute that passes.

Jude says, "Not yet. She'll probably need another before it takes enough out of her to let her sleep."

"Let's get her inside, then," Logan says.

There's a flurry of movement. A door closes, and arms wrap around me, guiding me off of Carter and into someone else's chest that smells like sandalwood.

Logan.

I twist my hand into his workout shirt, pressing my nose into the hollow of his throat and breathing deep without opening my eyes.

"Has she eaten?" Logan asks as he starts to walk. There's a soft no and then a mention of making something. Logan nods. His hold is careful, and I'm not jostled at all as he takes me to the condo and up the stairs to my nest. I open my eyes a fraction before immediately closing them again.

"Too bright," I mutter. There's movement behind me and then the soft shuffling of the curtains being moved.

"Better?"

I chance a look around the room, and I relax against him, nodding. He lays down with me, stretching out beside me, and I grab his hips, encouraging him to roll over so that he covers me, that haze settling over me again, my thoughts growing muddy. When he doesn't get his shorts off, I bite his shoulder, fisting his shirt in my hands and forcing it up to his neck, exposing the expanse of his torso. He sucks in a breath when I bite his chest.

"You need me, Red?" he asks, his lips brushing my ear, and I whine, arching into him, arousal racing through me until I feel like I'm burning with it.

I bite him again when he doesn't get rid of his clothes, the mark left on his skin making me smile. He doesn't waste any more time, pulling off of me only long enough to strip, his body hard and heavy against mine as he forces my legs wider, the head of his cock pressing into me. My nipples brush against his chest, and I suck in a breath, my skin oversensitized. His lips are on mine, his kiss stealing my breath as he pushes into me with one hard thrust, pulling a keening cry from me.

He isn't careful or calm or sweet like he's been the last several days since we knotted the first time. His hips snap into me, grinding against my clit with each stroke, and my legs tremble, sensation buzzing through my body. The haze overwhelms me, and I scratch at his back, my nails biting into his skin. I meet every stroke, trying to take him deeper, twisting my hands into his hair and forcing his mouth onto my neck, driven by a primitive urge I don't understand but crave nonetheless.

"Not happening," he mutters against my skin, his thrusts becoming faster, harder.

Tears inexplicably flood my eyes, a sudden sadness overtaking me. Logan kisses just under my ear. I tighten my hold on him, the tears spilling over.

He grunts, whispering, "No bonding without talking about it, Red."

I don't like that answer.

At. All.

I cling to him, trying to get him closer to me, my tears falling faster. The bed shakes from the force of his movements, and he buries his hands in my hair, keeping me from being moved up the bed with each thrust. He bites my neck as he comes, sucking on the skin, making my back bow as I cry out. His knot triggers another orgasm, and I jerk under him, my hands tightening in his hair again, my nails breaking his skin. He doesn't seem to mind, licking the spot of my neck he sucked, making me shiver. My body relaxes, exhaustion sweeping over me, and Logan presses gentle kisses across my jaw, the corner of my mouth, my cheekbone.

"Good job, Red," he murmurs even as my eyes flutter shut. "Love you."

I'm asleep in the next moment, the words following me into my dreams, and part of me wishes they hadn't been my imagination.

Thirty-One

CARTER

Logan tosses another blanket into the ensuite, and I nudge it out of the way, swapping the loads already running in the machines, folding the newly dried sheet and putting it in the closet behind the bathroom door. The smacking sounds of Jude fucking Faedra grow muffled when Logan closes the door behind him. He leans back against it, his eyes falling shut as he tilts his head back. Dark circles stand in stark contrast to his fair complexion. He blows out a hard sigh, and I press my palms into my eyes to keep from saying anything.

"This is worse than I expected," he admits after a bit.

I grunt. "It's definitely more extreme than normal," I say, making sure the sound is turned off on the washer before starting it. "It's been six days. Typically they've already surfaced by this point."

Faedra's keening moan cuts through the closed door, and we both relax at the sound.

"I can't imagine how this would have gone if there weren't all three of us," he mutters. "I'm a fucking athlete, and I can barely keep up."

"One of the reasons the Council has a minimum pack size, I imagine," I mutter, moving some of the dirty linens around to get the last soft fleece blanket out of the closet. Faedra's been demanding them after every knotting, growing distraught if there isn't one clean. It's something we'll need to make sure we have more of for the next time she drops into her heat.

Jude curses a moment before the noises of sex stop altogether. Logan takes the blanket from me and opens the door. We step into the bedroom without comment, trying to stay quiet so Faedra doesn't worry about keeping us satisfied, too. She panicked yesterday when Jude and Logan brought her a bit of food and we were still knotted, crying about how she didn't want to disappoint them by being with me.

Heats are something else.

Jude nuzzles her neck, running his lips down her throat, and she hums, arching into him, her eyes fluttering shut. There's a stillness to her this time that has me cautiously optimistic that she's nearing the end of her heat. Her breathing evens out, and Jude glances back at us, still locked with her.

"You find one?" he asks. When I hold up the blanket, he nods, dropping his forehead to rest on her shoulder, his weight held carefully off of her. It takes a few more minutes for his knot to release, and then he's walking to the bathroom, closing the door without any comment toward us. The shower turns on. Logan blows out another breath.

"Think it'll get less weird for her to fall asleep during it?" he asks, carefully wiping down her legs.

I shake my head as I cross the room, spreading the blanket over her. "Not for me."

He pulls his phone from his pocket, tapping a few times. "What do you want from JJ's? I'm going to order us dinner."

∼

Jude runs a hand over his beard, pushing away what's left of the dinner Logan ordered, his frown deep. He glances up toward the loft and freezes. I follow his gaze and cock an eyebrow when I see Faedra sitting at the top of the stairs. She's put on a slip from the dresser in her nest room, and her hair is braided around her head into a makeshift crown like when we were hiking.

"You alright, Red?" Logan doesn't miss a beat, standing up and heading for the stairs.

Faedra's blush is as swift as it is deep, and the heavy weight in my stomach loosens.

She's out of her heat.

Jude relaxes next to me, his gaze still fixed on her.

"Just dying of mortification," she says, leaning against the railing, her fingers running along the edge of the stair.

That has me pushing off the island and heading towards her, flanking Logan as we climb the flight of stairs. She traces the edge of her slip, biting her lip. Logan sits next to her while I crouch in front of her, taking her hands in mine. Her eyes flutter closed as she leans into me, resting her forehead against my sternum, and I drop her hands in favor of wrapping my arms around her and pulling her tight against me. Logan traces the hoop in her ear, and she shivers—though she doesn't scent.

"How long?" she asks, pressing her cheek to my chest so she can see Logan. When he tells her, she grimaces. "Definitely dying of mortification," she whispers. "That was..." She blows out a breath. "I don't even know."

Jude's silent as he climbs the stairs and leans over me, his touch soft where he trails it over her cheek.

"It was—" Logan tries to soothe, but she cuts him off.

Her voice is sharp. "Don't tell me it was normal. I've read enough to know that it wasn't."

Jude makes a noise deep in his throat, wedging a finger under her chin and forcing her to look at him. Logan drops his hand and palms her knee.

"You were told it would be more intense than normal," he says. She frowns, and I tighten my arms around her. "It wasn't what I would have wanted for your first heat. It was longer than typical, and your reactions were more acute."

She blows out a breath, pushing against me until I let her sit back up. Jude doesn't release her face, his palm moving to cup her cheek.

"Now that it's done, you can focus on becoming more comfortable with the daily aspects of being Omega off suppressants. We have another six months or so before we need to worry about what a typical heat will be like for you."

She holds his gaze for a long moment, her fingers picking at the hem of her slip again.

"Sounds like a plan," she says. She glances past me to the kitchen, her eyebrow ticking up as she licks her lips. "Any of that left for me? I'm starving. And then I need a shower." She adjusts how she sits, flinching a bit. "Or maybe a bath."

FAEDRA

I frown down at the letter again, taking in the watermark of the Council's insignia, faded enough to not interfere with the official notice typed on it.

Five days to finalize the match. Failure to do so will result in the Council reassigning me.

It should be easy to bring up to the guys. I've been in Denver for nearly six weeks. I've gone through my first heat, and they didn't back away or hold my ridiculous reactions against me. We're happy. And despite me still being convinced that Logan's words were just a figment of the heat haze, the reality is that I love them. All three of them.

I know the Council doesn't always get it right. It's why there's a system for being reassigned—and even for matches to be dissolved years later if necessary, like the more common divorce courts. But it feels like they've gotten it perfect for me.

Logan makes me laugh, a friendship dynamic I've never had before in addition to our physical relationship. Carter adores me and challenges me to think about the future. Jude and I are able to be scholars together in the middle of the night when the others are sleeping. All three of them support me and want me to go after my dreams.

So why is broaching the subject of filing the final bit of paperwork so incredibly *overwhelming*?

I don't have an answer as I unlock the condo's main door and slip off my sandals, taking my bag with me into the living room since it has my quilting hexagons in it. The guys are spread around the room, Jude in the large wingback facing towards the windows, Carter and Logan on opposite ends of the sofa. They glance up in near unison as I enter the room, and I can't help but blush under their collective attention.

Carter notices the letter in my hand and leans forward, his elbows on his knees, his hands steepled in front of him. "Everything alright, little Omega?"

A weight releases from me as his husky voice curls around my nickname.

I hold up the letter. "I got an official notice that we have five days to finalize everything, or they'll reassign me." My lips twist into a sardonic smile, and I scoff. "Not that they sent the paperwork with it. Just the reiteration that we're almost out of time."

Jude nods, glancing at the others before getting up and crossing the condo, taking the steps two at a time before closing the door to his bedroom softly behind him.

"How are you feeling, Red?" Logan asks once Jude is out of sight. "Confident in making everything permanent?"

My gaze catches on Jude's closed door.

"Not confident enough to talk about it with Jude upstairs," I mutter, and Logan laughs.

Carter holds out his hand, and I let him guide me onto the sofa between them. He presses a kiss to my cheek, and Logan palms my knee. I bask in the feel of them both, ignoring the anxiety simmering in my belly the longer Jude is upstairs.

The others don't seem to be in any rush to talk about everything while he's gone, and I follow their lead, pulling out my hexagons and working on a few of the larger pieces. Soft steps sound across the hardwood a few minutes later, and I look over my shoulder, setting down the fabric after tucking the needle away.

Jude perches on the coffee table in front of me, a nondescript black folder in his hand. He shares a long look with Carter, one of those unspoken conversations happening between them before he sets the folder next to him and holds his hand palm up toward me. I lace my fingers with his, and he tightens his grip. Logan moves until our thighs touch, his hand soft where it cups my knee.

I start before they can say anything.

"When I prepped for matching this spring, I didn't let myself think about what it might look like," I say, looking at Jude's hand intertwined with mine. He runs his thumb across my knuckles. "The Council sent all kinds of material to prepare me. The more I read, the fewer expectations I wanted to have going into the gala. It seemed like they would get crushed."

Carter palms my thigh, his finger tracing just under the hemmed slit of my skirt.

"I'm glad I didn't," I whisper, biting my lip before looking at each of them. "Because I don't think I would have been able to imagine a scenario like this. I know you guys have been through so much waiting to be matched."

Logan squeezes my knee. Jude's Adam's apple moves with his swallow.

"But it feels like the Council knew from the beginning of my designating that I was meant for you. It feels like it was always supposed to be you. And I can't imagine being matched with anyone else. I don't want to."

Logan grasps my chin, turning me to him, his lips soft against mine. I sink into the kiss, letting it be another method of conversation like it has been from the beginning, from that dance at the gala.

When he pulls away, he whispers, "You're it, Red. Always."

Jude leans forward, palming my waist. "I'd wait another four years if that's what it took, Fae," he says, stoic but with a thread of emotion that has butterflies welling in my belly.

"Little Omega," Carter murmurs against my ear. I turn to him, and he takes my face in his hands, kissing me thoroughly before pulling away. "I'm so thankful. You're perfect."

I'm not, but I let the words wash over me anyway.

Jude grabs the folder and pulls out an innocuous looking form before pulling a pen from his pocket.

"We'd thought about whether or not to make this part more public," Logan admits, running his hand up my thigh as Jude hands me both items. "But we decided we wanted it to be more intimate."

I quirk my lips, nodding as I look over the final form from

the Council. All three of them have already signed it, their signatures crisp and clean. And dated to four days ago, right after my heat ended. Their confidence is a balm to my soul, and I smile fully, carefully signing my name so it's as perfect as theirs so I can hang it in my room once the Council sends it back after we file it.

Jude's on me the moment I'm finished, but Carter grunts, interrupting our kiss before it can really even get started. Jude sighs but sits back on the coffee table, his eyes locked on me as Carter pulls something from his pocket.

Logan kisses the crook of my shoulder, his lips warm against my pulse point. My breath catches as Carter opens a black velvet box, the lights of the living room catching on the pear shaped sapphire, the bands of gold intertwining, forming leaves that are intermixed with small white diamonds.

It's beautiful.

It's exactly my taste.

It's...not what I was expecting.

I look up at Carter. "You got me an engagement ring?" I ask, wonder lacing my voice.

He tips one corner of his lips up, nodding.

One of the things the Council's pre-gala packets had mentioned was the tradition of gifting an Omega a set of stacking rings, one for each in the pack. I was ready for those, even though I would have had to field questions from my family about what they meant. Logan's lips are gentle against the shell of my ear, his breath ghosting across my skin, a shiver racing down my spine.

"We wanted something your family would understand, too," he murmurs. "They matter a lot to you. We didn't want to ostracize them. There'll be time to give you the more traditional stacking rings in the future."

That's one of the sweetest things I've ever heard. I smile, joy making me giggle, and hold out my hand. Carter doesn't hesitate, pulling the ring and sliding it onto my ring finger, kissing the knuckle above it before kissing me, too.

As they lay me out on the couch, arousal blooming through me, slick coating my thighs, I can't help but think that this is perfection incarnate.

Thirty-Two

LOGAN

Faedra's radiant tonight, her hair pulled into one of her claw clips, a simple golden necklace draping around her neck, the small green gem nestling into the hollow of her throat. She smiles as I take her hand, helping her out of the Jeep. The airport is especially crowded tonight, and I keep Faedra close to me as we navigate the main floor, finding the arrivals information.

"Oh shoot," she says. I squeeze her hand, and she offers me a tight smile. "There's a lot of people here. I didn't expect to need to deal with them for an extra half hour."

I feather a kiss over her temple and then guide her up another level. The crowds here are fewer and significantly more organized, people standing in lines to get checked in for their flights and sort out their baggage costs. I help Faedra into one of the seats looking out over the cargo shipping bay, but the moment I'm situated beside her, she crawls into my lap, tucking her nose into the crook of my shoulder, and I run my hand up her thigh.

"You good, Red?"

"Tired," she murmurs, grabbing my other hand and lacing her fingers with mine.

It's been nearly two weeks since we gave her the ring and signed the final bit of paperwork, but it still feels surreal to see her wear it. I run my thumb over the band of it, enjoying how she hums under her breath—this time a song I recognize *and* know the name of.

"I like that one," I whisper, tucking my hand under her skirt and running it up her bare thigh. Jasmine floats around us, and I smile into her cheek. She giggles.

Best damn sound I've ever heard.

"You got your information submitted for the school?" I ask after a bit, and she nods, squeezing my hand. "School doesn't start for a while, though, right? Jude's doesn't start for another six weeks."

"I think mine starts a week after his," she murmurs. "I'll double check when we get home."

She lets her legs fall open just a bit, and I run my finger along the crease of her thigh before tracing her hip bone. Jasmine mingles with my own sandalwood, and my cock twitches.

Probably not the smartest idea to put my hands on her while we're waiting for her friend.

"Have you thought about when you'd like to have the Pack Celebration?" I ask, tracing the band of her ring again.

She smirks. "You're full of questions tonight."

I shrug. "Maybe I'm being a good Alpha and keeping you calm in a way that won't make you feel self-conscious about your Omega nature."

She sits up, her eyebrows drawing low and her lips pushing into a pout.

I want to bite them. Or feel them around my cock. Instead of doing either of those, I press my thumb to them, and she kisses it, the concentrated look falling away.

"I'll allow it," she says, nearly wistful, "since it means I get to sit on your lap and do this."

She squirms against me, and my half-hard dick is suddenly at full attention.

I groan, grabbing her thigh hard enough that she gasps. "That's just mean. I'm trying to be polite, and here you are making it very difficult to remember why I am."

Her reply is cut off by the quiet chime of her phone. She reaches over and grabs her purse, causing her butt to press harder against my erection, and I groan, tipping my head back. Her cheeks are dark when she looks back at me.

"They've landed," she says, and I nod, closing my eyes and trying to think of anything that will get my body to cool off. Her lips are soft where she trails them up my throat, and I tighten my hold on her leg again.

"Not helping," I mutter.

She giggles, dropping her forehead to my shoulder. "I'll fuck you in the car to make up for it."

I clutch her tighter. Her soft voice saying things as crass as *fuck* makes me want to bend her over a chair.

"I'm sure security will appreciate that," I say, and she laughs. I let go of her leg, cupping her face and kissing her until she's breathless and jasmine surrounds me. I give her a half smile. "You're so bad about your scent blockers."

She shrugs as she stands and adjusts her skirt. "Maybe I brought them but didn't put them on yet," she says. She grabs her bag from beside my feet and turns for the restroom, her hips swaying as she offers a knowing smile over her shoulder.

I shake my head as I laugh, running a hand through my hair.

Once she's gone, I sigh and adjust my dick, using the walk to the restrooms to cool off.

Her smile as she walks out is just as radiant as before, and I'm struck with an inordinate amount of joy. Her fingers lace with mine, and she rests her head against my arm as we head down one floor and towards the main atrium. We're just rounding the last corner when someone yells.

"There you are!"

Faedra drops my hand, laughing as she rushes across the space, her arms wrapping around Violet even as she stumbles a bit. A tall man I've never met before helps steady the women, his brown eyes shrewd as he takes in the airport around him.

Jasper offers Faedra a quick hug when the women separate, and Rylan lifts a shoulder in greeting.

"This is Dominic," Violet says when I get close enough to hear, grabbing the third man's hand and lacing her fingers with his.

Faedra nods but doesn't extend her hand, and the man keeps his tucked in the pocket of his slacks.

"Let me see it!" Faedra says, and Violet laughs, rolling her eyes. She places her hand in Faedra's upturned palm. The light catches on a large solitaire emerald cut diamond. Faedra whistles. "Damn, girl! That almost makes up for it."

Dominic scowls, wrapping his arm around Violet's waist. I press a kiss to Faedra's temple, and she beams up at me, her eyes dancing with mischief.

"That look spells trouble," I mutter, and she winks.

"Well then, show me yours," Violet says, grabbing Faedra's other hand and twisting it so that her own ring is visible. "Holy shit, Fae. That thing is the size of my eye."

The exaggeration has me laughing, and Jasper shakes his head, a half smile on his lips.

"You're shocked?" he asks, bumping against Violet's

shoulder. "Carter has a damn Centurion, Violet. I'm honestly shocked it's a sapphire and not a red diamond."

"Red doesn't look as good against her skin," I comment, voice dry, as Dominic cocks an eyebrow. "And blue is her favorite color. But it's still a diamond."

Faedra turns to me fast enough that she almost hits my chin, her eyes wide.

"*What?*" Her voice is incredulous. "I thought it was a sapphire."

My laugh is low. "Carter was adamant, Red," I murmur as I kiss her cheek.

Jasper laughs, wiping tears from his eyes even as Rylan shoves him. Violet recovers after a moment, smirking.

"Let's get bags," she says, "and then I want to see your place before the guys force me to sleep."

"Sleep. Right. That's what we were going to suggest." Jasper rolls his eyes at Rylan's sarcastic comment.

Faedra laughs, shaking her head. "Alright, Vi. Let's go."

FAEDRA

"Of course, Mom. I'm more than capable of having safe sex," I say, rolling my eyes. Beside me, Violet laughs, though she does her best to cover it. A couple people give me odd looks as they pass us on the busy street crowded with artists and festival attendees.

Mom clicks her tongue, and I can practically see her hand on her hip despite her being over twelve hours away. No doubt she has that *look* in her eyes that used to make me choke on my own breath for fear of saying the wrong thing.

"You still planning on coming out next month to help with planning?"

When in doubt, distract.

"Dad's buying our tickets as we speak," Mom says, taking the bait. "We'll be out there the week before school starts. Have you looked at any of the ideas I've sent you?"

For all of my mom's worries over the guys, she's thrown herself head first into planning this Pack Celebration.

"Not yet," I admit, glancing at Violet. She sticks out her tongue, and I roll my eyes. "Violet's been out here the last few days. I promise to look at them all this week once she goes back to California."

Mom is quick to end the call after that, her focus switching to figuring out where her and Dad will be staying when they visit in another several weeks. Violet shakes her head, laughing without trying to hide it this time, and I sigh, tilting my head back and letting my eyes close, focusing on the warmth of the sun on my skin.

"She does understand that you've already submitted the paperwork, right?" Violet giggles, and I scowl at her. She has the gall to smirk, completely unrepentant. "Pretty sure two months into sleeping with someone is a bit late to be double checking if you're making smart birth control decisions."

I roll my eyes again, groaning. I'm pretty sure I'm the only twenty-two year old in a permanent relationship having to field *sex* questions from my mother.

"What were you wanting to show me before that lovely conversation happened?" I ask after a moment, stretching my neck and tracing my orbital piercing. Her eyes brighten, and she grabs my hand, dragging me about twenty feet farther down the road, pointing out one of the pieces of chalk art to our left. It's a life size whale and takes up at least three of the drawing spots that the artists have been given. Violet grins when I look at her with wide eyes.

"Told you it was impressive!" she says.

"That one's my favorite so far for sure," I say, and she offers an enthusiastic agreement.

She glances over her shoulder a moment later, grabbing my elbow as she waves to someone behind us. When I follow her gaze, I see the guys heading toward us, lunch in their hands. Violet steers us through the crowd, continuing down the row of chalk art instead of toward our men. Just as I'm about to ask her about it, I notice a group of tables just past this row of artwork, tucked under a couple trees that provide decent shade.

The light catches on one of her bond scars, and the question falls from me without meaning to.

"What's it like?"

Violet looks at me, her eyebrows bunched, and I lightly trace the scar that caught my attention where it straddles her collar bone. Her cheeks darken, and I laugh.

"Violet has been rendered speechless." I pat my hips as if my skirt had pockets. "Where's a phone? I need to document this."

Violet pushes me, shaking her head, and I laugh harder, my shoulders shaking. Someone bumps into me as they move by us, and I offer a quick apology, stepping closer to Violet.

"Sometimes it's annoying," Violet says once there's room enough for us to spread out again. "But mostly that's when Dominic is in a mood and the others have no patience for it."

I frown. "Wait. Everyone can feel...everyone?" That sounds asinine, but I don't try to come up with another way to say it. Violet nods, suddenly serious. She traces the scar I noticed, but there's another just under her ear, slightly more jagged.

"It was overwhelming at first," she explains, her eyes distant. "But after everything..." She shakes her head, looking at me again. "I can't imagine my life without them. Dominic and Rylan really wanted to bond. And after everything happened, it wasn't so scary to imagine them knowing everything about me. It felt...like the natural next step."

She flips her hair over her shoulder and adjusts her bag.

"Anyway, the bonding itself was intense but very fun." She winks, and curse it all, I blush like I haven't been all over—and under—my guys for the last six weeks. "Different from my heats. There wasn't that haze that happens when you're in heat. But the org—"

I cover her mouth with a high pitched yelp, and she laughs, biting the palm of my hand. A couple of men glance at us, their arms crossed. They lean into each other, muttering something under their breath, and then one rolls his eyes as they turn away. Embarrassment races through me, and I turn away from them, dropping my hand. Someone bumps into Violet, and she takes a step into me to let them pass. That horrible crawling sensation starts along my skin, and I glance back to where I saw Logan's blond hair sticking out among the crowd. He's still at least fifteen feet back, though they're working to close the gap quickly.

"I need to get out of this crowd," I whisper, running my hands over the front of my skirt and switching my bag to rest on my opposite shoulder.

"Give me two seconds," Violet says.

I nod, glancing back to Logan again, doing my best to stay calm. He isn't looking at me anymore, though. I turn, trying to figure out what's caught his attention, when Violet curses, someone knocking her to the side hard enough that she stumbles a few steps away from me. There's a commotion behind me, Carter's voice rising above the din of the crowd, and I frown, taking a step toward Violet to try and help her up.

"Red!"

Logan's voice is even louder than Carter.

"You ok, Vi?" I ask as she grabs my hand.

She nods. "Some jerk just decided I was in the way. You good?"

There's a sudden, hard slice of pain along my back, and I

gasp. Or try to. I twist, and there's a second slash of pain between my ribs.

"Grab her!" Someone is shouting instructions that I can't quite understand. "Don't move!"

My chest feels like it's on fire, a sharp, debilitating pain tracing up my back and into my left shoulder with each breath. I manage to turn around, hearing Jude's voice join the rush of sound around me as people are suddenly moving away from me.

All except one.

I come face to face with Harper, her shrewd brown eyes narrowed. I stumble a bit, my head growing light as my breathing shallows from the pain, and she pushes against me.

"Fuck off, bitch," she seethes.

Another sharp pain explodes across the front of my chest, just below my ribs. Frowning, I look down, confused over the red that's quickly staining my shirt. Somebody crashes into my shoulder, and I scream, white hot pain exploding down my side as I collapse to my knees.

There's a gust of breath against my ear, blonde hair falling into my face from whoever leans over me. "If I can't have him, there's no way you can, whore."

Thirty-Three

JUDE

"What the fuck?" Jasper is running beside me, his question quiet compared to the shouts surrounding us from the rest of our group. Rylan tackles the person in front of Faedra, covering them with his body to the point I can't accurately tell who it might be. The sinking sensation in my gut tells me it's not good, though. Before I can reach Faedra, Dominic is pulling the other woman off, restraining her in a matter of seconds, his movements precise, a controlled lethality about him that he isn't keeping as leashed right now.

I somehow manage to get to Faedra first, not that it does either of us much good. I'm a scholar of the ancient Near East, not a paramedic. Her eyes are glazed over, her chest moving with quick, shallow breaths. She collapses against me, her hands pressed against her ribs.

"Call," I tell Jasper as he moves around Dominic to grab

Violet. He's reaching for his phone when another man steps towards us, his phone to his ear.

"They're saying up to five minutes because of the road blocks," he says. "She ok?"

I shake my head as I see her back, blood soaking through her cropped shirt and dripping along the waistband of her skirt. Carter and Logan are crouching in front of me before the man can say anything else. Logan's focused on her back, pulling her shirt up enough to see what happened.

He scowls as he looks to where Rylan has one of the people pinned before he curses viciously. I follow his look, and my stomach drops.

"God fucking damnit," he mutters.

"Little Omega," Carter murmurs, and she sobs, the noise breathless and weak, flinching a second later. Logan shakes his head and focuses on Faedra, muttering something I can't quite understand. Someone is crying nearby, and the woman held under Dominic screams when she doesn't manage to break his hold.

"She deserved it!"

The voice cuts across the chaos surrounding me, shrill and cruel and horrifyingly familiar.

Fuck. Me.

"Shut up," Dominic growls.

Carter twists, fury etched in his face, but Rylan cuts him off before he can do anything that'll get him in trouble, grabbing him by the shoulder with a quick shake of his head, the knee that's holding Harper to the ground not moving an inch.

"She's going to need you with her, not warming a holding cell with these two." His voice is low but firm, and Carter tips his head back, his throat moving with his forced swallow.

Logan's lips flatten, but he doesn't look up from Faedra's back, his hands quickly becoming covered in her blood. There's finally sirens in the distance, growing louder with each thundering heartbeat in my ear. Jasper holds back Violet, her eyes wide, her hand covering her mouth. He pulls her to the side as three police officers come running through the crowd.

"Jude, is there another one on your side?" Logan asks, pulling me back to Faedra in my arms.

"Another what?" The words are growled, but Logan's lips thin at the thread of fear running through my voice.

"Another stab wound. She's still wheezing like there's another one."

The man who called for help steps forward as the third officer begins asking questions, the woman he's with holding out her phone, a video queued to be watched on the small screen. My stomach twists. Everything fades, the voices blurring together when I help Carter pull Faedra off of me so Logan can see her front. He hisses another curse.

Before he can tell me what to do to help, the sirens cut off, and there's a flurry of movement around us.

"Shit, Logan." One of the EMTs crouches next to him, deftly wedging between Faedra and Carter, and Logan shakes his head, not offering a response. "Weren't you supposed to be at the game tonight? What happened?"

Logan explains what we've noticed, and the EMT pulls Faedra from my arms, calling out for someone else.

"Ah shit," he mutters. He calls a code into the radio clipped to his collar, and Logan grunts. "We're going to need more space, guys. Finish whatever the officers need, alright?"

Logan blows out a breath. "Can one of us stay?"

The man nods. "Pick now. It's going to be fast."

Both of my best friends look at me. Behind Carter, Dominic eases off of Melanie as one of the officers handcuffs her. She locks eyes with me, hatred so pervasive in her gaze that I want to punch her.

"Jude goes." Carter's firm. My attention snatches back to the situation in front of me. "The second she's gone, you're going to make a poor decision," he says quietly. "You go. We'll follow once we know what's happening with the rest of it."

"Shit, Jasper, I can wait," Violet mutters. Another EMT evaluates her arm as Jasper shakes his head.

"Alright," the man says. "Here we go."

Two more people crowd around us, adjusting us all without saying a single word until we stand on the outside of them, their hands flying over Faedra, cutting away her shirt. I move to my left, blocking the last bit of space so no one can casually look over and see my Omega half naked.

"Faedra, right?" the first EMT asks Logan, glancing back at him.

"Let's tape down the posterior ones," a paramedic says. "We'll try for a typical occlusive on the anterior. She's going to need a thoracostomy either way."

"Yeah, her name is Faedra," I tell the man when Logan is pulled away by an officer before answering.

He holds her head between his palms, leaning over to catch her gaze. "Hi Faedra," he says. "I'm John. We're going to get rid of some of the pain, alright? And then we'll get you to the hospital so they can fix it."

She pants, the edges of her lips taking on a bluish tint that has my heart in my stomach. He looks up at me.

"She allergic to anything?"

Fuck if I know.

That's something I should know, right?

It's only been two months. Maybe it's not something I'm supposed to have in my back pocket.

Violet calls out a random antibiotic name. He glances over his shoulder. "Anything else? Any history of anaphylaxis?"

Violet shakes her head, pulling out of Jasper's grasp and

closing the distance between her and John. "Just really awful hives."

John nods.

"You take it, Marcus. You've done them more often than I have."

The second paramedic presses a large needle into the other's palm before cleaning Faedra's chest. Most of me wants to look away, nausea sitting heavily in my stomach and making my throat itch. But if I see Melanie again, I'm going to lose my shit. Faedra's glazed look catches on me, and her hand flutters at her side.

"One. Two. Three."

Faedra cries out, the sound crackling, and John palms her shoulder, keeping her still.

"Is that better, Faedra?" John asks. Her tongue brushes over her lips, her breathing growing marginally less shallow as she nods once. The others continue to work, and before I can decide where it's best to stand, more first responders are edging past me, helping get Faedra onto a stretcher. They have her up and into the ambulance nearby in a matter of moments. They're racing off before I can figure out where I'm supposed to be to join her.

"You're the fiancé?" a petite woman with ice blonde hair asks me, her blue eyes keen. Another woman stands behind her, both in the half uniform of the local fire department.

"One of them," I say. The taller woman cocks an eyebrow, but the other nods.

"I'm Tiffany," she says, holding out her hand. She nods to the other woman. "This is Elise. We'll take you to the hospital. Is the rest of your pack coming, too?"

Elise frowns, looking at Tiffany. I glance over at our disorganized group. Violet catches my look, and she shakes her head, waving me on while Logan and Carter are giving statements.

"They'll follow later."

LOGAN

Carter and Jude are still in the waiting room when I get back with dinner from one of the nearby restaurants. They glance up as I set the bag on the table between us, and that weight that's been sitting heavy in my stomach gets even worse.

"No update?" I ask.

Jude shrugs, opening the bag and pulling out containers, separating the orders without comment. His eyes are bloodshot, his hair disheveled. And despite having a new set of clothes, he looks like he hasn't gotten a moment of peace since everything happened several hours ago.

Carter says, voice low, "Doctor just went in a few minutes ago. Nurse has been in and out. Dominic made Violet take a walk after she got her arm stitched."

"Rylan and Jasper go to the game?"

Jude nods.

"Detective called." I offer after a moment, picking at the food. "The judge has denied them bail."

Carter's eyes sharpen. "Good."

A door down the hall opens, and we all look up. Faedra's doctor heads towards us, her steps long and sure, her face a careful neutral that has that weight clogging my throat. We don't offer a greeting. We've been here long enough that they know who we are.

"Gentlemen," the doctor murmurs. She pulls a chair from the other table and sits. The nurse stands behind her, hands in her pockets. Before anyone can offer something, a beeping goes off, and the nurse walks away with a murmured apology.

"Faedra is awake and responsive," the doctor offers after a moment. "She is incredibly lucky at this point."

I nod. Punctured lungs are nasty.

"A few ground rules," she says, cocking an eyebrow, "to help protect her lung while everything heals. She needs to stay calm as best as possible. Anything strenuous before the sutures heal could lead to the repair work rupturing. This includes laughing along with heavy lifting or twisting."

Jude sets his chin on his palm.

"She's newly off suppressors, so the possibility of heightened emotional response is much greater. If she can't tolerate having all of you in the room, we'll have to adjust visitor limitations." Carter rubs his neck, and I offer a nod. "And just so it's clear: *nothing* that will make her breathing quick or shallow that you have control over. Her chest tube will hopefully be removed in a few days. Until then, she'll need help doing pretty much everything. If you're uncomfortable or not confident in being able to help with whatever she needs, call for the nurse. We don't want to have to replace the tube if possible."

We murmur our agreements. When she stands, nerves race up my throat, and I swallow to try to ease them.

"You're more than welcome to see her when you're ready. I don't think she's ordered anything to eat yet, but there's no restrictions. Feel free to get her whatever she would like." She tucks her hands into the pockets of her jacket. "Let the nurse know if you have any questions or concerns. I'm happy to help."

"Thank you," Carter says, holding out his hand. She takes it easily enough and then heads out of the department, pulling out her phone as she heads deeper into the hospital.

Jude gathers up the food without comment, tucking everything back into the bag before standing up. We pass by the nurse's station, and she offers a smile and wave.

"Text Violet and let her know she can come back," Carter tells me.

Jude's pushing open the door to Faedra's room by the time I have my phone put back away.

Faedra looks over as we step inside, her hair a mess behind her. She picks at the tube of oxygen where it sits beside her, the canula perched delicately under her nose. The hospital light has her even more pale than normal, but it doesn't decrease the relief I feel when I see her rosy cheeks and pink lips.

"Fae," Jude murmurs, hesitating just inside the room. "Fuck, Fae. I'm so sorry."

Her eyes well with tears, and whatever hesitation had overtaken us is gone. Carter makes it to her first, his hand covering hers as he kisses her temple.

"I'm so sorry, little Omega," he murmurs, and she hiccups a sob, flinching at the sudden intake of breath.

Jude comes up on her other side, his hand gentle on her forearm. "It's alright, Fae. Don't cry. It kills me when you cry."

She gives a sardonic smile before wiping the tears from her cheeks. The IV in her hand catches on the oxygen tubing, and she grimaces. I set the food on the table in the corner and then rush to the other side of Carter, helping her undo the twisted lines before her IV gets ripped out and they have to place another one.

"You need anything?" Carter asks on a whisper, and she shakes her head, the tears coming faster.

"Red," I murmur, and she looks up at me. I wipe away the tears, cupping her cheeks before kissing her once, so soft it's almost a brush of our lips. "I love you."

She hiccups another sob but doesn't flinch.

Jude palms her neck. "We've got you," he says, leaning in the moment I've pulled away from her, resting his forehead against hers. Carter rests his hand on her thigh, the blanket pulling down a bit from the weight of his touch. She worries at her lip, biting it until it starts to bleed, and she curses.

"Are they—"

"They won't hurt you again," Carter says, voice dropping. She shivers, and I wrap her fingers in my hand, squeezing lightly.

"You ok, Red?" I ask. "You're not in pain?"

She's quick to shake her head, wiping away the bit of blood off her lip with the blanket.

"We brought you food." She gives me an unsteady smile, and I squeeze her hand before walking to the table and digging out the food for her. Carter and Jude each take a moment with her, their murmured affection tender, but Faedra doesn't relax the way she has the last two weeks during moments like this since finalizing everything with Council. Where she normally cuddles into us, she instead grows more reclusive, pulling her hands into her lap, her eyes growing reserved.

"Faedra," I say, stopping at the foot of the bed. She looks up at me, her eyes wide. "What is it?"

Her hands tremble against her belly—and that's the least like her I've seen. After an agonizing silence, she blows out a cautious breath.

"The…" She licks her lips and shakes her head, dropping her gaze. "The doctor just said something."

Jude glances at us both, his frown set deep, his jaw clenched. Her murmured words are almost too soft to hear, but they ring through me like a death knell all the same.

"I'm, uh, pregnant."

Thirty-Four

FAEDRA

My chest aches, and the spot between my ribs where the tube that's keeping my lung from collapsing again sits itches like hell. My hand with the IV burns, and I can't seem to feel like I can get a deep enough breath without it shooting a pain through my sternum. And yet none of that competes with the nerves settling heavily in my stomach and making my throat itch with nausea.

"What?" Logan asks after what feels like forever.

Did he really not hear me? I guess I did say it pretty softly. I lick my lips and try again.

"I'm pregnant." It's still much too quiet for it to be anything other than a whisper. It feels just as surreal to say it as it did to hear the doctor tell me. When the guys don't say anything, I continue. "She said they run a standard blood work panel, and that's one of the things they screen. It came back positive." My voice is scratchy, and I twist my hands into the blanket at my waist to keep from picking at the tape on my hand.

Logan sets the takeout container on the end of the bed, carefully avoiding my feet, and then grabs his hair. His eyes are wide, his mouth slightly ajar. Jude is eerily still beside me, but Carter doesn't miss a beat, squeezing my thigh and taking my hand in his, running his thumb over my knuckles.

"What do you want to do?" he asks after a minute.

I frown. "Like right now? I'd really like a shower and for someone to help me with my hair."

Carter's lips tick up in a small half smile, but he shakes his head. "Not what I meant, little Omega."

I mess with my tragus piercing, twisting the small flower around, unsure what to say.

"Carter's trying to be tactful, Red. It's in his blood." Logan blows out a breath, but his eyes stay locked on me, his shoulders dropping. "Do you want an abortion?"

My knee jerk reaction is to say yes, but I keep from saying it out loud. It feels like something we should all agree on together. It's not like I got into the situation on my own.

Right?

I bite my lip again, the pain from where I previously split it open grounding me in a weird macabre way that has me even more unsettled. Carter runs his thumb over my knuckles again, his touch soft, and the confusion sitting on my chest like a freight train doubles.

"What do you want to do?" I ask after a moment, my voice breathless, scratchy.

Logan shakes his head. "Not our choice to make, Red. It's your body."

My stomach flutters, and I swallow around the lump in my throat. It feels too overwhelming to think about right now. I don't want to have to make the choice on my own.

"But we're a pack," I say, trying to convince them to help me decide. "It's not a decision that just impacts me."

"Faedra," Jude murmurs, and I swallow again, my mouth suddenly dry. He tucks his finger under my chin and tilts my head back until our eyes lock. "If this isn't something you want and we pressure you into it, you will spend your life resenting us. Do not ask us to consent to that. You need to make the right choice for you."

Curse him for being logical.

"I..." I lick my lips, and Carter tightens his hold on my fingers. Too much has happened today for me to be able to think objectively about any of this. "I need more time."

Logan pulls the chairs from the table, offering one to both Jude and Carter before stepping out to the hallway. He's back a minute later with the nurse who smiles at me while grabbing a set of gloves from the boxes arranged on the wall.

"You're wanting to take a shower, Faedra?" she asks. I glance at Logan, blushing, and he shrugs. When I nod, she maneuvers around Carter, messing with the equipment next to the bed, and then helps me stand, going slow enough that I don't feel out of breath.

Fifteen awkward minutes later, Logan sits beside me feeding me bits of their dinner, Jude holds my non-IV hand, and Carter checks his phone from where he perches on the sofa under the window. There's a soft knock on the door, and Carter crosses the room to open it.

"Is now a good time?" Violet's question is soft, hesitant, and it has my gut clenching all over again. Violet is neither of those things. Logan offers me another piece of dinner, and I smile, nodding when Jude tightens his hold on my hand.

"Come in, Violet," Jude says a moment later. There's shuffling behind Logan, but I can't see beyond the machine that's hooked up to my IV. Carter leans against the wall, his hands tucked into the pockets of his jeans, his polo unbuttoned, his wavy hair messier than normal. Violet's changed into a set of black shorts and a band tee—this one Lana Del Rey. Her eyes are red and puffy, like she's been crying the entire afternoon since everything happened at the festival.

I hold out my hand to her, and she steps up beside Logan, taking my outstretched fingers in her grasp, beyond gentle in her touch, and my throat feels tight.

"You're alright?" she asks after a minute, her eyes scanning me twice before settling on my gaze. When I nod, she looses a deep breath that has me jealous, and a tension leaves her body, her shoulders relaxing.

"This was definitely not what I had planned for the week," I admit, and she rolls her eyes. "Sorry your trip got messed up."

She snorts, waving her hand in dismissal. "You've got stitches all over and a tube sticking out of your ribs, and you're apologizing to *me*? Fae, you're ridiculous sometimes."

I don't take back my apology. I *do* feel bad that her trip has gotten thrown off because of this whole mess.

Logan feeds me the last bit from the takeout container and then stands, pressing a kiss to my temple. Jude kisses my knuckles, and Carter palms my ankle through the blanket, his touch warm despite the barrier.

"We'll be back, little Omega," he murmurs, and I nod, holding out my hand for him. He laces our fingers together for a heartbeat, and then the three of them leave, shutting the door quietly behind them.

"What's wrong?" Violet asks the moment we're alone, her eyes sharpening on me as she takes over Logan's seat. "You have that vacant look that you'd get every time we had to do something unsavory as R.A.s at school. Like when that freshman got kicked out."

I laugh. I can't help it. Shooting pain races up my chest, and I grimace, palming my sternum as if it will help. "Shit, Vi. I'm not supposed to laugh."

She frowns. "That wasn't supposed to be funny, so that's on you, not me." She touches her industrial piercing before asking me about what's bothering me again.

I expect her to be shocked when I tell her, but instead of her eyes widening and her shoulders dropping, her gaze grows keen, her head tipping a bit like she's thinking hard about something.

"Talk me through it," she says after a bit.

I frown, and she sighs.

"You're conflicted," she says, "which isn't abnormal. So talk through it. What part of it is keeping it from being an immediate yes? Not a simple yes, but a confident one."

"It just feels like there's things I'd be giving up, and I don't know if I'm ready for that."

She nods. "Like what?"

For the life of me, I can't remember anything beyond the photography degree. When I tell her, her lips purse.

"Could you opt for something online? Or what about hiring a nanny?"

"I...don't know," I say after a while. "Why are you trying to talk me into keeping it when you're so staunchly *against* having kids?"

She pats my leg. "I am so confidently childfree *because* I had this conversation. I looked at all the options, all the ways my life could look, and decided on the one I liked the best." She lifts a shoulder. "And then matching made it to where I had to compromise a bit."

"Kids were an eventually thing," I say after a bit. "Not a right away thing. I didn't expect my birth control to fail, you know? And now I can't even remember why."

Violet shakes her head. "Let's make a list. All the things you want to do at some point. You can look at all the things and decide which ones are musts and which ones aren't." She cocks an eyebrow and flips her hair over her shoulder. "You would be surprised what surfaces as musts when you're pressed to actually think about it."

She says it with an air of experience that has me wondering just how much happened between her and Dominic that she didn't tell me. My thoughts are scattered, though, and I can't seem to focus enough to put any of my ideas into a semblance of order.

"Is there paper on the table?" I ask her. She nods, grabbing a small pad with the hospital's logo and the single pen with it.

"Tell me your dreams, Fae," she says, setting the paper in my lap. "I'll braid your hair while you do."

Thirty-Five

FAEDRA

"Hey, we're back," Logan calls after he shuts the door. I slip off my sandals and set my sunglasses in my bag, dropping the whole thing unceremoniously to the floor. The breathlessness has gotten better over the last week and a half, but the walk from the garage to the condo is still rough. Logan turns back to me, lifting me bridal-style into his arms before I can protest. Not that I would at the moment. Instead, I let my head settle into the crook of his shoulder, breathing in his sandalwood scent, and close my eyes. Footsteps sound from the upper floor as Logan carries me further into the condo.

"Everything alright?" Carter's voice drifts to me, even and smooth in that intentional way he uses when trying to hide that he's worried. I've heard a lot of that tone in the last week since I've been home.

"Doctor said everything is looking fine." Logan turns around, walking backwards, but I keep my eyes closed. "Stitches dissolved the way they were supposed to. Breathlessness will get better with time as her lung finishes healing. Mentioned it could be another eight weeks before she feels like her breathing is back to normal." Logan rattles off the main points without missing a beat. He brushes his lips against my jaw, arms tightening around me, and then asks, "You good, Red? Jude's just about finished with lunch."

With a small nod, he starts walking again. His footsteps echo against the hardwood, and I can hear Carter crossing the main floor behind us. Pressing my palm to his sternum, I open my eyes.

And come nearly face to face with Jude's bright green ones, eyebrows furrowed as he assesses me. He traces his thumb over my cheek, and I can't help but smile, leaning into the touch. His lips tip up in a half-smile before he drops his hand. Logan moves carefully past him, helping me sit on the cool stone of the island's countertop. Goosebumps cover my legs as I shiver.

"You good?" Logan asks, hand splaying across my waist, thumb brushing the smaller scab along my ribs. His throat moves with a hard swallow, and I can't help but lace my fingers with his, setting a soft kiss to his lips.

"I'm good." I assure him, pulling away.

With a nod, he grabs dishes to prep for lunch. Carter steps into the kitchen a few moments later, brown eyes intent on me. He leans against the fridge, hands tucked into his pockets, looking way more delicious than he has a right to. I hold out my hand, and he blows out a breath before pushing off the appliance and walking over to me.

"I miss you," I whisper against his lips, wrapping my hand around his neck, twisting my fingers into the black strands of his hair.

He hums, stepping into me, and I spread my legs without hesitation, encouraging him to press fully into me.

"I swear to God, Carter, I will kill you if you get her worked up right now," Jude threatens behind me. A giggle leaves me, bordering on hysterical.

"The doctor said sex is fine," I say against Carter's lips, still smiling. Jude curses behind me, and then I hear him crossing the space. A moment later, his hand is on my thigh, his thumb brushing the hem of my skirt.

"You could have led with that, Logan," Carter says, clearly bemused, a smirk on his lips. I giggle again, shaking my head.

"I needed to get her somewhere central before I let you descend on her like rabid dogs," Logan says, voice dry. His hand cups my knee a second later, and I look over at him. He gives a soft smile, running his thumb over my lips.

We'd almost lost this. So soon after getting it, too. I don't want to take any of our time for granted.

You would be surprised what surfaces as musts when you're pressed to actually think about it.

Violet's words float through my mind, and I tighten my grip on Carter's hand and grab Logan's, too. I look at Jude, and my breath catches in my throat.

"I want to bond," I tell him, my voice firm, clear. He takes a half step into me, his Adam's apple moving with a swallow. "Is... is that something we can do now? Or is it something that has to wait until, um, after?" I ask, dodging actually saying the word out loud, not sure I can without crying, and I don't want to panic them unnecessarily.

Carter hums, and my gaze flicks to him. He gives a small shake of his head, a lock of hair settling on his forehead.

"Bonding can be something we do at any point," he says, voice dropping, scraping along my skin.

I nod once, swallow the sudden lump in my throat, and adjust my hold so that my hand is sandwiched between Carter's and Jude's on my thigh.

"What is it, Red? What has you so nervous?" Logan

murmurs, his soft voice a balm to my soul, settling my nerves without him trying. I swallow again and then let the words fall out without thinking them through.

"Just trying to decide how to convince you to bond right now," I say, and all three of my Alphas growl a bit, stepping into me, their bodies pressing into mine. "And feeling grateful I won't have to wait nine months."

Everything freezes, and I hold my breath, waiting to see how they'll respond to my decision. Jude cups my chin, turning me until our eyes are locked.

"That's what you want?" He double checks. "You want to have a baby?"

I blow out my breath, a part of me just thankful that I can do it again.

"I'm not going to lie. I'm terrified," I tell him, my voice wavering despite my best intentions.

His eyebrows furrow, a frown pulling at his lips. I continue, ignoring how my hands start shaking just a bit.

"Of how it'll change me. Of how it'll change us when we've only just figured out an us. I don't feel like I've lived enough to do any of it properly."

A slow breath in to control the trembling in my body. Logan runs his hand up my thigh, and Carter spreads his fingers across my hip, anchoring me.

"But I don't want to look back in five years and regret missed opportunities because I kept waiting for the perfect timing."

Jude's eyes flash, and I know he's thinking about Iris and her list. I think about the list shoved into the top drawer of my dresser that Violet wrote with me while I could barely breathe.

"And..." I swallow before licking my lips. "And I think I would regret not having a baby."

Jude's eyes are glassy, and he doesn't bother with trying to blink away the tears before they fall over his lashes and down his cheeks. He doesn't say anything before his lips are on mine, slow and soft and infinitely gentle, and the care he takes breaks my heart. I pull away from him and reach into my back pocket, grabbing the thin piece of paper and pressing it against my stomach.

Logan frowns.

"What's that?"

"Something the doctor did for me while you were taking that phone call," I say. The column of his throat moves with his swallow, and Carter's hand spasms against my side. "She said it isn't nearly as good as an ultrasound tech could do, but..." I shrug and flip the paper over, resting it in my lap so they can see it.

I don't know what I'm expecting, but complete silence greets me, and I squirm as my nervousness grows.

"She said I'm about eight weeks, so it would have happened before my heat." I swallow and mess with the corners of the ultrasound picture. "Which she explained is probably why I didn't drop into it on my own. Officially I'm due mid-March, but she said that they'll probably come closer to early February—and harped on me for getting in to see the proper doctor soon."

Logan blows out a breath. "They?" he asks, his voice shaking. "As in more than one?"

"It's apparently something that's more common when a hormonal birth control fails." I point to each of the small bean shapes from the ultrasound. "She can't tell if they're identical, but there's some testing we can do if we—"

Carter cuts me off with his mouth on mine, his hands cupping my face and tipping it towards him. Someone takes the ultrasound picture and sets it on the counter beside me. A moment later, Carter has my legs wrapped around his hips as he takes me toward the bedrooms, lunch all but forgotten.

"Mine, please," I whisper against his lips between kisses.

He lays me out on my bed, standing at the foot of it, and I rush to take off my shirt, throwing it towards the closet on the other side of the room. Logan's already stripped by the time I'm pulling off my bra, and Jude isn't far behind. Carter hesitates, his eyes roaming over me, catching on the scabs from the knife wounds, his gaze pausing longer on the scab left from where my chest tube was placed.

Logan climbs up beside me, nuzzling my neck, nipping at my throat hard enough that heat races through me, slick pooling between my legs. Jude groans, flanking him, kissing just under my ear.

"Right here," he murmurs. "I've wanted to mark you right here since that first night you were in my bed."

I tip my head back, giving them both more room, anticipation making my heart race. My scent drowns the room, overpowering both of theirs, and I twist my hands into the sheets to keep from reaching for them, wanting them to explore me without my urging.

And still Carter pauses.

I hold out my hand for him, palm up, and he takes it in a steady hold, his fingers lacing with mine, but he doesn't move towards me. Doesn't strip out of his clothes. Doesn't set a knee on the bed.

His face is full of emotion, awe and devastation and joy, and I tighten my hold on him in silent question.

"I am so incredibly lucky, little Omega," he murmurs, voice thick with the same mix of emotions. I squeeze his hand and pull him towards me.

This time he doesn't hesitate, setting a knee on the bed while stripping out of his polo. He kicks off his slacks and boxer briefs in the next moment, and then he's on me, pushing me back into the bed and covering me with his body. He strips me of my skirt and underwear so fast I gasp. Jude and Logan back away as

Carter sinks into me, driving into me with hard thrusts that have my hips lifting off the bed with need.

This isn't a seduction. It's a primitive need, similar to my heat but infinitely more at the same time. He sets small bites along my sternum, and my orgasm rises, his movements so precise that they have me writhing in pleasure in a matter of moments. He tips my chin back, his eyes full of desire, and then sets his teeth on my throat. My body is alive with pleasure, and one expert flick of his thumb over my clit, and I'm falling over the cliff, my body locking as wave after wave of my climax races through me. He bites hard enough to break my skin at the same moment, and I cry out, my hands scratching into his back hard enough that I pull blood.

His satisfaction is suddenly simmering in my blood, so visceral I almost don't notice him pulling out and coming across my belly. He runs his tongue over the bite, and my core clenches around nothing, more slick rushing down my thighs. Before I can settle into the afterglow of the orgasm—and the bond with Carter—he's moving away from me, adjusting until he lays next to me, breathing heavily. Logan pulls me against him, rolling me onto my side so that we're looking at each other, lifting my leg as he slides in with a single, seamless push, and I groan, dropping my forehead against his, the sensations overwhelming me as he sets his thumb to my clit and encourages me to the brink of awareness again. He hums as he kisses the spot just under my ear, the same spot he bruised during my heat when the need to have him bond with me rode me hard.

"Love you, Red," he murmurs, his lips skating over my ear. All I manage is a moan, my body awash in goosebumps as he drives into me harder, faster. He pinches my clit, and I'm *gone*, drowning in another unending wave of bliss. His teeth sink into that spot, and I cry out, clinging to him as his emotions roar through me, his happiness and soft, tender affection. Just when I think he's going to knot with me, he pulls away, his cum landing across my clit and hips, his breathing ragged as he takes my lips in his, his tongue twisting with mine.

I've not yet come down from the high when a firm hand grasps my ankle and pulls me away from Logan, flipping me onto my back as I'm moved to the edge of the bed. Jude wraps my knees around his hips, one hand on the base of my throat as he pushes into me with a hard thrust, his face tight with desire. His eyes never leave mine, even as he forces me closer to the edge of the bed, bringing one leg to rest over his shoulder.

"Fae," he murmurs, and I shiver. I don't know how I'm still capable of responding to his touch, to his systematic claiming of my body. Lightning ripples through me, and I clench around him, pulling a groan from deep within his chest. He leans over me, his teeth brushing along the delicate, sensitive space just under my left ear, left devoid of either of the other claiming marks. He pulls the skin into his mouth, sucking gently, pressing his thumb against my clit and rubbing quick circles around it.

I fall apart in his arms, my entire body trembling, over sensitized from the three orgasms they've pulled from my body in quick succession. His teeth break my skin, and my back bows, my keening cry echoing off the windows.

His love overwhelms me, his bone deep gratitude keeping me from floating away entirely on the wave of sensation that ripples through me as his knot locks us together, his grunt against my throat making me clench around him again. He runs his tongue over his mark before pressing a kiss so gentle it feels more like a whisper of his lips against it.

His eyes are bright, tears lining the bottom lashes when he pulls away, cupping my cheeks and kissing me until I'm gasping for breath, my body igniting under him again. Carter and Logan flank me, their lips soft against my temples, and I lace my fingers with theirs, holding them both over my belly, drowning in the overwhelming sense of them within me. Jude pulls back, rising above me until he can spread his palm over my pelvis, his fingers stretching to my belly button.

"You're ours, Fae," he says, emotion making his voice crack.

Carter whispers in my ear, "Always, little Omega."

Logan hums, biting my ear before murmuring, "Our perfect Red."

Joy floods through me, wholly my own, and I press my heels into the small of Jude's back, encouraging him over me again.

"I love you," I tell them, and my heart is full when they murmur it back.

Epilogue

ONE YEAR LATER

FAEDRA

Doug's all smiles where he stands at the trailhead, his pack already adjusted, his hand entwined with a smiling woman's. Her eyes are bright blue, her dark brown hair pulled into a braid.

"You made it!" Doug says, waving at me as I round the back of our new SUV. The woman beside him waves, too, and they head towards us, crossing the parking lot before Carter and Jude manage to get out of the Jeep beside us. He offers me a quick side hug. "Everyone else is working on getting ready to go."

I glance around the parking lot, my smile growing as I realize he's right. Violet glances up at me from where she's adjusting something in her pack, her lips pursed. Jasper steps in front of her before I can ask what's bothering her, helping her into the pack and adjusting everything until she smacks his hands and kisses him.

"Faedra Rose, there you are." My mom's voice carries across the lot, and I turn towards it, smiling when I see her standing with Dad and Aiden, their packs already adjusted. She walks over to me, enveloping me in a hug as Logan opens the back of the SUV, his hand gentle where it runs across the small of my back.

The soft hiccuping cry from the SUV has me pulling away from her, twisting until I can see Jude holding Rose, her strawberry blonde hair peaking out from the top of the baby carrier. He looks up as he gets her settled against his chest, her small cries calming once he's done finessing the straps. Heat blooms in my belly at the promise in his gaze. Logan hands him his pack, breaking the moment of tension, and he has it adjusted before I even grab mine from the back of the SUV.

Aiden is quiet beside me. "Congratulations, Faedra," he murmurs. I glance up at him, and he smiles, pulling on one of my braids. "I hear you sold your entire portfolio from last semester. Good job."

My grin is wide, and I murmur a thanks as I hug him. He helps me put on my backpack without further comment. Doug and my father start up a conversation as I focus on getting my pack comfortable, adjusting the waistband to accommodate the changes from having the girls. The last time I wore this pack, I was very pregnant.

"Faedra mentioned this is your first time," Doug says, and my father offers an agreement. "It's a good one to start with. Rocky Mountain National Park is gorgeous!"

Violet comes up next to me, her hand twisting the industrial piercing in her ear. "Do you have any extra studs? Mine apparently got left at the condo." She rolls her eyes, and I laugh.

"I don't, but I bet Ashlynn does," I say, looking out over everyone. Ashlynn catches my gaze at just the right moment, and I wave her over, asking her the same question Violet asked me. She's quick to pull a few from her car, offering them to Violet along with an alcohol pad.

"Damn it!" Gina curses from the other side of the car, and we all look over. My eyebrows furrow. She's standing with Carter, her hands in the air as he shakes his head, a half smile on his lips.

"There'll be plenty of time to pass the babies at camp tonight," Carter says, his movements confident as he adjusts the baby carrier, and I smile. Gina pouts as she crosses her arms, and Ashlynn laughs, shaking her head.

"So insistent on baby cuddles," she murmurs, quietly enough that only Violet and I hear her, "and yet she's convinced she doesn't want another one."

I laugh and elbow Ashlynn in the side. "That's because you told her she had to do the work this time and then offered to have her watch the twins be born. I'd be terrified too after that."

I can still feel the contractions and the burn if I stop to think about it, so I don't. If I do, I won't be brave enough to try for a third, and that would result in my not having an exact replica of Carter, too. Violet cocks an eyebrow. Dominic comes up behind her, their height difference meaning that her backpack doesn't get in the way of him pressing a kiss to the crown of her head.

"I'll leave all the cuddles to you, then," she murmurs after a moment. "No children for me."

Ashlynn smiles. "Sounds great."

Doug calls us all towards the trailhead, and Logan grabs my hand, pressing a kiss to his bond scar, his happiness a warm stream in my chest.

"Alright. So altogether it's about a thirty mile loop. Should see some pretty great things, including Brianna's favorite waterfall. Good luck trying to beat her to it."

Everyone laughs as he winks, and I lean my head against Logan's arm. Jude and Carter come up behind me, each resting a hand on my waist.

"Our goal for today is eight miles. If you're feeling like you're dragging, make sure you've had something to eat within the last half hour and that you've been actively drinking your water.

Don't be discouraged when the Bennetts outpace you despite having babies strapped to their chests. This is a warm-up trail for them."

My dad looks over his shoulder, surprise written all over his face, and I blush. Mom grabs his hand, and he refocuses on Doug at the front. Jude grunts, and Carter chuckles, moving until he's standing next to me. My gaze catches on my daughter's bright green eyes, the exact same as Jude's.

"For the love of all that is good, please don't do anything stupid. The only doctor we have is a pediatrician. He'll be great for the twins. Awful for the rest of us."

Aiden laughs, shaking his head, and Doug grins. Violet twists so she can see me.

"Is thirty miles really a warm up for you guys?" she whispers.

I shake my head. "Not for me."

Logan shrugs. "We've done thirty mile days before to get ahead of weather. Not our favorite, but it's manageable. We averaged about twenty miles a day before Faedra."

Jasper mutters a curse.

"And you don't want Logan having to patch anything." Doug continues, his voice going dry. "He deals with professional athletes. He'll have no sympathy for your idiotic decision of trying to jump the ten foot cliff gap."

There's a round of laughter through the group, and then Doug claps his hands. Another man steps up next to him, about three inches shorter than his average stature, his hair nearly all gray, his brown eyes bright.

"Before Doug can kill us with his crappy humor, let's get a couple group photos and then get started. I promised Brianna I'd kiss her under her waterfall, and I need to make sure I beat Willa to it, or she'll keep Brianna to herself all night." He winks, and I can't help but grin.

The group photos are surprisingly easy to take, and Gina

passes the camera the guys gave me for my birthday back to me once they're finished. She purses her lips, eyeing up Carter again, and I shake my head, running a hand across Iris's cheek.

"You good to go, Red?" Logan's question is a murmur against my ear.

When I nod, he kisses his scar again.

"I love you," I tell my Alphas. They close in around me, kissing whatever part of my neck and face they can reach, and I can't hold back my grin.

"Always, little Omega," Carter says, running his thumb over his scar, his gaze hot.

"Another thing off your list, Fae," Jude murmurs. "I'm proud of you."

Jude takes my hand, leading me onto the trail, his joy so strong that I know the others can feel it, too. I let my own mix with his, and Logan and Carter both laugh behind us as we take the front of the line, leading our friends and family into the forest.

Content Warnings

ON PAGE

- Discussion of Abortion
- Dubious Consent
- Toxic Relationships
- Knife Violence

OFF PAGE

- Parental Death
- Sibling Death
- Death by Cancer
- Death by Drunk Driver

Acknowledgments

Thank you so much to my husband for keeping me afloat when it felt like I couldn't get this story to figure itself out. You are a beacon of light in my world, and I am forever grateful that you decided my brand of crazy was just right for you.

Thank you to my wonderful Book Chat besties! You have been so supportive this entire time, and I am so grateful to each of you.

Thank you to my beta readers. You are a gift that I will never be able to adequately repay, and I am forever grateful for you taking a chance on me.

Thank you to the wonderful book communities on both Instagram and TikTok for taking me in with open arms despite my chaotic, unhinged postings and general unorganized disaster approach to social medias in general. I am only here because of you all!

Special shoutout to the wonderful artists who are always so excited to work with me and are cheerleading so incredibly loudly for all of us small baby authors!

About the Author

Jillian has been crafting stories since she was a young teen. She's always had a soft spot for heroines thrown into the deep end without any prior training. And while she, like most of Booktok, loves the dark-haired love interest, she secretly enjoys the blonde, Golden Retriever heroes. Other secret indulgences include the miscommunication trope, surprise or secret babies, and arranged marriages with age gaps.

Jillian enjoys soaking up the sun in Colorado. She can be found most days keeping the children and animals alive. During the summer, she enjoys testing the limits of her ADHD by seeing how far into July she can remember to water the flowers and veggies in the garden. She spends most of the winter chasing after her snow loving children while silently cursing that she lives somewhere that actually gets cold.